"Ready to go in?"

Conall rose to his feet in a smooth motion and held out a hand.

Touching him might be…risky. Still, Lia reached out and let his hand close around hers.

And knew immediately that she'd been right.

His warm clasp felt better than almost anything she could remember. Strong, safe… and yet not safe.

With a gentle tug, he boosted her to her feet. They ended up no more than a foot apart. Her breath caught in her throat. Neither of them moved. He didn't release her. She wanted, quite desperately, for him to pull her closer, until her body bumped up against his. She wanted him to kiss her.

And she knew letting that happen would be stupid. He was here only for a little while, and she suffered enough every time a child left her. She couldn't bear anything else temporary in her life.

Yet the temptation…

Dear Reader,

I find myself feeling a little sad at introducing
Conall MacLachlan to you, because it means saying
goodbye. I don't know when I've been as drawn to
my characters as I was writing this trilogy. I fell in
love with each brother. Their shared childhood meant
they all had major issues, but not the same ones.
Conall was the youngest, the most vulnerable, when
his family dissolved and the big brother he'd adored
sacrificed all to keep the boys together—but in doing
so became a tyrant.

In his head, Conall knows that his brother saved him;
at twelve, Conall was angry, constantly in fights,
drinking alcohol, even going so far as stealing a car.
He was in trouble because neither of his parents
cared enough to stop him. Duncan did care—but
Conall grew to hate his brother's rules, his brother's
rigidity...his brother. When *The Call of Bravery* opens,
Conall hasn't been home in over ten years. He'd never
intended to come home, but his job brings him back.
And now everything he remembered, everything he
believed, gets shaken up and settles in a different way.

Of course, a woman has something to do with that.
No surprise that Conall has vowed never to have
a family—not when his memories are so terrible. I
figured he needed to confront his worst fears in a
big way, so I made him move in with a beautiful,
generous, compassionate woman who has a houseful
of foster children—including two recently orphaned
boys who remind Conall of himself.

Oh, I loved shaking up this man who believed himself
invulnerable and who turns out to be the most
vulnerable of the three MacLachlan brothers! Wow.
Making the hero of my next book measure up is going
to be a real challenge.

Good reading!

Janice Kay Johnson

The Call of Bravery

Janice Kay Johnson

TORONTO NEW YORK LONDON
AMSTERDAM PARIS SYDNEY HAMBURG
STOCKHOLM ATHENS TOKYO MILAN MADRID
PRAGUE WARSAW BUDAPEST AUCKLAND

Recycling programs
for this product may
not exist in your area.

ISBN-13: 978-0-373-60694-8

THE CALL OF BRAVERY

ABOUT THE AUTHOR

The author of more than sixty books for children and adults, Janice Kay Johnson writes Harlequin Superromance novels about love and family—about the way generations connect and the power our earliest experiences have on us throughout life. Her 2007 novel, *Snowbound,* won a RITA® Award from Romance Writers of America for Best Contemporary Series Romance. A former librarian, Janice raised two daughters in a small rural town north of Seattle, Washington. She loves to read and is an active volunteer and board member for Purrfect Pals, a no-kill cat shelter.

Books by Janice Kay Johnson

HARLEQUIN SUPERROMANCE

HARLEQUIN ANTHOLOGY

SIGNATURE SELECT SAGA

*The Russell Twins
**A Brother's Word

Other titles by this author available in ebook format.

PROLOGUE

CONALL MACLACHLAN SLUMPED on the bathroom floor, his back against the tub, a wet washcloth pressed to his face. One eye had already swollen shut, and the other lid barely opened. His nose wouldn't quit gushing blood. He could taste it in his throat, and thinking about it, he lunged forward barely in time to retch into the toilet. Afterward he stumbled to his feet to rinse his mouth out and then brush his teeth. Neither helped much when blood kept pumping from his nose and running down his upper lip.

He wet then wrung out the washcloth again and lifted it to his face. His hand paused briefly as he caught a glimpse of his face with the swelling, bruising, a puffed lip, two black eyes that were going to be hideous, blood…and tears.

He didn't cry. He didn't! He was nine years old, way too old to weep like a little girl. But he felt… he felt… A sob tore its way free and he crumpled again, pressing the cold cloth to his face to stifle blood and tears both.

He'd been beaten up before. He was a shrimp

for his age, and hated it. When other boys shoul-dered him aside or knocked him down for the fun of it, he hit back. Every time, he knew he'd lose, but he couldn't seem to help himself. He was so full of rage, even he didn't understand it.

And it wasn't fair that he was small. His broth-ers weren't; Duncan at fifteen didn't have a man's muscles, but he had a man's height. He had to be six feet tall. And Niall wasn't far behind at twelve. Their mother always said he was growing like a weed. She'd sigh, because usually she was no-ticing that his jeans were too short. But then her gaze would stray to Conall, the runt of the litter, who *wasn't* growing like a weed. Sometimes she looked…he didn't quite know, and wasn't sure he wanted to identify her expression. It was too much like she couldn't figure out where he'd come from. As if he'd followed Niall home one day like an abandoned puppy and moved in without her no-ticing, until recently, that he was always there.

It was getting worse, too. Not that long ago, she would have yelled at him when she saw him like this, but she also would have hustled him upstairs, cleaned him up and gotten him a bag of frozen peas or corn for his face.

Today when he'd stumbled in the door and Mom saw him, she said, "Not again. What is *wrong* with you?"

When he fled toward the stairs, he saw his father step out of the kitchen. What was Dad doing home this early? Had he lost his job? Or quit? The surprise on his face changed to disgust, and Con knew what he was thinking.

What's wrong *with you?*

He didn't *know* what was wrong with him, why he couldn't be like Duncan, who was smart and athletic. Nobody would be stupid enough even to *try* to beat him up. Not Duncan. Anyway, Conall's big brother didn't get in trouble. He was too controlled, too focused on what he wanted.

And Niall…well, Niall did screw up. He used to be a good boy, too, until Dad got out of prison and things weren't the same. But even so, he was also the star forward of the middle school soccer team *and* the basketball team. Dad liked Niall because he played the bagpipe like Dad. In fact, he was better than Dad, Con privately thought, maybe because, like Duncan, Niall had that ability to focus so intensely, he shut the world out.

Niall had Duncan, too. They were friends. When Mom and Dad started yelling, they often disappeared together. Con would look out his bedroom window and see them walking down the sidewalk to the school, one or the other dribbling a basketball. They didn't seem to remember he was here.

Like they'd waste time teaching him, the runt, to play basketball. Not that long ago, Dad had said,

"Usually a boy can start playing the bagpipe by the time he's nine or ten, but you won't be able to." He'd snorted and turned away.

The nosebleed had finally stopped. Conall washed his face again, and decided he really needed ice. He could hardly see at all.

He'd made it most of the way downstairs when he heard Dad yell, "Why are you blaming me? You're supposed to be raising the damn kids, aren't you? If that pathetic excuse for a boy is anyone's fault, he's yours."

Conall froze, steps from the bottom.

"Mine?" Mom screamed. "You know I never wanted him. *You're* the one who insisted we have another kid. God knows why, when you can't be bothered doing any *real* parenting. Conall wouldn't be such a mess if you did."

"What am I supposed to do with him? Teach him how to be a man?" Dad laughed as if the idea was unbelievably stupid. That laugh sank into the very marrow of Conall's bones, becoming part of him. "He doesn't have it in him." His voice became ugly. "Is he even mine, Laura? Because I sure as hell don't see myself in him."

This time Mom's scream was wordless. There was a metallic crash as if she'd thrown something like a pan. Ceramic splintered. Dad bellowed in fury; there was another crash and then a thud, the screams and yells continuing.

Conall whimpered. Feeling the way with his foot, he retreated up a step, then another. *Please don't let them hear me. Please don't let one of them come out of the kitchen.*

When terrible weeping replaced his mother's screams, he turned and fled, stumbling, falling, banging his shins but scrambling up the stairs. He raced into his room and shut the door. Quietly, so carefully.

I sure as hell don't see myself in him.

I'm glad, Con thought fiercely. *I wish he* wasn't *my father.*

You know I never wanted him.

He wished *she* wasn't his mother, either.

Conall cried again, and was ashamed. The snot he wiped away with the back of his hand was mixed with blood, and he didn't care.

Sometime in the next couple of hours, all his rage and bewilderment and hurt hardened until his emotions felt petrified, like a slice of smooth stone he had on his desk that had once been wood. At first the sensation was uncomfortable, but that wasn't surprising, was it? Think how compressed the wood must have been to become stone. All moisture squeezed out. After a while, the glossy, hard surface in his chest felt okay, and he could replay what he'd heard his parents say without feeling anything in particular.

He did stiffen when he heard footsteps on the

stairs and his bedroom door opened. By this time he couldn't open his eyes at all. If Mom pretended to care now, he didn't know what he'd do.

But it was Duncan who swore, and said, "Have you put ice on your eyes?"

Conall shook his head.

"I'll get you some."

Duncan's footsteps retreated. Eventually he came back with a bag of frozen vegetables and a washcloth to wrap it in. He said, "There's a lot of blood in the bathroom," and Con shrugged.

"Nose," he mumbled, and grabbed for the bag as it slipped.

"Don't suppose you want to tell me what it was about."

He shook his head.

"Did Dad do this to you?" Duncan's voice had changed a while back to sounding almost like a man's. Now it was so hard, so unforgiving, that change was complete. "Or Mom?"

"No," Con whispered, wincing when he realized one of his teeth was loose. He wriggled it with his tongue.

"I saw the kitchen."

"They were fighting. This was a couple of guys."

Duncan sighed. His weight compressed the edge of the bed as he sat. "You know, you can run away instead of getting into it every time."

Conall shook his head.

"Sometimes it's better to be smart than brave."

He got it, he really did. But…there wasn't much to him. Pride was about it. If he ran, he wouldn't even have that. He wasn't like his big brother.

He told himself he didn't care, and almost believed it.

Conall shrugged again. Duncan tried to talk to him for a bit, then finally gave up and went away.

Alone again, Con realized that today, for the first time, not caring was easy.

CHAPTER ONE

DOMINGO GARCIA STAGGERED toward the storefront and artistically fell against the large window, which shivered from the blow but didn't break. He slid to a sitting position on the sidewalk.

Crouching on a concrete staircase dropping to a basement apartment not thirty feet away, Conall MacLachlan watched with admiration. Garcia played a homeless guy like no one else; Conall didn't even want to know what he'd rolled in to make him stink like that. The sacky army fatigue jacket did a great job of hiding a bulletproof vest.

As they'd hoped, the steel door to the storefront slammed open. Two big men appeared, one with a snarling Rottweiler on a leash, the other using his body to prop open the door.

Clutching his bottle of cheap wine in a brown paper bag, Garcia peered blearily at them. "Hey, dudes." He pretended to look alarmed. "Your dog won't bite me, will he?"

The handler laughed and told Garcia in obscene terms that yes, indeed, the Rottweiler would rip him to shreds if he didn't move on.

Garcia whimpered and got to his hands and knees, coincidentally a few feet closer to the door and the dog's frothing muzzle. Then he demonstrated his one true talent. Everyone had to have one. Garcia's was handier than most, however, for a special agent with the United States Drug Enforcement Agency. He could puke at will, assuming he'd primed his stomach in advance. Conall had sat with him an hour ago while he consumed two huge burritos in green sauce at a little Mexican joint a few blocks away.

Now, with sound effects and spectacular retching, he brought them back up. Vomit spattered the dog handler's shoes and pant legs; even the Rottweiler backed up in alarm. Garcia managed to drop the wine bottle and shatter it, adding to the mess and stench. The other guy swore. All their attention was on the stinking pool of vomit and the seemingly drunken homeless man crawling on the sidewalk. The dog whined and scrabbled backward toward the door.

Conall murmured into his transmitter, "Now," and moved, coming in fast while Johnny Harris did the same from the other direction. At the same time Garcia sprang to his feet, his Sig Pro pistol in his hand.

"Drop your weapons! This is a police raid. Drop them now!"

Conall slammed the doorkeeper to the sidewalk

and went in first, low and fast. Garcia leaped over the dog and was on his heels. Reinforcements sprang from a van parked halfway down the block and within seconds were on the two guards, dragging them away from the window glass in case of flying bullets before cuffing them.

The interior was poorly lit, the window having been covered with butcher paper, the bare overhead bulb maybe forty watts. Two men burst from a rear hallway, firing as they came. Conall took one out with his Glock while Garcia brought down the other. They kicked weapons away and plunged down the hall. The back of the store was the drug distribution facility; the guys packaging coke were already wild-eyed at the spray of bullets and had their hands up before Conall went through the door.

Garcia and Harris checked out the bathroom and office while Conall kept his gun on the pathetic trio in front of him. Within moments, other agents arrived to cuff and arrest.

It was all over but the cleanup. Conall's experienced eye weighed and measured the packets of cocaine, leaving him disappointed. They wouldn't be taking anywhere near as much off the street as they'd hoped. Either this operation was more small-time than they'd realized, or a shipment was due and their timing had sucked.

That was life, he thought philosophically, holstering his weapon.

And I'm bored out of my frigging skull.

As he all too often seemed to be these days.

LIA WOODS SAT on the middle cushion of the sofa, a boy perched stiffly to each side of her, and watched *Transformers*. She'd seen bits and pieces of it before; Walker and Brendan were addicted. This was the first time she'd sat down with the intention of watching beginning to end.

In her opinion, the movies were too violent for the boys at eight and ten, especially as traumatized as they were. But their mother had given them both the first two Transformers movies on DVD, and Lia couldn't criticize Mom, even by implication. Not when she'd died only three days ago.

Besides, she could see the appeal of the movies to the boys. Chaos erupts, and regular, nerdy guy seizes control and ultimately triumphs. The fantasy must be huge for two boys who'd now lost both parents, who had no idea what would happen to them. For them, it was a fantasy worth clinging to.

The sound of a car engine outside made her frown. People didn't drop in on her unexpectedly. Her farmhouse on ten acres was reached by a dead-end gravel road she shared with five other houses. Only one was past hers. There were new neighbors there, renters, Lia thought. She hadn't tried to get to know them. She'd as soon keep her distance from all her neighbors, and was glad the men she'd seen coming and going weren't friendly.

Or nosy.

This car, though, had definitely turned in her driveway. She touched each of the boys reassuringly and murmured, "I'd better go see who's here."

Walker turned his head enough to gaze blankly at her before looking back at the TV; Brendan kept staring as if she hadn't spoken.

Lia left them in the living room and paused at the foot of the stairs, listening. Quiet. Arturo and Julia must still be asleep. Thirteen-year-old Sorrel was most likely lying on her bed listening to her iPod, or prowling the internet on Lia's laptop. Maybe harmless, maybe not, but Lia couldn't watch her 24/7. She could and would check later to see what websites Sorrel had visited.

Outside, a car door slammed. She opened the front door and had a freezing moment of panic. The dark sedan, shiny except for a thin coat of dust from her road, was clearly government issue, as was the man walking toward her, wearing a suit, white shirt and tie. If he was from Immigration, she was screwed. There was no time to hide Arturo and Julia.

He paused at the foot of the stairs. "Ms. Woods?"

"Yes." She stepped onto the porch and drew the door mostly closed behind her. "What can I do for you?"

He was a large man, in his late forties or early fifties at a guess, with a receding hairline and the beginning of a paunch. "I'm with the United States Drug Enforcement Agency. I'd like to talk to you."

Lia knew she was gaping. "To *me?*"

He smiled. "You're not under suspicion, I promise you. I'm hoping that you can help us."

"Help you." She must sound like an idiot, but… wow. She'd never even smoked marijuana. Excessive drinking had been a way bigger problem in her high school than drug use. Her crowd in college hadn't been into drugs, either. Was there any chance he was lying and really with Immigration after all?

"May I explain?" he said.

She blinked. "Yes, sure. Why don't you— Actually, let's stay out here on the porch. Give me a moment to check on the kids."

He remained politely outside while she dashed in, peeked at Walker and Brendan, then tore upstairs to Sorrel's room. The teenager was indeed using the laptop.

"There's a government type here I have to talk to," Lia said. "Will you listen for the little ones and take care of them if they wake up?"

"I guess so." Sorrel wrinkled her nose. "Unless Arturo's diaper is gross. I don't want to do gross."

"They should keep sleeping for another hour. But just in case. Okay?"

She shrugged, her attention returning to the monitor. "Okay."

The teenager didn't know that two-year-old Arturo and eight-month-old Julia were in this country—and being harbored by Lia—illegally; Lia made sure her legitimate foster children never had a clue. Kids came and went here. There was no reason any of them would question why one social worker brought some of them to her door and a different one the others.

Then Lia bounded downstairs and went out on the front porch, closing the door behind her this time. The man turned to face her.

He held out his badge. "I'm Special Agent Wes Phillips."

She scrutinized the badge, as if she'd know a fake if she saw it, nodded and said, "Please, sit down."

He gingerly settled into one of the pair of Adirondack chairs. She took the other one.

"I'd invite you in, but I'm a foster parent and have kids napping. Plus, I thought maybe you'd rather we weren't overheard."

"I'd definitely rather not be overheard by children." He hesitated. "This is actually a matter that concerns your neighbors to the south."

Her first reaction was relief. It was hard to make herself think, to orient herself. The south? "That nice place? Someone new is in it. I'm afraid I haven't even met them."

"Have you noticed them coming and going?"

"An occasional car. Either there are several men living there, or else whoever is renting the place has lots of friends."

He nodded. "We have reason to believe the house is being used by members of a drug distribution network."

"You're not talking about methamphetamine, are you?" she asked in alarm. "Are they making it there? Can't it be really volatile? Are my kids in danger?"

"No, no. We're frankly not sure what's up in that house, but don't believe meth is involved."

Wariness returning, Lia straightened her spine. "How is it you think I can help you?"

"I came out to determine whether the house can be viewed from yours." He had his back to it currently, although from here woods blocked all but the rooftop and a corner of the enormous garage. "We'd like to place it under surveillance. Yours is the only building within visual range. What we'd like is to, er, rent your house from you for a period of time."

"A period of time."

"It may be weeks to several months."

She didn't even have to think about it. "No."

"I'm sure we could provide you with—"

"No. This is my home. I'm currently caring for five traumatized children. Two of them lost their mother to leukemia this week. One is a teenager prone to acting out. This is their home, too, the only security they have right now. I will not uproot them."

Plainly, he didn't like that. "You don't mind that your nearest neighbors may be dealing drugs?"

"Of course I mind. But what you're asking is impossible."

He studied her. "This is a large house."

Oh, damn. "Yes, it is," she said cautiously.

He seemed to ponder. "Perhaps it would work best if your neighbors see life continuing as usual here."

She waited.

"Do you use your attic?"

She'd known that was coming. After a hesitation, Lia admitted, "No. It's pretty bare-bones up there, though."

"Would you consider allowing two agents from the DEA to conduct a stakeout from your attic?"

She queried what that meant; he explained. Assuming there actually *was* an adequate view from upstairs, they would use advanced surveillance equipment to watch the nearby home from the attic windows. The agents could sleep up there as well. He did concede that they'd need to use a bathroom if one wasn't available in the attic.

"There isn't," she said flatly.

"It would also, er, be convenient if you could be persuaded to provide them with meals. We'd give you reimbursement for groceries and an additional stipend, of course."

The entire time he talked, Lia thought furiously. Would the DEA have any reason to investigate which children had legitimately been placed in her home? Perhaps Arturo and Julia could be moved. They were short-term anyway; she didn't expect to have them for more than a week or two. Their mother had been swept up in a raid on a tulip bulb farm here in the county and immediately deported. Supposedly a family member would be coming for them if the mother couldn't make her way back quickly.

Lia might look more suspicious if she refused than if she agreed. And she did hate the idea of something like cocaine or heroin being sold from her next-door neighbor's house. The whole idea was surreal; she might have expected it in New York City, but not in rural Washington State.

But...weeks or months?

"Would these agents be...respectful?" she asked

slowly. "I'm a single woman, and I currently have a thirteen-year-old girl living here."

Phillips's smile held the knowledge that he was about to get what he wanted. "I guarantee you have nothing to fear from our agents."

Oh, yes, she did, but she couldn't say that. Lia sighed and stood. "Then let me show you the attic and you can see if it's suitable. Please try not to wake the children."

She felt nothing but apprehension as she led the way upstairs, shaking her head slightly at Sorrel's startled look when they passed her open bedroom door. At worst, the resident government agents would discover that she regularly harbored illegal immigrants. At best...well, having two strange men—or maybe a man and a woman?—living in her house, sharing one of only two antiquated bathrooms, expecting to be fed, would be a horrible inconvenience. Never-ending houseguests she hadn't exactly invited in the first place.

But...how could she say no?

She couldn't. And that's what, in the end, it came down to, wasn't it?

CONALL COULD NOT BELIEVE he was here, driving through the town of Stimson where he'd grown up. Out of the twenty-one domestic divisions of the DEA, the Seattle division, covering Washington, Oregon and Idaho, was the only one he would have balked at being assigned to. When he left home, he'd never intended to come back.

He hadn't even come home for his brother Niall's wedding. The pang of guilt was unavoidable; he knew Niall had wanted him to be there. He might even have made it if he hadn't gotten shot two weeks before the wedding. Yeah, he'd been out of the hospital and could have come anyway, but recuperation seemed like a good excuse.

A good excuse for him, that is, not his brother. He hadn't told Niall about his near-death experience. In their every-few-months phone conversations, Conall tended to keep talk about his job light, even though Niall was a cop and would probably be able to handle the grimmer aspects of what Conall did. Maybe.

His fingers tightened rhythmically on the steering wheel as his attention was arrested by an obviously official, handsome brick building. Oh, damn. That was the new public safety building right there, housing the police station and city government. It was linked to the equally new courthouse by a glass-enclosed walkway.

The knowledge that Niall and Con's big brother Duncan might be in there right this minute unsettled him more than he wanted to admit. God. Was he going to have to see Duncan?

He knew the answer. Yes. This was his operation. He had an obligation to liaise with local law enforcement. Which meant newly appointed Police Chief Duncan MacLachlan.

The sense of unreality swept over Conall again. Was God playing a nasty prank on him?

He'd tried to say no to this assignment. The suits upstairs didn't like the word. Yes, they understood that he'd applied for a position with FAST—the Foreign-Deployed Advisory and Support Teams— that were interjected where needed abroad. The decision would not be made immediately. Even if he was chosen, the transfer could wait.

Somebody, somewhere, had noticed that he was, apparently, the only agent within the entire DEA from this particular corner of Washington State. Con had no idea why the fact that he'd gone to high school here was considered to be an advantage. He wouldn't be conducting some kind of deep cover investigation that required him to have to act like a local. Good God, he'd fail if that was the object; he didn't recognize half the businesses he was passing on the main street of the modest-size county seat.

The man who had ridden for the most part quietly in the passenger seat beside Conall said now, "Do you have family here?"

Conall wanted to lie, but knew he wouldn't get away with it. "Yes," he said shortly. "Two brothers. One is the police chief."

Jeff Henderson looked thoughtfully at him. "Handy."

Conall grunted.

He didn't know Henderson, had never worked with him, but hadn't learned anything bad about him, either, when he asked around. Henderson had been dragged in from the El Paso division. Apparently Seattle was currently conducting some major, named operation that had everyone excited and left them understaffed when something new cropped up.

"We're not stopping?"

Oh, crap, Conall thought. They should. Or he should have set up a meet.

"No. I'll call Duncan. I don't want word to get around that a couple of DEA agents are in town."

Henderson nodded, apparently satisfied. "You know your way?"

"Yeah." He was a little startled to realize how clearly he remembered every byway in the county.

The town proper fell behind them, although they didn't leave the city limits, which had been drawn by an optimist. Or maybe, he discovered, a realist after all since they passed several major new housing developments and an elementary school that hadn't been here in his day.

They did shortly find themselves on a typical country road, however, with a yellow strip down the middle and no shoulders to separate road from ditches. Homes were on acreage now; animals grazed behind barbed wire or board fences with peeling paint. The countryside was pretty, though, the grass lush, maples and alders bright with spring greenery, a scattering of wildflowers adding cheer to the roadside. Deciduous trees gave way to forests of Douglas fir and cedar in the foothills, above which glimpses of white-peaked Cascade Mountains could be seen.

Henderson kept his thoughts to himself, although he eyed the scenery with interest. Conall found himself reluctantly wondering about his temporary partner. Normally he tried not to get personal, but this was the kind of job that would have them spending long hours together. They'd get to know each other one way or another.

"You married?" he finally asked.

Henderson glanced at him. "Yeah. I have two kids, four and six. You?"

"No. No wife, no kids." God forbid.

"You know this house is stuffed full of kids."

That snapped Conall's attention from the road ahead. "What?"

"You didn't know?"

He frowned. "I got pulled in at the last minute. All I was told was that the home-owner is willing to let us use the attic and will feed us."

"She runs a foster home. Records show she currently has three kids, but I guess from what she told Phillips, she has another two on a real short-term basis."

"*Five* children?"

"That's the word."

Conall groaned. "Does the attic door have a lock?"

"If not, we may want to install one," Henderson said, faint amusement in his voice.

"If we have to deal with kids, you're the specialist."

"Okay." He leaned forward. "Is that the street?"

It was. Conall slowed and put on the turn signal, even though he hadn't passed another car in the past five minutes.

The road was gravel and made perilous by potholes. Conall drove at the pace of a crawl. The shocks were none too good on this aging Chevy Suburban, borrowed from the fleet of seized vehicles kept for occasions when agents wanted to be inconspicuous. Conall had been assured that, belying the appearance of dents and a few pockets of rust, there was plenty of power under the hood if he needed it.

A small grunt escaped Henderson when the right front wheel descended with a clunk into a particularly deep crater. "Why the hell isn't this road paved?"

"It's private. Only five houses on it." Conall had counted the mailboxes out at the corner. "Too expensive to pave, even if the residents could all agree to share the cost."

"The least they could do is fill the damn holes."

Conall didn't bother to explain what a headache it could be for residents to coordinate on even such a relatively modest project. A couple of the households might be short on bucks; the home-owners closest to the county road might not feel their share should be equal. Probably the only ve-hicles that used the road belonged to home-own-ers or visitors; kids would have to catch the school bus out at the main road, and obviously the post office had declined to deliver off the pavement. Probably even garbage cans had to be hauled out to the main road for pickup.

Which gave him the idea that, once he knew what day was garbage pickup, he'd wander out here and investigate the neighbor's cans. If they were smart, they wouldn't be careless enough to dump anything but kitchen garbage and the like in their cans, but you never knew. Crooks were often stupid, a fact for which law enforcement person-nel gave frequent thanks.

Last driveway on the right, his directions had said. No house number was displayed at the head of the driveway he turned down. Scruffy woods initially screened the house from view; alders, vine maples, a scattering of larger firs and cedars, scraggly blackberries and lower growing salal. At least there were no potholes here, instead a pair of beaten earth tracks separated by a grassy hump.

They came out of the woods to see fenced pasture and, ahead, a white-painted farmhouse that probably dated to the 1920s or 1930s. Red and white beef cattle grazed the pasture on one side of the driveway, while on the other side a fat, shaggy Shetland pony and a sway-backed horse of well-used vintage lifted their heads from the grass to gaze with mild interest at the passing Suburban.

As they neared, Conall could see that the house had two full stories with a dormered attic to boot. Several of the wood-framed, small-paned, sash windows on the first floor boasted window boxes filled with bright pink and fuchsia geraniums. The wide, covered front porch with a railing looked welcoming.

The one outbuilding, probably a barn in its past, apparently served now as garage. The double doors stood open and he could see what he thought was a Subaru station wagon in the shadowy interior.

The setup was good, he reflected; they'd been lucky to find a neighbor willing to cooperate with a surveillance team, and even luckier given that this one and only suitable house happened to have an unused attic that offered a perfect vantage point. Still, he studied the facade nervously, half expecting children to swarm out like killer bees from a hive. God, he hoped there wouldn't be babies squalling all night. Although babies might be preferable to kids of an age to be curious.

No one, adult or child, swarmed out. Or even peered. Lace curtains didn't twitch.

"This woman expecting us?" Conall asked.

"So I'm told." Henderson glanced at his watch. "It's nap time."

"Is that like the eye of the hurricane?"

His partner's raw-boned face split into a grin. "That's one way to describe it."

They parked beside the barn and pulled out a duffel bag each before starting across the yard to the house. They could come back later for their equipment.

Walking across the lawn, Conall realized he felt no sense of anticipation whatsoever. Okay, this might not be the most exciting operation ever; surveillance gigs never were. Even so, he used to feel at least mildly stirred at the beginning of any new challenge. Lately…

He shook off the momentary brood. He liked action, not sitting in the middle of a cow pasture watching grass grow. No wonder he wasn't worked up about this particular assignment.

Somehow he hadn't convinced himself. Boredom wasn't the whole problem. His dissatisfaction had other causes. He just hadn't nailed them down yet.

There was no doorbell. Henderson rapped lightly instead. Conall thought he heard a TV on somewhere inside. They waited, finally hearing the sound of someone approaching.

The door opened and a woman stood there. Behind her was a girl—maybe a teenager?—but Conall was only peripherally aware of her. He couldn't tear his gaze from the woman.

He hadn't come into this situation with any expectation, so he didn't know why he was so startled. Then he barely stopped himself from grimacing. Of course he knew why; what he hadn't expected was to find himself sexually riveted by their reluctant hostess.

She was average height, maybe five foot five or six. Slender but strong, her curves subtle but present. Her feet were bare, her jeans fit snugly over narrow hips and fabulous legs. Her yield-sign yellow T-shirt fit even better, displaying a narrow rib cage and high, apple-size breasts to perfection.

Her face…well, damn, she was beautiful. Stunning. High, winged eyebrows, a model's cheekbones, a luscious mouth and small straight nose. Her eyes were an unusual mix of brown and green. The colors were deep and rich, not like the typical hazel. And her thick, wavy hair was midnight-black and hung loose to her waist.

God help him, he wanted to grab her, carry her

upstairs and find a bedroom. And they hadn't even said hello.

Man. This wasn't a good start to what promised to be a lengthy stay. Conall had the wry thought that the stay might be considerably shortened if she noticed he was aroused.

And maybe that would be a good thing. Right this minute, Conall couldn't imagine living in close proximity to her without breaking down at some point and coming on to her.

Way to lose his job.

His jaw flexed. For God's sake, if he was that desperate, he'd look for a woman while he was in town. Any woman but this one. Get laid.

He realized how long the silence had stretched. Conall cleared his throat. "Special Agent Conall MacLachlan from the DEA. This is Jeff Henderson. I believe you were expecting us."

CHAPTER TWO

HENDERSON HAD BEEN gaping, too, but he managed to snap out of it and offer his hand. They shook. Conall offered his badge instead of his hand. He didn't dare touch her.

She examined it briefly, then glanced at their duffel bags. "That's all you have?"

"We have more stuff in the car. We thought we'd find out where we're to set up first."

She looked past them to the gray Suburban. "At least you don't have one of those government cars. That would have given you away in a heartbeat."

Jeff's face relaxed into a smile. "True enough, ma'am."

"No ma'am." She moved back to let them in. "I'm not old enough to be a *ma'am*. Call me Lia."

Lia Woods. That was her name. Was Lia Hispanic? Only partly, he thought, given the delicious pale cream of her skin where it wasn't tanned, as her face and forearms were. And her eyes were a remarkable color.

"Lia," he said politely.

"This is Sorrel," she said, "my foster daughter."

The girl was pretty, in an unfinished way. Skinny but also buxom. She had her arms crossed over her breasts as if she was trying to hide them. Blond hair was pixy-short, her eyes blue and bottomless, her mouth pouty. Blushing, she mumbled, "Hello," but Conall had the impression she hadn't decided how she felt about their presence.

They stood in a foyer from which a staircase rose to the second floor. The television was on in a room to his right. He could see the flickering screen from here. To the left seemed to be a dining room; a high chair was visible at one end of a long table.

Lia crossed her arms, looking from one to the other of them. "You understand that I have a number of foster children."

"Yes."

Both nodded.

"The two little ones are currently asleep. Chances are you won't see much of them. Julia is a baby, and Arturo a toddler." She pronounced *Julia* the Spanish way.

They both nodded again. Sorrel watched them without expression.

"Let me take you on a quick tour and introduce you to the other kids." Lia led the way into the living room, where two boys sat on the sofa watching TV.

The room was set up to be kid-friendly, the furniture big, comfortable, sturdy. The coffee table had rounded corners. Bookcases protected their contents with paneled doors on the bottom and glass-fronted ones on top. Some baby paraphernalia sat around, but Conall didn't see much in the way of toys. Did she let the kids watch television all day?

"Walker," she said in a gentle voice. "Brendan. Would you please pause your movie?"

One of them fumbled for the remote. Then they both gazed at the men. They had to be the two saddest looking kids he'd ever seen. Grief and hopelessness clung to them like the scent of tobacco on a smoker. Their eyes held…nothing. Not even interest.

They were trying damned hard to shut down all emotional content. He recognized the process, having gone through it. He didn't know whether to wish them well with it, or hope someone, or something, intervened.

His child specialist was staring at them with something akin to horror and was being useless. *Somebody* had to say something.

Apparently, that would be him. "Walker. Brendan. My name is Conall. This is Jeff."

After a significant pause, one of the boys recalled his manners enough to say, "Hi."

"I know we'll be seeing you around," Conall said awkwardly.

The same boy nodded. He was the older of the two, Con realized, although they looked so much alike they had to be brothers.

Lia guided the two men out of the living room. Behind them the movie resumed.

She hustled them through the dining room and showed them the kitchen.

"I serve the kids three meals a day and can include you in any or all of those," she told them. "If you'd rather make your own breakfasts or lunches, just let me know in advance and help yourself to anything you can find."

She didn't say whether those meals would be sugary cereals and peanut butter and jelly sandwiches. Right this minute, Conall didn't care. He kept his voice low. "What's with the boys?"

Her glance was cool. "Their mother died five days ago. She had adult-onset leukemia. Six weeks ago, she was healthy. She went downhill really fast."

"They don't have other family?" Jeff asked.

"No. The boys barely remember their father, who abandoned them a long time ago. If there are grandparents or other relatives on that side, no one knows anything about them. The boys' mother grew up in foster care."

"So now they will, too." Conall wasn't naive; in his line of work, he didn't deal much with kids, but sometimes there were ones living in houses where

he made busts. He'd undoubtedly been responsible for sending some into foster care himself.
He'd never had to live with any of those children
before, though.

"Yes," she said. "Unless they're fortunate
enough to be adopted."

He didn't have to read her tone to know how unlikely that was, especially with the boys as withdrawn as they were. And being a pair besides. Or
would they end up separated? That was an idea
that he instinctively rebelled against.

He and Henderson both were quiet as she
showed them a home office on the ground floor,
and opened the door to a large bathroom and, at
the back of the house, a glassed-in porch that was
now a laundry slash mud room.

"You can do your own laundry, or toss your
clothes in the hamper and I'll add them to any
loads I put in."

They nodded acknowledgement.

Upstairs was another bathroom and bedrooms.
Hers, one with a closed door that was apparently
where the little kids slept, a room shared by the
boys, and a smaller one that was obviously the
teenager's. It was little larger than a walk-in closet;
maybe originally intended to be a sewing room
or nursery?

"Sorrel understands that the attic is off-limits,"
Lia said, her tone pleasant but steel underlying it.

The teenager looked sulky but ducked into her bedroom as Lia led the way to the door at the end of the hall. Like all the others in the house, it had an old-fashioned brass knob. It also had an ancient keyed lock with no key in it.

Behind it was a staircase steep enough Conall wouldn't have wanted to navigate it after a few beers. Lia's hips swayed seductively at his eye level as she preceded him up.

Don't look.

He couldn't not.

It was a relief to have her stand aside at the top, where a huge open space was poorly lit by only four, smallish dormer windows. The dormers would allow them to stand upright in front of the windows, but the men especially would have to duck their heads in much of the rest of the space.

"Yesterday I washed those windows on the inside." Lia sounded apologetic. "I can't even get my hose to squirt that high on the outside."

The two light fixtures up here didn't do much to illuminate the attic, especially around the edges where the ceiling sloped sharply down. As in many old houses, it was cluttered with unwanted pieces of furniture, piles of cardboard boxes filled with who knew what, more modern plastic tubs stacked closer to the top of the staircase, and a few oddities and antiques. A naked female clothing mannequin with a bald head stared vacuously at them. Conall saw an old treadle sewing machine cheek by jowl with a gigantic plastic duck.

Lia's gaze had followed his. "I think the duck rode on a Fourth of July float every year until my uncle died."

"The mannequin?"

"My aunt owned a small clothing store in town." She looked around as if she hadn't thought about the contents of the attic in ages. "I don't actually know what's up here. Someday I should go through it all, but I always seem to be too busy."

"The animals out there yours?" Jeff was peering out one of the windows.

"The horse and the pony are. They're fun for the kids. I rent the other pasture out. Keeps it from growing up in blackberries."

Conall found himself curious about her and wanting to ask questions, but none of them had anything to do with the job. Had she inherited the house? Why did she foster kids instead of having her own? Why wasn't a woman who looked like that married?

Focus, he told himself. Lia Woods wasn't the point here. Her neighbors were.

He walked to the second of the two windows looking to the south and saw immediately that they had a bird's-eye view of the target. Except for the film on the outside of the glass, it couldn't be better.

"Do these open?" he asked.

"I have no idea."

From the reluctance of the latch to give way, he could tell no one had tried in years. He muttered a swear word or two under his breath, scraped the latch open and heaved upward at the sash window. It groaned, shuddered and rose two inches before jolting to a stop.

"Hell."

"Is this not going to work for you guys?" Lia sounded hopeful. And why shouldn't she? She'd probably rather they got in their Suburban and drove away never to be seen again.

"We'll loosen it up," Conall said. He saw that Henderson was using his muscle to work on the other south-facing window. They'd need the damn things open, if only to get some air flow up here. Not surprisingly, the attic was stuffy and warm, and that was on a cloudy day with the temp reading sixty-nine when they passed a bank in town. If this op dragged on long, with spring edging into summer, it could turn hellish up here.

He was starting to turn away from the window when movement caught his eye. "Damn," he muttered, and Henderson joined him. Oh, yeah, the neighbors definitely had a dog.

"You know those folks have a Doberman?" he asked.

Lia hurried over, catching a glimpse before the

dog trotted around the corner of the other house. "No." She sounded worried. "Maybe they put up an invisible fence of some kind. I haven't seen it in the pasture. If I do, I'll have to talk to them—" She looked fiercely at the two men. "I'll have to do something if that animal scares my horses or attacks them."

"Let's worry about that if it happens," Conall said.

She didn't look happy, but finally reverted to tour guide, pointing out the bed she'd set up in the far corner. She had the polite thing down pat, and he imagined her giving much the same spiel to newly arrived foster kids. Except she'd probably offer it to them with more warmth than he was hearing. No, she wasn't thrilled about their presence, the subtext was there. "I set it up yesterday and put fresh sheets on it. I gather that you won't be sleeping at the same time?"

Conall said, "No."

She nodded. "If it gets uncomfortable up here, there's a twin bed in the room Julia and Arturo are in right now. I don't expect them to be with me over a week. You can have that room once they're gone."

Right across the hall from hers. Conall imagined sleeping that near to her. Oh, yeah, that would be restful. He shot a narrow-eyed glance at Henderson to see if he was thinking the same, but he was looking around the attic with curiosity. Beyond his initial reaction, he hadn't registered a lot of awareness of her. Conall's shoulders relaxed slightly, which had him frowning. Another surprise; he hadn't liked the idea that his partner might be slavering over her.

Like I am?

She was a sexy woman. So what? He'd had plenty of sexy women before. Getting them seemed to be one of *his* talents. Maybe it was the appeal of a man who didn't really give a damn one way or the other. If a woman who attracted him made it plain she wasn't available or interested, he shrugged and moved on. There were plenty of fish in the sea. Conall didn't remember ever feeling anything approaching jealousy.

Lia might have a boyfriend or fiancé. He wondered if Phillips had thought to ask. A regular visitor here could threaten their anonymity. If that regular visitor was a man who felt possessive of her, he wouldn't like their presence.

Conall wouldn't like his, and definitely didn't like the idea of a man having the right to go into her bedroom with her and shut the door.

"Do you have regular visitors? Family? Friends? Boyfriend?" His tone was abrupt.

Her chin edged up slightly and he saw a flare of irritation in those richly colored eyes. "Are you wondering how I'll explain you?"

"Something like that."

"These people next door are strangers. None of my friends have anything to do with them."

"Are you so sure? Chances are they shop for groceries locally, pay their utility bills in town, wander the aisles in the hardware store, pump gas at the Arco or Shell station, stand in line to buy stamps at the post office. All they have to do is overhear a snatch of gossip. Maybe a word of concern about Lia, stuck with those feds doing a surveillance."

She stared at him mulishly, but he could also tell that what he'd said had registered.

"What we need is zero gossip. No one can know we're here." He hesitated. "Our first and biggest problem is the kids. I presume they're still in school."

"The boys have been out the past two weeks. We're close enough to the end of the school year, I think I'll keep them home. You saw them. They're not ready to go back."

Good. Great. That left them with a teenage girl who would like nothing better than to have a dramatic story to share about the two federal agents spying on the neighbors from her foster mom's attic.

"Sorrel…" Lia hesitated.

"Can you guarantee she'll keep her mouth shut?"

She glared at him. "Maybe your advance guy should have nixed my household."

Conall said bluntly, "He probably would have, if there'd been any other options at all."

Her fingers flexed into fists, then relaxed. "I'll talk to her."

"Can you keep her home from school?"

"I have my teaching certificate. I can homeschool the boys, but I'm not certified for secondary education." She looked past him toward the mannequin. He could tell she was thinking. "I don't actually think she'll be a problem. Sorrel came to me only a month ago. She hasn't made friends yet. She claims no one will even talk to her."

He remembered middle school and high school all too well. "All the more reason for her to be delighted by an attention-grabbing story."

Frustration showed on her face. "What do you suggest?"

"I'll talk to her." Seeing the way her expression changed, he corrected himself. "*We'll* talk to her."

"All right." She looked from him to Henderson and back. "Is there anything else you need from me right now?"

"Maybe a key to the front door? Although we won't be coming and going much. We don't want to draw any attention."

"I have extra keys."

"You didn't answer my question about visitors."

Annoyance flared in her eyes again. "I gather I'm supposed to curtail all social life."

"It would be helpful if you could conduct your social life elsewhere." He was going for law enforcement formal, but had a bad feeling he was coming off sounding like an ass instead.

Yep. Her expression morphed into active dislike. "Consider it done." With that, she turned and left them alone in the attic.

"Way to get the lady on our side," Henderson remarked mildly.

Conall gave him a cold look and said, "Let's get the rest of our crap."

DUNCAN MACLACHLAN sat behind his desk and tried to concentrate on the document open on his computer. The Vehicle Impoundment and Inventory Procedure did not qualify as riveting reading, but he'd made it his mission to review and potentially revise all the department procedures and policies, from Field Training to Case Tracking. None had been reworked in at least ten years, and police work had changed, if only because of technological and scientific advances.

He kept thinking that if he hung on for another hour, he could take an early lunch with Jane and Fiona. He'd promised to bring takeout from the Snow Goose Deli to Jane's store, Dance Dreams. Owning her own business meant his wife could take their now five-and-a-half-month-old daughter to work with her. They wouldn't have to think about looking into preschools for at least another year.

Duncan realized he was smiling fatuously at the framed photo of his wife and daughter that sat on his desk. There were times he still didn't understand how it had happened to him—falling in love, getting married, starting a family. He'd never intended to do any of those things. And here he was, still crazy about his wife, and head over heels in love with their daughter, a cherub with her uncle Niall's red hair.

Damn, he thought, and focused his eyes again on the computer monitor.

When an officer impounds a vehicle, the officer shall complete the Vehicle Impound Report indicating the reason for impoundment in the narrative portion at the bottom of the form.

Did they absolutely have to use the word *impound* three times in one sentence?

Clarity, he reminded himself, was the goal, not elegant writing.

His phone rang, and feeling embarrassingly grateful for the interruption he grabbed it.

"MacLachlan."

His administrative assistant cleared his throat. "Chief, you have a caller who says his name is, er, MacLachlan. Conall."

Duncan's youngest brother hadn't spoken to him in over ten years. And he was calling now?

"Put him through," he said brusquely. What could have happened that would have motivated his angry brother to be willing to talk to him? When he heard the click of the call being transferred, he said, "Conall, is it really you?"

"Yeah, it's really me." Startlingly, his voice hadn't changed at all. It sounded a lot like Niall's, maybe a little huskier.

"Damn."

"That's friendly."

"You've caught me by surprise."

"Yeah, I imagine I have." There was a momentary pause. "I'm actually calling on official business. Believe it or not, I'm here in Stimson pursuing an investigation. I'm going to be conducting a surveillance within your city limits."

Duncan stiffened. "Are you."

"That's the plan."

"Do you have a warrant?"

"If I had a warrant, I'd go in and toss the place. What I have is permission from a home-owner to use her premises to watch her neighbor's house until we see something interesting enough to justify that warrant."

"Why is this the first I'm hearing about it?"

"I don't know," his brother said. "I got pulled in late. I've been working out of the Miami Division."

"So Niall said."

"I'm currently on loan to Seattle. They've got something big going and needed extra manpower."

"Are you already here?" he asked.

"Yeah. Flew into Seattle last night."

"Does Niall know?"

"He's next on my list. I figured I owed you a courtesy call first."

Because he was police chief, not because they were brothers. That stung, although it shouldn't have after years of estrangement.

"All right," Duncan said. "Do you plan to come by the office to give me the details?"

"I'd rather not. I'm trying to fly below the radar." Conall was quiet for a moment. "I'm hoping we can meet somewhere that looks unofficial."

"You can come by the house." The words were out before he could recall them. "You know I'm not in the old place."

"I did know that. You sent me a check for part of the proceeds when you sold it."

He had. Duncan had insisted on splitting what he made on their parents' house, little though it was after the mortgage was paid out. Still, it was the closest thing any of them had to an inheritance from their worthless parents.

"You can meet my wife."

"I meant to come to Niall's wedding."

"Then why didn't you?"

This silence was a long one, and heavy with everything that hadn't been said in the past decade. Or perhaps that was in his imagination.

"I was wounded," Conall said finally.

Duncan's reaction was visceral. It had been his greatest fear that one of these days he'd get a call from some higher-up at the DEA letting him know that they were very sorry, but his brother Conall had been killed in the line of duty. Niall was the one who talked to Conall from time to time, and he'd admitted he sometimes thought their youngest brother had a death wish. At the very least, he was a cold-blooded son of a bitch who lived for the adrenaline rush risk-taking gave him. Duncan wondered how much else he was capable of feeling.

If that wasn't a chilling thought.

"You didn't tell Niall."

"I didn't want to worry him. Especially right before his wedding." Conall laughed. "Both of you married. Blows me away."

"You know I have a baby daughter now."

"You sent me a birth announcement."

"Thanks for the congratulation."

"Did you expect one?" His brother's voice hardened.

"No." Shit. He bent his head and pinched the bridge of his nose. "Maybe hoped." His own voice had come out rougher. "Whether you know it or not, I've missed you."

It was so long before Conall responded, Duncan thought he'd lost him. *No, I lost him twenty years ago, when I had to rein him in. Become the father he didn't want.*

"You think I don't know what you did for us?" Tension threaded every word. "Of course I do. That doesn't mean I have to like you."

God. Damn. Duncan hadn't hurt like this in a long time, not since he'd almost lost Jane before he could even tell her he loved her. He had to swallow before he could say with relative calm, "No, it doesn't."

"Oh, hell." Conall sounded ragged. "I didn't mean to say that."

"It's okay."

"Listen, I have to talk to you about this investigation. Can we keep it to that?"

"Sure. Do you want to have coffee somewhere? Or shall we meet up on a deserted road?" he added dryly.

"No. It would look best if I do come to your house. Gives me an excuse to be in town."

That ticked Duncan off some. Good to know he was worth something to this brother he'd raised from age twelve on.

"Fine." He gave Conall his address. "Jane and I don't go out much. I'm home by six most nights."

"I'll make it this evening."

"Fine," he said again, and hung up the phone.

He sat there for a long time, unable to decide how he felt about Conall's call. Or maybe what he couldn't decide was which emotion was paramount. Anger? Hurt? Resentment? Or the astonished gratitude that might even have been happiness, because he'd heard Conall's voice again. He was going to *see* him.

Tonight.

He looked at the computer monitor and realized there was no way in hell he could concentrate on impoundment procedures now.

What he was going to do was take an extra early lunch and go spend time with his wife and baby girl.

CALLING NIALL WAS ANTICLIMACTIC. Conall almost didn't, almost put it off until tomorrow. But he didn't want his middle brother to hear from Duncan that he was in town. He and Niall had been…friends, maybe, for too long. Niall was the only family Conall had accepted after he left home. It was bad enough that Niall had cooled toward him since his wedding last fall. The one Conall had failed to show for.

He didn't have to identify himself. Niall listened in silence to his brief explanation of his presence in Stimson.

"You're in town" was said in disbelief.

"Weird but true." He was actually sitting outside on Lia's porch, on an Adirondack chair painted a glossy, cherry red.

"Does Duncan know?"

"Yes."

Niall made a sound that might have been a laugh, might have been a grunt. "You planning to meet with him face-to-face?"

"I'm going by his place tonight. If anybody hears I'm in town, they need to think it's to see the two of you. There can't be any talk about this operation."

"You'll meet Jane."

"Yeah." Conall made himself say it. "I want to meet your Rowan, too."

"I haven't told you she's pregnant. We, uh, didn't want our kids too far apart in age."

Our kids. He must be talking about Rowan's two. And a baby. Another little MacLachlan. This was getting surreal, Conall thought. His brothers had gone and turned into average joes. How had that happened?

"I'm glad for you," he made himself say, "if that's what you want."

"It's what I want."

No hesitation. The coolness was still there, too, the one he'd heard ever since he called to apologize for ducking out on the wedding. He'd told himself

Niall wouldn't give a damn if he wasn't there, but Conall knew even then he'd lied to himself. He hadn't ever been the one who'd made the effort to stay in touch, although Niall and he had gotten close after their father went to prison and their mother walked out on them. After Duncan sacrificed too damn much for them and turned into a tyrant. No, Niall was the one who had made the calls in the first few years. Who'd flown to wherever Conall was a few times. The one who seemed to need the connection.

Sitting here on the porch, gazing sightlessly at the old barn and the pasture and woods that lay beyond it, Conall had an uncomfortable insight.

He'd needed that connection, too. Maybe needed it more than did Niall, who had held on to a relationship with Duncan. Conall hadn't admitted it to himself, but he'd been grateful every time he heard his brother's voice.

He had somebody. One person who cared.

And he hadn't realized how much *he* cared.

This unexpected homecoming, he thought, was going to be a bitch.

CHAPTER THREE

LAST NIGHT LIA had come upstairs, knocked briskly and then set two covered plates on the floor along with a couple of cold beers. "Dinner," she'd said then left. If she'd been a waitress, she wouldn't get much in the way of tips with that attitude.

This morning Jeff had gone downstairs and come back reporting that she made damn good waffles. By the time Conall got down to the kitchen, it was apparently closed. He found cereal in the cupboard and called it good, eating a solitary meal in the dining room.

They'd fended for themselves for lunch.

Tonight, he didn't want to show up at Duncan's anywhere around dinnertime; he hadn't been invited and wasn't sure he'd have accepted if he had been. So when Henderson said, "I had a decent breakfast and you didn't. Why don't you go down and eat with them?" he nodded.

"I'll bring something up if Lia doesn't."

He left Henderson scanning the neighboring property with a scope that had both night-vision and digital filming capability. So far, nothing had happened over there. Literally nothing. No one had so much as stepped outside, although some-one had to be letting the dogs—turned out there were a pair of Dobermans—in and out, or was at least feeding them. Tomorrow Conall planned to do some prowling. He wanted to see the back of the property, too.

This view was ideal, but unfortunately the neighbors were keeping their blinds drawn. Shad-ows occasionally passed in front of the windows. Any vehicles were hidden in the triple car attached garage, which had a single window covered inside with what looked like a heavy tarp.

The dogs definitely complicated things. He or Henderson could have slipped a few listening devices beside windows or on the porch if they could have gotten close enough. Somehow he sus-pected the Dobies wouldn't prove to be tail-wag-ging friendly.

You wanted a challenge, he reminded himself. *Consider yourself lucky.*

Conall went downstairs to find Sorrel setting the table. A baby had already been placed in the high chair. The little girl had spiky black hair and eyes almost as dark. Her cheeks were fat and she grinned at him with no inhibitions at all, banging a spoon hard on the tray in emphasis. He retreated hastily, going to the kitchen where Lia stood over the stove, from which really good smells emitted. She glanced at him, expression shuttered.

"Are you eating with us?"

"If that's okay."

"Is Jeff coming down, too?"

Jeff. Good friends now, were they?

"No. With rare exceptions, one of us will be at that window all the time."

She took a tray of big rolls out of the oven. Hunger pangs hit Conall and he had to swallow.

"Sorrel," she called, "set a place for Conall, please."

So he was on a first-name basis with her, too. Ridiculously, he was pleased.

The answer floated back. "Okay."

"Here." Lia had dumped the rolls in a huge basket and thrust it at him. "Will you put these on the table?"

Without checking to see whether he obeyed, she disappeared toward the living room. A couple of minutes later, she steered the two boys ahead of her into the dining room and set the toddler she'd carried on her hip onto a plastic booster seat at one place.

"What's for dinner?" one of the boys asked. Brendan, Conall thought.

"Sloppy joes." Her eyes cut to Conall. "Nothing fancy."

"It smells amazing," he said honestly.

Her expression didn't soften. She finished bringing the food to the table, including a bowl of peas. "Picked an hour ago," she informed everyone.

Conall waited and sat at the same time she did, feeling some alien need to display good manners. She—or maybe it was Sorrel—had placed him at the opposite end of the table from Lia. Mother and father, children ranged between them.

He couldn't remember sitting down to a family dinner like this since he was… Good Lord, maybe seven or eight. Before one of Dad's prison terms. After that, nothing was ever the same. One thing he did know, though, was that conversation should be flying and the kids more animated than these.

Baby Julia was the only cheerful one, banging and chattering unintelligibly. Little Arturo, chubby, too, focused entirely on his food and didn't say a word. Neither did either of the older boys at first. Sorrel watched Conall surreptitiously, blushing when his gaze caught hers a couple of times.

They passed around the food—those homemade rolls straight out of the oven, sloppy joe sauce to go over them, and peas. He'd forgotten how good peas fresh from the garden could be.

Lia presided over the meal with grace and warmth, refusing to let the kids stay entirely closed off. Brendan, it turned out, was the older one. She got him talking about the *Transformers* movie and why the theme appealed to him. Conall was pretty sure he'd never considered that movies *had* themes when he was that age.

"Do you like it?" the boy asked him shyly.

"Yeah, actually I enjoyed all three of the movies," Conall admitted. "Not that they're—"

Lia shook her head, her gaze fierce.

"Uh, they're fun," he said. "You like 'em, too, Walker? Or do you watch what Brendan says you have to watch?"

The younger boy looked confused. After a minute he said softly, "I don't care what we watch."

Oh, geez. "I had—have—two older brothers. I pretended I liked whatever they liked because I wanted to hang around with them."

It was the first time Walker had actually seemed to see him. "I like to hang around with Bren."

"He seems like he's pretty good to you." Conall found himself speaking gently.

The boy nodded.

"We're brothers," Brendan said.

"I can tell. You look alike." He hesitated. "Lia told me about your mom. I'm sorry."

They both ducked their heads. Walker blinked furiously. Oh, hell. He'd probably blown it. Why hadn't he kept his mouth shut?

And then he opened it again. "When I was twelve, I lost my parents." A fireball of alarm exploded in his chest. What in God's name was he doing? But something on those two boys' faces when they looked up drove him on. He cleared his throat. "They didn't die. My dad went to prison and my mother decided she didn't want the responsibility of kids anymore. She packed up and left."

There was an appalled silence. Conall didn't let himself see the expression on Lia's face.

"She left?" Brendan whispered. "On *purpose?*"

"Yeah. I'm guessing you know your mom would have done anything in the world not to leave you."

He could see in their eyes that it was true.

If he'd been into greeting card moments, he would have gone on and said, *You're lucky because you'll be able to remember your whole lives how much your mother loved you.* Fortunately, he wasn't, and he didn't.

But they understood anyway. After a moment they both nodded.

It was Sorrel who asked, "How come your dad got put in prison?"

"He sold illegal drugs."

"My friend Rochelle's does sometimes, too. At least, she thinks so. She hasn't seen him in a long time."

"I haven't seen mine since I was twelve."

"Is he still in prison?"

"I don't know," he admitted.

"Did you have to go to a foster home, like us?"

Conall looked around the table. They were all

staring at him except Arturo, who kept eating, messy but getting the job done. Julia beamed at Conall, her four teeth cute accents in that broad smile. The other kids had expressions that said, *Are you one of us?*

He shook his head. "I told you I have two brothers. My oldest had turned eighteen. Mom and Dad let him keep the house. He got a job and took care of my other brother and me." He was getting a lump in his throat. Man, this was stupid, but right this minute he couldn't help seeing the past in a different light. Yes, he knew he'd been lucky to have Duncan, but seeing the faces of these kids brought it into sharp focus.

He would have gone to a foster home if Duncan hadn't given up his dream of going off to college, Conall knew. Or his stay would have been short. He'd been too big a screw-up, as young as he was. He'd already stolen a car and gotten caught. He'd gotten so drunk a couple of times, he'd blacked out. He'd smoked marijuana, tried cocaine. He'd have ended up in a group home if he'd gotten his act together at all, in lockup if he hadn't.

Dad and me.

He didn't like acknowledging it, but he owed Duncan big-time. Not the mood Conall wanted to be in for this reunion.

"What kind of job did he get?" Brendan asked.

Conall blinked. "Ah...construction. He'd been

doing it summers anyway. He managed to get his college degree, too, mostly with evening classes. Duncan was really motivated." He heard how sardonic that sounded. *My brother who could move mountains.*

"Duncan?" Lia said sharply. Her eyes were wide and astonished. "I should have realized."

"Realized?" he said warily.

"Your brother is the police chief."

"He's a *cop?*" Sorrel exclaimed.

"Yeah, he's a cop." Didn't she realize he was, too? "So is my other brother, Niall. He's a detective with the police force here in town." Conall could feel how crooked his smile was. Ah, the ironies of life. "Our dad was in and out of prison, and all three of us went into law enforcement."

The teenager stared at him with open astonishment. "But…"

"We don't have to follow in our parents' footsteps, Sorrel," Lia said. "I think that's what Conall is telling you."

Actually, it wasn't, but he didn't argue. What had he been trying to tell her? He should know, but didn't. Truth was, he'd stumbled into law enforcement, not chosen it as Duncan had. Conall had looked for something exciting, out of the ordinary. What he'd found suited him perfectly. He was good at undercover work because he was a hell of an actor. Always had been. The job didn't require him to make emotional connections; in fact, his ability to feel nothing was useful. Going deep for months at a time was hard if you identified too closely with your role. If you started caring about the people you were there to bring down. That wasn't a problem he'd ever had.

He hadn't set out to do battle with all drug dealers because they symbolized his father. He wasn't aiming for atonement. The idea was ridiculous. You had to care, if only in a negative way, to draw in a face on the paper target at the shooting range that you intended to pump full of bullet holes. Conall didn't do that. His paper targets stayed faceless.

He was aware, though, of some tension he didn't understand. He was frowning, he realized. Probably because thinking about either of his parents always made him edgy.

Then don't.

Easier when he was far, far away from his not-so-beloved hometown.

He tuned in to discover that the others were talking, sounding more normal than they had earlier. Lia laughed at something Sorrel said, and he found himself staring. The sound was unexpectedly throaty and…honest. Most people tried to rein themselves in when they laughed. They didn't surrender to the moment. Her head fell back and she shook with it. Amusement seemed to light her from within. His body tightened in automatic re-action and he made himself look away.

She was still smiling when she scanned the faces at the table. "Blueberry cobbler, anyone?"

Conall almost groaned. He'd intended to take off, but...homemade cobbler? "With ice cream?" he asked hopefully.

She laughed again, the first genuinely warm look she'd ever aimed directly at him. "Vanilla."

"Then wow. Yes for me."

Chortling nonsense sounds, Julia whacked her spoon on the tray. She was already a mess, sloppy joe sauce smeared on her fat cheeks. He could only imagine what blueberries would do to her.

Turned out Lia was smarter than that. The baby only got ice cream, her brother ice cream with a few berries stirred in. They both seemed satisfied. Everyone else ate with gusto and enthusiasm, even Walker and Brendan. It was hard to be depressed when every bite you put in your mouth was bliss on the spoon. This, he thought, was Lia's talent. Or one of them, anyway. The ability to soothe and inspire and heal by the food she put on the table.

And with her smiles, too, unbelievably gentle for all the kids, a little different for Sorrel, as if with the tilt of her lips she was implying some-thing conspiratorial: *we girls are in this together*. Her smiles for him were considerably more cautious, conventional. Conall didn't blame her. She *should* be cautious around him.

He scraped his bowl clean and resisted the temptation to lick it even cleaner, then grinned. "That was the best thing I've eaten since I can remember. Thank you."

Unless it was his imagination, a tiny bit of color touched her cheeks. "You're welcome."

"If I may be excused, I'm off to see my brother."

"Duncan?" Walker asked.

"Yeah. Duncan."

"Oh." The boy ducked his head. When everyone waited, he asked, "Will he ever come see you here?"

"Ah...probably not." Definitely, hell no, not.

The boy's shoulders seemed to sag slightly. "Oh. Okay."

Conall was still asking himself what that was about when he stuck his head upstairs to tell Henderson he was going, then walked out to the Suburban. What would Walker think if Conall told him that, after all his big brother had done for him, he hadn't spoken to him in years? No mystery there—the kid wouldn't understand.

Conall didn't totally understand.

Brooding, he hit the first pothole out on the gravel road too fast, and thought for a minute he'd broken an axle and maybe a tooth.

Goddamn it, concentrate. This was a job. He hadn't come home to muck around in the past.

Duncan, he discovered, had a pretty fancy place. Nothing cookie-cutter about it—angles and planes and shingled siding, very Northwest. Spectacular garden, too. The wife's influence, maybe?

Conall didn't suffer from nerves, but he felt a few twinges after he rang the doorbell. He rotated his shoulders to reduce the tension there was no reason to feel.

Even so, when the door opened he was balanced on the balls of his feet as if anticipating an attack. Ready for the worst, but making sure his body language looked relaxed. Acting.

When he saw the man in the opening, Conall thought, *Damn.* He would have known Duncan anywhere, but he'd changed, too. Aged. Well, of course he'd aged, but Conall was shocked to see that he had threads of silver in his dark hair. Not many, but a gathering at each temple. Of course, he was heading toward forty now.

In fact, he was close to the age of their father when they'd last seen him. And…the same age Mom had been? Was it possible?

The craggy face that looked more like Conall's own than he was comfortable acknowledging was almost as expressionless as he remembered. But…not quite. He'd loosened up in some indefinable way.

"Conall." He stepped back. "Come in."

Conall dipped his head and walked in. He followed his brother past the living room to the kitchen, where a woman closed the dishwasher then turned to study him.

"Another MacLachlan," she said with a small laugh. "Nobody could mistake you."

He stiffened at that, but only said, "You must be Jane."

"Yes. I'll leave you two to talk, but I wanted to meet you." She smiled and came to him, her hand outstretched. "Hello, Conall."

She was a beauty. Not like Lia, but definitely classy. She moved like a dancer, toes slightly turned out, had a mass of glossy brown hair bundled carelessly at her nape, and deep blue eyes that were friendly but also watchful.

Suddenly amused, Conall suspected that if Duncan hadn't been present, she'd have issued dire warnings. *Hurt my husband and you're dead meat.* Strangely, he was pleased. She loved his big tough brother, who was a lucky son of a bitch.

Conall took her hand, but instead of shaking it he drew her to him and kissed her cheek. "It's a pleasure, Jane."

She eyed his deliberately charming smile with suspicion as she withdrew, heightening his amusement. Yeah, she might even be a match for Duncan. Go figure.

She excused herself, leaving the two men alone.

"Have you eaten?" Duncan asked.

"Yes."

"Coffee?"

"Thanks." He sat on one of the breakfast bar stools and rested his elbows on the counter. "Nice place."

Duncan nodded.

"Baby asleep?"

"Yeah, she just went down for the night."

"There's a baby at the place I'm staying." He didn't know why he'd said that. "Eight months, I think. Happy little thing."

"Fiona isn't quite that."

He knew exactly how old Duncan's daughter was. He'd looked at the baby announcement in amazement when it arrived, and later the one photo Duncan sent. Until today, Duncan never commented on the fact that he didn't hear back from Conall. Into the vacuum he kept sending a very occasional letter, things like the wedding invitation and then the birth announcement, sometimes a Christmas card. Conall had never figured out why he bothered.

Now…he thought maybe they were a trail of bread crumbs, offering a way home. The idea unsettled him, maybe because here he was.

Not home. Not anymore.

It hadn't been in a long time. The trouble was, he didn't exactly have a home. He'd never made one.

Didn't want one.

"I'd like to see her." Strangely, he realized he really did. See what MacLachlan blood wrought in the next generation.

"How long are you going to be around?"

"I don't know. It depends on what we find. Or don't find."

Duncan inclined his head. He brought two mugs of coffee to the bar and sat, too, a couple of stools away from Conall. "So tell me about it."

They talked then, both professionals, Conall expressing some of his irritation with the vagueness of the information he'd been given. "You know anything about the people in that house?" he asked.

His brother shook his head. "No. The owner does something in the oil business. He worked up at the refinery in Anacortes, but I hear he got transferred to Texas, and couldn't sell the house as quick as he needed to. Real estate is slow right now."

Real estate was slow right now everywhere.

"So he and his wife are renting the place out for now. It can't be cheap, that's a big house."

"You actually know it," Conall said slowly.

Duncan's eyes, razor sharp, met his. "I've driven or walked every street in my city."

"You didn't herniate a disk driving that one?"

Duncan grinned. "A few potholes? Are you such a city boy now you can't deal with 'em?"

"These damn things have to be a foot deep. I'd kick in some bucks to the cause of filling them, except I don't want Lia to have to go knocking on her neighbors' doors right now."

"Lia?" His brother frowned. "Lia Woods? That's who you're staying with?"

"That's her."

"Foster kids?"

"Unfortunately."

"Huh." Duncan became pensive.

"What? You know her?" He set down his cup hard enough to splash. "You had a thing with her?"

That earned him a startled look. "God, no. I've never met the woman. At least, I don't think I have. No, I heard something." He hesitated. "Probably nothing I should repeat."

Conall snorted. "Hell, no, you're not doing that. You think I can't be close-mouthed?"

"I don't want you, as a federal agent, to feel like you have to do something about it."

About…what? He sifted through the possibilities. Lia wouldn't still be licensed if this had anything to do with the children in her care. Say, an accident, or alleged abuse, or…

"She's got more kids than we were told she had." Duncan's gaze, steady, met his. "Hispanic?"

"Yeah." Conall laughed. "Oh, man. They're illegals."

"I, uh, heard a rumor and made the decision not to check it out. Most of the time we don't get involved in immigration issues. I don't want anyone to be afraid to talk to us because they think we'll get them deported."

Conall nodded. Maybe that was why Arturo hadn't spoken at all at the dinner table. If he was Spanish-speaking, he probably hadn't understood a word anyone said.

"I assume the county or whoever licenses her doesn't know this."

"I assume not. And that's if it's true. It may not be."

"Oh, I'd bet it is. Phillips didn't know anything about the two littlest kids she has, except that she told him they were real temporary. He figured it was a receiving home thing." Conall laughed again. "No wonder she hasn't been as warm and welcoming as she could be."

"She can't be thrilled with the arrangement anyway. She's got two men moving in with her. Must be awkward as hell. You're extra work, could be a bad influence on the kids. Worse yet, what if the bad guys next door learn you're there? Your presence could put those kids in danger."

Conall couldn't argue. In fact, offhand he couldn't think of an upside for Lia. When he thought about it, he guessed maybe she'd been decent to the two strange men she'd been saddled with.

Should he try to reassure her that they weren't interested in immigration issues, either? Was there any way to do that without letting her know that she was on the local law enforcement radar? Without scaring the crap out of her?

No. There wasn't.

He'd keep his mouth shut, he decided.

"Let me know if there's anything I can do to help," Duncan said. "We could maybe find a reason to knock on their door without making them suspicious."

"Not yet. Sooner or later they'll show themselves. If we can get some photos, identify faces, then we'll know what we're dealing with."

"Okay," Duncan said.

Conall recognized a signal and slid off the stool. "I'd better get back."

"Jane will want to have you to dinner."

Conall depended on his instincts, developed over years of perilous undercover work. What he didn't often do was pause to think, *How do I feel about that?* His stride checked briefly when he discovered he didn't recognize what he was feeling. Something was going on inside him, but he didn't know what. It seemed that he was okay with the idea of socializing with his brother and sister-in-law. And *that* was worrisome. This whole experience was like being flipped upside down and given a good hard shake. Things weren't settling back into the right places.

Remembering the look of warning his sister-in-law had given him, he said, "I'd actually like that. I told Niall I want to meet his wife, too. And their kids."

"We'll do a family get-together." Did Duncan sound as bemused as Conall felt?

Maybe.

Needing to get out of there, Conall departed after only a few more words, all polite and shallow as a coat of paint.

Where was the bone-deep anger? The resentment? The intense gratitude he'd hated most of all?

Nowhere to be found.

There was a whole mess of stuff going on inside him, but none of it was familiar. That left him unsteady, a stranger to himself. Not a sensation he liked.

LIA DIDN'T MAKE IT OUT to feed the horses until dark. The younger kids were all in bed. Having Sorrel was something of a blessing right now, as Lia trusted her enough to believe she'd respond to sounds of distress. Otherwise Lia wouldn't be able to linger outside, as she was doing tonight.

She'd quartered an apple and brought that out,

too. She loved the feel of the soft lips on her palm, the whiskers tickling her. Noses butted her chest and she laughed aloud.

Eventually she returned to the porch, where she'd probably hear any cries as she'd left the living room window open to the night air. She chose to sit on the porch with her feet on the top step, her arms wrapping her knees. She didn't even kid herself that she was here to enjoy the solitude.

She was waiting for Special Agent Conall MacLachlan.

He wasn't quite what she'd first thought. Although she wasn't sure what that was. He'd both stirred something in her and scared her from first sight. She told herself she didn't like him.

The other agent—Jeff Henderson—seemed like an okay guy. Almost too normal to be a federal agent. When she'd asked at breakfast this morning about his family, he had whipped out a photo of a blonde woman who was plain but nice-looking and two kids. The boy looked a lot like his dad, which probably meant his hairline would recede early, too. Jeff glowed with pride.

MacLachlan, though, was another story. He was…maybe not handsome, but definitely sexy. The air all but shimmered around him from a mixture of charisma and testosterone. She could see even Sorrel reacting to it, which worried Lia. That was one of the reasons she wanted to talk to him privately. The boys were another. He'd awakened their interest, which could be good for them or very, very bad.

Mostly, she wanted to know who he was. If that story he'd told at dinner was true.

When he'd first arrived, she thought he was cold. He had a tempting smile that didn't reach his gray eyes. His expressions were fleeting and hard to read. He was an enigma, and she'd been forced to take him into her house. She didn't see how she could prevent contact between him and the kids.

And then, what did he do at dinner but discombobulate her utterly. He'd talked to the boys as if…well, as if they were *people*. Not the way most adults dealt with children. He'd been kind and honest—she hoped—and known exactly the right thing to say.

Lia wanted to know how that could be. Jeff had told her his partner wasn't married. "No kids," he'd said, shaking his head as if baffled that a man wouldn't want them. If Conall had the background he said he did, how did he know what Bren and Walker needed to hear?

Please, God, it wasn't all an act designed to gain their confidence, to get them to talk to him. About *her*. What if he wasn't with the Drug Enforcement Agency at all, but was really with Immigration? Or cooperating with them? She shivered and hugged her knees harder.

I'm paranoid. That's all. Surely nobody would care all that much about what she was doing.

Still. Why, oh why, was it taking so long to find a place for Julia and Arturo to go? Didn't Mateo understand how dangerous her situation was? The whole network could be at risk.

The deep sound of an engine made her stiffen. As she saw headlights turn into her drive, she was glad she hadn't turned on the outside light. She'd have felt unbearably exposed.

It wasn't too late to go in, before he saw her.

No. This was a good time to talk to him, to feel him out, and she had determined to seize it.

The Suburban rolled to a stop by the barn. A moment later it went dark and silent. The door slammed, and Conall strolled across the yard toward the house. One of the horses whickered softly and Conall's head turned but he kept walking.

She knew the exact moment he saw her.

CHAPTER FOUR

HE DIDN'T SAY anything until he reached the foot of the steps. She could see him better than he could probably see her, as light shining through the living room window fell on his face as he stopped.

His voice was deep and quiet. "Enjoying some peace and quiet?"

"Something like that. I actually came out to feed the horses."

"Kids okay?"

She liked that he asked, but didn't trust him. "All asleep except Sorrel."

His shoulders moved slightly. "Teenagers tend to be night owls."

"She's only thirteen."

"She looks older," he said thoughtfully.

"She, um, acts older than that in some ways. Younger in others."

"Is that a warning?"

Lia frowned. "I suppose it is. She's rather drawn to men."

"Ah."

She hesitated, unsure whether to say more. Sorrel was in counseling. Lia didn't like exposing her kids' problems to anyone unnecessarily. Surely neither of the two men, federal agents, would behave inappropriately toward a thirteen-year-old girl.

After a moment, she said, "What I really wanted to talk to you about is the boys."

Hearing how aggressively that had come out, she winced. His expression had been reserved; now it closed completely. Bang. All access denied. She'd blown it.

"I'm sorry," she said hastily. "That didn't come out the way I meant it to. The thing is, they're... vulnerable."

"And I should have kept my mouth shut at dinnertime." His tone was resigned. "Understood."

"No." She bent her head and bumped it on her crossed arms, then lifted it again. "It's not that at all. Everything you said was...right. They opened up to you."

He stared at her. She imagined he'd tensed, but couldn't be sure. He was very, very good at hiding what he was thinking.

"Okay," he said slowly.

"I don't want you being nice to them if you don't mean it." She'd gone from belligerent to fierce and didn't regret it. "If you keep being nice, they're going to—" She had to swallow, and still her voice came out small and cracked. "Depend on you."

"And I won't be around for long."

"It's not that," she said again. "I won't be a permanent part of their lives, either." Why did saying that out loud make her feel as if her heart was breaking in two? Kids came, kids left. That's what she *did*. "They know you're only here for a while. What would be bad is if you talk to them, spend time with them, and then blow them off."

"I see." He paused. "Let me think about it, okay?"

"Okay." She hugged her knees harder. "Was what you told them true? About your parents and your brother?"

Still he didn't move, his expression didn't change. His eyes were too shadowed in the limited light for her to read them, assuming she could have.

"Yes."

Lia nodded. "I'm sorry."

"Thank you, but sorry isn't necessary. I haven't been a kid in a long time."

She wondered if he'd ever been a kid after his mom walked out. Or was he even before that? His couldn't exactly have been an ideal family.

"Even so."

"All right." He finally put a foot on the first step. "You planning to stay out here long?"

"Maybe a few more minutes."

"Do you mind if I sit down?"

Her pulse stuttered. "No, of course not."

He settled at the top of the steps a few feet away, leaning against the post opposite hers. He stretched out his long legs, looking relaxed and comfortable. For some odd reason, Lia had a suspicion he was neither.

"Having us here must be a pain."

"An inconvenience," she corrected.

His mouth twitched. "Is that all?"

"A worry."

His gaze suddenly felt more intense. "Why?"

Because I'm doing something illegal and I'm afraid you'll notice? "Because I have to think about your influence on the kids, of course. Sorrel and the boys all have big problems. I know I can't shield them completely, but I try."

"So I've noticed." He sounded amused. "The glare you gave me at dinner was a clue. Why wasn't I supposed to criticize the movie?"

"Their mom gave them the DVDs. They've been watching them over and over."

"Ah. Gotcha." He thought about it. "There are worse movies they could be clinging to."

"Bambi?"

He grunted; maybe laughed. "Yeah, that one would suck."

They sat in silence for a minute or two, Lia gazing out into the darkness, Conall—she thought—still looking at her. The sounds of the night were quiet, familiar: the soft, distant hoot of an owl, a whicker from one of the horses, the rustle of grass. None of it felt peaceful, not with him here. Not knowing *why* he was here.

Finally she couldn't stand it any longer and started talking. "I take it you grew up locally. Are you glad to be home?"

"No." For the first time, that deep, husky voice sounded harsh.

Startled, Lia turned her head. "Your memories are that bad?"

"Yes."

Okay. She groped for a response and came up with nothing better than another, "I'm sorry."

For the first time, he reacted visibly. Not much, only shifting, but the movement was jerky for a man who customarily moved with the lithe ease of a hunting cat.

"I shouldn't have said that." He inhaled; let it out audibly. "Oh, hell. There's nothing secret about it. Being back here has unsettled me, that's all."

"You went to see your brother, didn't you? Did something happen that bothered you?" she asked, genuinely puzzled.

He laughed, but the sound wasn't pleasant. "I haven't seen Duncan since I graduated from college, and that was a long time ago. I never intended to set eyes on him again. It's my luck that I got stuck with this operation, and that Duncan is the police chief."

"Never see him again?" She was hung up on that part. "But…you said he raised you. You made it sound like a good thing."

"It was a good thing. He was noble." Bitterness roughened his voice now. "You don't have to tell me. Duncan MacLachlan always does the right thing, whatever the sacrifice he has to make. He saved my ass. I know that." He was breathing hard. "Oh, hell," he said again. "I shouldn't have gotten started."

"I don't mind listening if you want to talk."

He was quiet so long she thought he would rise to his feet any moment and say good-night. And really, why would he talk to her? They were strangers.

But Conall shocked her by speaking after a minute. "He did save me. I'm not kidding about that. I wasn't like Brendan and Walker. I wasn't a good kid who could have gone to a foster home like yours. Nobody would have wanted me. I cut classes, smoked pot, got drunk, was in constant fights. I stole a car before my twelfth birthday."

Shocked, she was the one to stare now.

"I guess you could say I was acting out." He laughed again. This time he almost managed to sound amused. "My middle brother, Niall, wasn't much better. I guess Mom ditched us for a good reason."

"No," Lia whispered. The single word held so much fury, it burned her throat. "No. What she did is awful."

He leaned his head against the post, and she saw his eyes close for a moment. "Yeah. You're right. It was."

Lia was beginning to feel cramped, but she couldn't make herself stretch out her legs. She needed to stay…contained, to hold herself tightly together. Stupid, but she couldn't make herself move.

"My point was that neither Niall nor I rallied willingly behind big brother." Conall's voice came out low now. "Oh, we were good as gold at first. For a couple of months."

"Scared."

"Oh, yeah. After that, we…challenged him." Strangely, Conall was smiling now. "He figured the only way he could get us to toe the line was to scare the shit out of us. So he did."

She stiffened in outrage. "How…?"

"Doesn't matter. He didn't hurt us, if that's what you're asking. But you have to understand, neither of our parents had ever bothered being authority figures. All of a sudden Duncan, who was supposed to be one of us, our brother and buddy, became this…" He paused and she knew what word he was about to say. "This tyrant. I didn't take it well."

"What about your brother?"

"He wasn't so happy about it, either, not at first. What I never understood was that instead of rejecting big brother the despot the way I did, he gradually went over to the dark side." Another laugh. "Or maybe it was the glorious and good side, I'm not sure. The two of them became friends again. They stood up for each other at their weddings. Niall's a cop, too. I said that, didn't I? But him, he followed in Duncan's footsteps."

"Didn't you?"

His head clunked a couple of times against the post. "Not long ago I'd have said 'hell no' to that, too. Now…" He shrugged. "Truth is, I don't know. I'm not exactly in the same line of work as they are."

Which was splitting hairs, but she suspected he knew that.

"I don't know," he repeated. "I'm not sure I want to know."

"I can understand that." She knew why she did what she did, but didn't like to dwell on the past, either.

They sat in a considerably more peaceful silence for a bit. Finally he asked, "What about you, Lia Woods? Did you grow up around here?"

"Down in the Kent Valley. My parents have

moved recently to Arizona. I ended up here because my great-aunt on my dad's side didn't have any kids and left me her house when she died. I could have sold it and gone on with my life, but it seemed like the perfect opportunity to do something I'd always wanted to and take in kids."

"You don't hold an outside job?"

She shook her head and felt her braid bump on her back. "Not anymore. Some foster parents do, of course, but I tend to take the really troubled kids. Or ones like Walker and Brendan who need some special attention. While their mother was in the hospital, we spent as much time there as we were allowed. A nine-to-five job wouldn't have been compatible with what they needed from me."

"What's next for them?"

That question surprised her. She'd expected something along the lines of *Why foster?*

"They'll go up for adoption. As I'm sure you've guessed, their chances aren't great. They'd be better if they get split up, but…God. I can't imagine. They *need* each other."

With quiet force, he said, "It would be an abomination to tear them apart."

She swallowed emotion trying to spill out. "Yes. It's not in my hands, although I'll express myself forcefully if anyone suggests they be separated. I may never know, though. Usually I foster fairly short term. They might get sent elsewhere.

It's possible they'd thrive in a more typical family situation, or that their caseworker will decide they need a father figure. I tend to get more girls than boys."

"Will they survive one more change?"

"I don't know," Lia whispered. "They're…withdrawing." It took her a few deep breaths to calm herself. "You got further with them tonight at dinner than I ever do. So maybe they *do* need a father figure."

"But from what you said, they only had a mother. Why would they relate to a man?"

"I don't know," she admitted.

He frowned but didn't move. He'd be a heck of a poker player, she found herself thinking. No tells. Did he ever fidget?

"I won't have a lot of time," he said abruptly. "I can't make promises."

Promises?

"But when I have a minute, I'll try to talk to them." The lines on his face deepened, or perhaps it was a trick of the light. No, not of the light; the dark. "They remind me of myself. They're…trying to quit feeling anything at all."

Dear God, Lia thought. Had this man *succeeded?* The idea appalled her, but in the next second she realized, *no*. No, of course he hadn't, or they wouldn't be having this conversation. He wouldn't have spent however many years he had running away from home. He wouldn't worry about two little boys he'd barely met. He was a federal agent, he might be a threat to her, but Lia suddenly knew with absolute certainty that he was also a good man.

His brother might have dealt him wounds that still ached when he moved wrong, but Duncan had truly saved an angry boy and helped him become this man.

She'd seen Duncan's picture in the newspaper and thought he looked cold and unlikeable. How wrong could she possibly have been?

"Yes," she said on a sigh, "I think that's exactly what they're trying to do."

Conall rose to his feet, a smooth motion. "I'd better go relieve Jeff." He held out a hand. "Ready to go in?"

She gazed warily at his hand for longer than was probably polite. Touching him might be… risky. Still, she reached out and let his hand close around hers.

And knew immediately that she'd been right.

His warm clasp felt better than just about anything she could remember. Strong, safe…and yet not safe. She lifted an astonished stare to his, to see…something on his face. Something fleeting, but she thought it might be surprise.

So he felt it, too.

With a gentle tug, he boosted her to her feet.

They ended up no more than a foot apart. Her breath caught in her throat. Neither of them moved. He didn't release her. She wanted, quite desperately, for him to pull her closer, until her body bumped up against his. She wanted him to kiss her.

And she knew letting that happen would be stupid. He was only here for a little while, and she suffered enough every time a child left her. She couldn't bear anything else temporary in her life. He could hurt her if she let him.

So I won't.

She eased her hand free and said, "Good night, Conall." Lia was proud of how firm she sounded. How unaffected.

Proud, that is, until he said, "Good night," and sounded so utterly indifferent, she knew without question that she'd imagined any chemistry between them.

Grateful she hadn't given herself away, she preceded him into the house. By the time she turned the dead bolt, he was already halfway up the stairs.

CONALL HEARD THE SOUND of a vehicle engine first. Noise traveled well at night in the country. There wasn't much traffic out here at—he pressed a button to illuminate the numbers on his watch—3:18 in the morning. Conall guessed he was hearing a pickup truck, maybe diesel; the roar was too deep for a car. From this window he couldn't see the gravel road, but he expected to see some suggestion of headlights through the woods. Nothing.

Not another neighbor coming home late, though; this truck or SUV had passed the other driveways, then Lia's. The Dobermans began to bark and raced to meet the... Yeah, a dark colored pickup with a black canopy. Using night vision, he watched the vehicle roll to a stop in front of that triple car garage. No headlights.

"About time," he murmured. Somebody had come calling.

And was expected. One of the garage doors rolled up. A light was on somewhere inside, probably a single bulb. Two men came out, one of them speaking sharply to the dogs who both dropped to their bellies. Passenger and driver's-side doors opened and the two newcomers got out. They went around to the back and opened the canopy on the pickup. After some conversation, all four began unloading...something.

Conall felt a chill. The wooden crates they carried in didn't look as if they contained drug manufacturing paraphernalia and seemed unnecessarily large and sturdy to hold packets of cocaine or heroin ready for distribution. He had a really bad feeling about this. Those crates looked to him as if they held guns. Big guns, and a hell of a lot of them.

He rubbed his burning eyes briefly, and resumed watching. Faces weren't real distinct, but he was letting footage roll so he could watch it again and try to zoom in on the scene: on the faces and in search of any marks on the wooden crates.

One of the men looked familiar. Conall couldn't swear to it, but a couple of times... The way the guy turned his head, gesticulated, hunched his shoulders like a bull ready to charge... "Goddamn," he said under his breath. "I've seen him before."

It would come to him. It always did. He had a near-photographic memory, another of his strengths. He could almost always get the girl, he rarely forgot a face and he was an icy-cold son of a bitch, which meant fear had no hold on him. He took risks the agents with families waiting at home wouldn't.

Images of Lia whispered through his mind. The woman who seemed to have a bottomless heart. He and she were polar opposites. She cared, he didn't.

He had to keep his distance. Conall did try not to hurt women. He steered clear of the home and hearth kind. She wasn't quite that, though; he wasn't sure he'd ever encountered a woman exactly like her, willing to give endlessly of herself to other people's children. At the table tonight, he kept watching her thinking, *What's in it for you?*

He still didn't know. Money? The state did pay her to care for each kid, but was it only a job for her?

Focus, he snarled at himself. The men all disappeared inside the garage. The dogs stayed where they were. Half an hour passed, one breath at a time. Conall waited with the patience of any hunter.

Behind him Jeff let out a couple of snorting breaths and then covers rustled as he rolled over in bed. They had no damn privacy up here at all. Conall for one was looking forward to the day little Julia and Arturo went away and freed up the bedroom. Conall didn't sleep well when he wasn't alone. He rarely stayed the night with women.

This time it was Lia's bed that slipped unbidden into his mind. A couple of times her bedroom door had been open when he passed in the hall. He hadn't been able to help looking. The room wasn't any fancier than the rest of the house, but it unmistakably belonged to a woman. To Lia. She wore bright colors, and she decorated with them, too. He hadn't seen any lace, but the duvet cover was a print of bright red poppies and green leaves against a white background. Puffy white and red pillows were heaped against a white-painted iron bedstead. Men never bothered with non-utilitarian pillows. That was a woman thing. The hardwood floor beside the bed was softened by a flower-shaped rug in the same poppy red. It was made out of torn strips of some soft fabric and he bet he'd sink ankle-deep in it.

He *wanted* to sink ankle deep in it while he was on the way to her bed, where she sprawled waiting for him. His body tingled as he imagined it. Her hair was loose…no, he wanted to take it out of the braid himself, comb out the curls with his fingers. Those glorious green-brown eyes were sultry…

He jerked and then swore when someone walked out of the garage. Two men. The dogs leaped to their feet but stayed silent. The two men got in the pickup, the garage door came down and a moment later he heard the muted roar of the engine. They drove away, still without turning on their headlights.

Conall hadn't seen any sign the visitors had brought groceries or dog food. No packages of toilet paper. Sooner or later whoever was staying in the house would have to go out. Lia had said she'd seen them come and go. She said she'd waved at first but quit bothering when they ignored her. Idiots. That's not how you went unnoticed in small-town or rural America.

After a couple of minutes, the dogs rose and trotted off, one around the house, the other loping along the fence line. Both wore thick collars and avoided the perimeter of the property, which likely meant they got shocked when they went too close. At least Lia could relax about her ancient horse and butterball pony.

Conall yanked at his hair. Why the hell couldn't he keep her out of his head? He'd been here three and a half days, spent less than two hours in her company, and she was already a big-time distraction.

This wasn't like him. He should be speculating on where he'd seen the one familiar face before. He'd encountered gun runners before, if that's what these men were. He should be trying to figure out how to get into that garage. He should be thinking about anything but the home-owner who so happened to be a beautiful woman.

Who loved children. Who'd rip his heart out and fry it for breakfast if he did one single thing to hurt the children she guarded so fiercely.

Not his kind of woman.

It was…unfortunate that he had the hots for her. He gave a soft grunt. No, it was worse than that. She drew him in an unfamiliar way. From first sight on. Now that he knew her a little better, it was even worse. The way she'd said, *I'm sorry.* Sitting here alone but for a few snores on the other side of the attic, he could hear her voice, soft but tangible as a touch. People didn't always mean it when they said that, but she had. She'd felt something genuine for him.

And that scared the crap out of stone-cold

Conall MacLachlan. He was trapped, living in a house with a gorgeous woman who cared like no one else he'd ever met, a woman he had wanted the moment he saw her.

People were rarely what they seemed, though; he knew that. Lia Woods wouldn't be. She had to be a fake. Maybe decent to the kids, but doing it because she saw fostering as an easy way to pay the bills. He'd catch her saying something cutting to one of them when she thought no one else was listening, and he would be cured of this uneasy fear that he'd found… What? The perfect woman?

Not for him. His perfect woman enjoyed hot sex when he happened to be in town and didn't ask when she'd see him again.

Forget Lia. Think about the fun in store for him: a family reunion. All three MacLachlan boys, two accompanied by wives and children.

Now, *there* was a nightmare.

Conall MacLachlan. He was trapped, living in a house with a gorgeous woman who cared like no one else he'd ever met, a woman he had wanted the moment he saw her.

People were going to be surprised, though he knew that. Oh, words would fly. She had to be a fake. Maybe he sent to the kids, but doing it

CHAPTER FIVE

"So, LITTLE ONES," Lia said. The day was so nice she'd brought Julia and Arturo outside, where they sat on the lawn at the edge of dappled shade. After wondering stares, Julia had become fascinated by the grass and now had her plump fingers knotted in it. "Do you miss your mama? I think you'll see her soon. Arturo, don't pull your sister's hair."

"You're speaking Spanish to them." Conall sounded thoughtful.

Lia jumped and swiveled on her butt to glare at him. "Don't sneak up on us."

"I'm a special agent," he said in apparent amusement. "That's what we do. Didn't you know that?"

"You'd better tell Jeff. I can always hear him coming."

"Heavy feet." He shook his head in disapproval. "I'd better report him."

She puffed out a breath. Her heartbeat was settling into something approaching a normal rhythm. Not quite normal; it wouldn't while he was standing there, she was afraid, looking unbelievably sexy and relaxed, that smile lingering around his mouth even as he watched her. His jeans were well-worn, cupping his— No, she would *not* notice that part of his body. A faded T-shirt clung to powerful muscles. His feet were bare. Was he unarmed? She'd caught glimpses a couple of times of a shoulder holster beneath a loose denim or twill shirt. But surely he didn't *always* carry a gun.

"Aren't you supposed to be spying?" she asked. "Or sleeping?"

"I just woke up. Made myself a sandwich and saw you out here."

"Oh." Brilliant. "Did you say hi to Walker and Brendan?"

"I suggested they come out, too."

Fat chance of that. She nodded.

"You're fluent," he observed.

"You mean in Spanish?"

"Yes."

Lia shrugged. "You can't tell I'm Hispanic? My mother's Mexican. She came up here illegally, worked as a maid until she met my father who married her." She winced inwardly at her tone of defiance. She should have told the story casually. She'd meant to. Lia didn't kid herself that Conall hadn't had her investigated, if that Agent Phillips hadn't already done it. She needed to appear open. Nothing wrong here, nope.

"I thought you might be," he said slowly. "I I

heard you singing a lullaby in Spanish last night."
He began to sing softly in a deep, lazy baritone.
"*Buenos dias, buenos dias, como estan? Como
estan? Estamos muy contentos, estamos muy contentos, din don dan, din don dan.*"

Julia and Arturo gazed at him, rapt. Goose-
bumps had risen on Lia's arms.

"Very nice," she said. "You speak Spanish?"
Dumb thing to say; his accent was as authentic
as hers.

"*Sí.*" He smiled and sat down, grinning at Arturo. He pointed toward the pasture. "*El caballo.*"

The little boy bounced.

Conall pointed the other direction, toward the
grazing cows. "*La vaca.*"

"*La vaca,*" Arturo agreed intelligibly.

"I didn't think to ask whether they spoke English or Spanish at home," Lia said. "When Arturo
was so quiet, it finally occurred to me he probably
speaks Spanish."

"Insofar as a kid this age speaks anything."

Indignantly, she said, "He's got a good vocabu-
lary for his age." She touched a finger to her nose
and asked in Spanish, "What's this, Arturo?"

"*Nariz,*" he shouted.

His sister giggled in delight.

Lia sang "Head, Shoulders, Knees and Toes" in
Spanish and soon had Arturo touching the parts

of his body with her. Julia clapped her hands and vocalized.

"I know how to sing that," Walker said. "'Cept not in Spanish. That's Spanish, isn't it?"

Startled again, Lia turned her head to see that both boys had approached unheard. They looked pinched and pale as if they hadn't seen sunlight in months, but they'd come outside willingly.

She willed her smile not to tremble. "Yes, I finally figured out that Arturo understands Spanish and not English." Actually, she'd gotten caught speaking it to him, which wasn't quite the same thing.

Please, Mateo, come and get these children.

"How come?" Walker asked.

"There are quite a few people in this country who speak a different language," she said. "America is made up of immigrants, you know. Everyone is descended from grandparents or great-grandparents or great-great-grandparents who came from somewhere else. Everyone except the native Americans who lived here first."

The boy nodded. "Mom said that our father's grandparents came from Poland. Only…" Uncertainty entered his voice. "I think they went back."

She nodded matter-of-factly. "Adjusting to a place where everyone speaks a different language and eats unfamiliar food and thinks differently would be hard, wouldn't it?" She knew; oh, she did.

Both boys nodded.

"Why don't you sit down?" Conall suggested.

They looked at each other in silent communication, then dropped to the grass side by side, maintaining some distance from the others. Brendan, she suspected, didn't want to be here at all. His little brother had talked him into coming out. It was Walker who'd opened up to Conall at dinner the other night, too, she remembered. It was Walker who now asked, "But how come Arturo's mom doesn't learn to talk English, since she lives here?"

No mention of dad; in Walker's world, kids didn't have a father.

Lia smiled at him. "She might not have been here very long. Or she spoke English when she was at work and Spanish at home. She might have wanted her kids to grow up bilingual. Speaking two languages," she translated.

"She might even be here illegally," Conall remarked. He'd stretched out on his side and his head was propped on his hand. It was her he was watching, not the boys. Although his tone was still lazy, his eyes weren't.

"But if the children were born in this country," Lia shot back, "they're American citizens."

He murmured wordless agreement, but she didn't like the sharp way he continued to watch her.

"I don't actually know much about their parents," she lied to the boys, trying to focus on their faces and not his. "They're only supposed to be here for a week or two. There was some kind of family emergency." She shrugged.

"Like their mom is dying?" Brendan asked, in the same tone another kid might have said, *Like their mom went to the grocery store?*

Pity leapt to her throat. "No, honey. No, their mom will be back."

"After she wades the Rio Grande," Conall said *sotto voce*.

Dear God, he knew. Somehow he knew.

"Do they have a dad?" Conall asked.

"Yes," she snapped, knowing her cheeks were flushed. "Actually...I'm not sure. It was the mom who...had something happen." Got deported.

He nodded.

"Mr. Henderson said he has kids," Walker reported. "Only I guess he doesn't live with them." The faintest quaver in his voice said, *Why doesn't he? Do* any *kids have a dad who cares?*

Oh, dear God, how did she answer the unspoken?

She was surprised when Conall sat up and reached for Walker. "Come here." He handled him with ease, man to boy, scooting him over so they were hip to hip. He kept an arm slung over his shoulder. Not cuddling exactly, but...holding him the only way an eight-year-old boy would accept.

Brendan stayed, stiff and frozen, where he'd been, watching Conall as if he were a timber wolf, creeping through the grass toward Pepito, the Shetland pony.

"Jeff does live with his kids," Conall told the boys. "He really loves them. You know when we're upstairs, it gets pretty boring." Even Brendan nodded. "He talks about them all the time. His wife and kids. He misses them."

"Then how come he's not with them?"

"Because this is his job. Sometimes it means being away from home for a few weeks at a time."

"Do *you* have kids?" Walker asked.

"No."

"So you don't have anybody to miss."

Conall got the strangest expression on his face for an instant. Not long enough for her to pin down. It was as if…he'd been shocked by some realization.

"No," he said, a little huskily. "I guess I don't."

"That's good." The boy's throat spasmed. "Cuz… Cuz…"

Lia was appalled to realize that her vision had misted. She wasn't sure she could have said anything, and was grateful when Conall nodded.

"It hurts when you miss someone. I know."

"*How* do you know?" The boy looked up at him in entreaty. "If you don't have anyone? Is it cuz of your parents going away?"

She could see him choking on that one. Over the top of Walker's head, Conall's eyes met hers. *Bail me out,* he was demanding.

"Even if Agent MacLachlan doesn't have anyone right now... A wife or kids or—" Best let that go. "If you've ever loved somebody, you've had times you missed them. Like his mom and dad. I miss my parents because they've moved to Arizona and I don't see them very often anymore. That's not the same as the way you miss your mom, because I know I'll see them again. But... sometimes I really wish my mom was here, so I could tell her something."

Walker bent his head. "Oh."

Conall ruffled his hair. "Hey. It's getting hot out here."

It *was* unseasonably warm, but Lia wouldn't have described a day in the upper seventies as hot. She was enjoying the feel of the sun on her face.

"You got a sprinkler?" he asked her. "I'm thinking Walker and Brendan need to get wet." Then he grinned. "Maybe you do, too."

She gaped at him. "You think we should run through a sprinkler?"

"Yeah, why not?"

Why not indeed?

"What do you think, boys?" he asked.

"I guess," Walker said uncertainly. His gaze strayed to his brother's. Again there was that moment of silent communication. "It might be fun," he said doubtfully.

Conall had them organized before she knew it. He hauled a hose and rotating sprinkler out of the barn, where they'd been since last fall, hooked the hose up to the faucet on the side of the house and had the sprinkler merrily turning in no time.

"But we're dressed," Brendan objected.

"What's a little water?" Conall strode to the porch steps where he stripped off his T-shirt. If she hadn't been watching closely, she wouldn't have seen him pull an evil-looking black hand-gun from his back waistband and slip it under the shirt. That distracted her—although only momentarily—from the sight of his lean muscles and the dark hair on his chest. "No shoes," he said, shaking his head as the two boys looked at the sprinkler as if they didn't know what to do with it. "Gotta have bare feet. No shirts, either."

Uncertainly, they pulled their matching, striped T-shirts over their heads to expose skinny, fish-belly-white torsos. Both sat to take off socks and shoes. "But our jeans will get wet," Brendan objected.

"Do you have another pair to change into?"

"Well...yeah."

"Does Lia mind if you get these wet?"

Smiling, she shook her head. She now held baby Julia in her lap. Both the little ones were watching wide-eyed as Conall dashed recklessly through the spray.

Shaking his head like a wet dog on the other side, he grinned at Brendan. "Dare you."

The solemn boy nodded, gulped as if for courage, then ran through the water. He let out a squawk as cold water fountained over him. Laughing, Conall called, "Now you, Walker."

"Is it cold?"

"Yes!" his brother exclaimed, skinny arms wrapping around himself.

"Do I hafta?"

"You hafta," Mr. Special Agent MacLachlan told him, that utterly irresistible grin turning his face into one guaranteed to make any woman's knees weak.

"Okay." The boy squeezed his eyes shut. His hands knotted into fists at his side. Then he ran right through the sprinkler, screaming all the way.

On the other side, Conall hoisted him triumphantly into the air. "Now wasn't that fun?"

"Yes!" For the first time since Lia had had him, Walker smiled. Really smiled. "It was fun, wasn't it, Bren?"

Conall grabbed the older boy's nape with rough affection, said, "Let's do it again," and all three of them bolted through the water laughing.

Laughing. Two boys who had hardly talked in the weeks they'd watched their mother die and in the days they'd mourned her. And now this amazing man had reminded them that there were still reasons to laugh.

Oh, blast it. She *was* crying now, and she never cried.

She sniffed, swiped away the moisture, and found all three of them arrayed in front of her, soggy jeans clinging to their legs, the laughter still on their faces.

"You, too," Brendan said.

"Yeah!" Walker grinned at her. "I bet even Julia would like it."

Julia liked everything. She was babbling and bouncing.

Conall scooped up Arturo then grimaced. "He's already wet. What's a little wetter?"

"I can't take off my T-shirt," Lia protested weakly.

Conall's smile became wicked. "Ever hear of a wet T-shirt contest?"

"I'd lose."

His gaze lowered to her breasts and there was a glint in his eyes. "Oh, I don't know about that," he murmured.

She glowered at him, but let the boys pull her to her feet, Julia on her hip. She was kicking off her flip-flops when Conall swung Arturo onto his shoulders, made sure he was gripping his hair, then raced through the water. Arturo chortled the entire way. The boys were right behind them. Resigned, Lia followed. The minute she discovered how really, *really* cold the water was, she squealed and sped up.

"Like a girl," Conall told her when she emerged from the spray.

"It's *cold,*" she said indignantly.

Conall's gray eyes strayed to her breasts again. Very quietly, for her ears only, he told her, "You win."

She looked down. Oh, heavens! She'd gotten soaked. Worse yet, her bra was *not* doing its job. Her nipples were poking out. She wanted to believe it was because of the cold water, but couldn't be entirely sure she wasn't reacting to that very sexual appraisal.

From a man who was a threat to her. She couldn't forget that. More of a threat than ever, now that he'd hinted he knew.

Even so… The boys were laughing and cavorting, darting in and out of the sprinkler, letting Conall roughhouse with them. They were having fun, when she hadn't been sure they ever would again. Arturo had Conall's sopping wet, too-long hair gripped tightly in two fists, and he was laughing in belly-shaking delight. Julia strained toward the sprinkler, her babbling gaining in volume.

"Oh, all *right*," Lia muttered, and raced through

again. This time, it almost felt good. She'd forgotten the pleasure of wet grass slick beneath her toes.

It didn't last long; it couldn't, when the day wasn't really hot at all. Pretty soon the boys were shivering and Lia announced that they were all going inside to dry off and change clothes.

Conall turned off the water and moved quickly to grab his T-shirt and the weapon it concealed before the boys could reach the porch steps. They groaned loudly as they climbed, trying to pluck the wet jeans from their legs.

"Take them off before you go inside," Lia told them. "Then use the downstairs shower."

They did, leaving on only their white briefs, their jeans in a sodden heap on the porch. Conall lifted his dark eyebrows. "What about me? Should I take mine off, too? What about you, Lia? Are you planning to drip all over the floor?"

Heaven help her, she was blushing. "I'm not getting undressed in front of you."

"Aw," he complained. He was laughing at her, but his eyes were warm, too. Usually even when he smiled, those gray eyes stayed cool, but not now. He was attracted to her, and letting her know.

And she did not dare do anything about it.

"I," she announced, "claim the upstairs bathroom. Julia and I are taking a shower, too. I think the hot water tank can handle two showers running at once."

"Wait. What about me?" His smile became ca-
joling. "What about Arturo?"

She made her own smile evil. "Wait your turn."

"But…"

Lia paused on the doorstep then turned back.
"Thank you, Conall. That was…really nice of
you."

Between one second and the next, he shut down
any real emotion. What was left was practiced
charm, and she didn't like it at all. He was still
smiling, but it wasn't the same.

When he didn't say anything, she nodded and
went in, leaving him dripping on the porch with
a happy little boy riding his shoulders.

TRYING TO PRETEND that Henderson wasn't there,
thirty feet away, sitting in profile to him at the
window, Conall lay in the dark and stared up at
bare rafters. That stupid display he'd put on this
afternoon kept running through his head.

From the minute Lia had thanked him, panic
had clenched in his gut. He still didn't know what
had gotten into him. Yeah, he'd figured he could
be nice to the boys; what would that hurt? But
when he had looked up at them standing there,
stiff and awkward and sad, some alien force had
overtaken him.

He didn't like that he'd acted so out of character. Sure, he'd spent time with kids before; some-

times when he was playing a part he had to. But this was different. It hadn't been *intentional*. He'd been friggin' possessed.

At a rustling sound, Conall turned his head and saw Henderson stretching before he hunched forward again.

Conall had eaten dinner up here. Brendan had delivered his meal, knocking on the door at the foot of the stairs, the covered plate held with self-conscious care.

"How come you can't eat with us?" he'd asked, craning his neck to see past Conall.

Conall had forced a smile. "It's Jeff's turn. Not fair to shut him up here 24/7, is it?"

"No, but—"

"It's my job," he'd said gently.

The boy nodded, turned and walked slowly away.

Conall squeezed his eyes shut now and contrasted that slow, mechanical gait with the joyous run through the sprinkler.

He pictured himself running through it, and for an instant thought he was identifying with the kid. But, no. He *was* the kid. Scrawny, shorter than Brendan. Laughing, feeling the sensations of hot summer sun, freezing cold water, short spiky grass under tender feet unaccustomed to going barefoot. It was extraordinarily vivid. Niall was there, too, not any huskier but way taller, and Duncan, soaking wet in shorts that clung to his hips and thighs. He was taunting his brothers, chasing Niall, turning back to grab Conall and hold him as the water caught them.

The feelings inside him were powerful. His brothers were including him, doing something because they thought he'd have fun. For that brief hour, he'd been happy.

Oh, man. Conall had a lead weight on his chest. Now he knew who he'd channelled today. Duncan. The ghost of what had been, too rarely. The brother he'd loved so desperately, emulated even as he knew he'd always fall short—Duncan Mac-Lachlan.

Today, he'd acted out a scene from his past. He had to have been about Walker's age, maybe eight or nine. He'd seen himself in those two boys' hopeless eyes and he had known how he could reach them.

The weight that kept him from breathing freely grew heavier, not lighter, and the knot in his belly made him regret the beef Stroganoff.

If there was one person in the world he didn't want in his head, it was his big brother. Conall was freaked by the idea that he had, unknowingly, taken Duncan as his role model and in so doing connected with a pair of wounded kids in a way he himself would never be able to manage.

Didn't *want* to manage.

They're not my responsibility.

What he'd done was no biggie, he tried to tell himself. He'd given them a little fun. Like Duncan had given him some fun, that long ago day. That hadn't meant anything, either.

But that was a lie, he knew. It *had* meant something. It always did. Duncan had been more of a father to him than their biological father ever was.

Yeah, he'd wanted more from Duncan than he ever got. He cringed at the memory of himself, so hungry for affection, desperately soaking up what he did get.

In the end, though, Duncan had become his father in every meaningful sense. By then, he'd have sneered at the idea of running through the sprinkler on a hot day with his brothers. He was too tough for that, too alienated, too angry.

And so Duncan had done what a father should do: he'd forced compliance, he'd scared Conall into toeing the line. There were years Conall had been grimly focused on only one thing: getting the hell away from home. He'd been a shit, he realized in retrospect, still angry for reasons he no longer understood.

He hadn't wanted to be a responsibility. He'd wanted to be loved.

Would he have accepted affection if Duncan offered it? Conall asked himself and knew the answer.

No.

Would Duncan have taken on the responsibility of his brothers, the burden, if he hadn't loved them?

Maybe. Duncan was the kind of man to see life as a series of responsibilities. He'd never evade one.

Panic was curling tighter in Conall's belly. He lay absolutely still in bed and his heart raced as if he'd just slammed through a locked door with gun drawn.

Hell, yes, Duncan had loved them.

Why had Niall been able to see it and I couldn't? Why did it still matter?

Especially now? Why did those two grieving boys make him feel as if he was being gutted? Why did he feel as if Lia was seeing more than anyone else ever had when she looked at him?

And why did she scare the crap out of him?

"You awake?" Henderson murmured.

"Yeah."

"Our neighbors didn't forget to take their trash out after all."

Conall swung his feet over the side of the bed, intensely glad of a distraction. "They didn't want to put it out too early."

"Most people don't wait until the middle of the night."

"Most people aren't worried about someone

going through their garbage." He stopped beside Henderson, who still had his eye to the scope. "How many cans?"

"Only one."

He grunted. "As soon as he gets back, I'll go take a look."

They could both hear the pickup driving out to the paved road; pausing, then coming back. The pickup pulled into the garage without allowing a good look at the driver's face.

"Damn it," Henderson muttered, as the garage door came down. "You want me to go out there?"

"Nah, I'll do it," Conall said. And after sitting up here in this damn attic for nearly a week, he was desperate to take action—even if that action was digging through someone's potato peelings and empty soup cans. In sudden amusement, he said, "I take it our neighbors don't recycle. Tut, tut."

Lia, of course, recycled religiously. Aluminum cans, paper and cardboard, plastic. She even cut the tops off her soup cans and ran them through the dishwasher so her recyclable goods were *clean*. As a result, she'd put out two containers: one garbage, one recycling. She was the first person he'd ever encountered who was so conscientious, and yet also willing to break the law.

He pulled on jeans and jacket, stuck his gun at the small of his back and slipped out of the house as quietly as possible. He carried a key so he could lock behind him. He didn't like the idea of leaving the inhabitants of this house vulnerable.

When he got out to the corner, he had to poke through several cans before he found the right one. Fortunately, the other neighbors on the road thought nothing of throwing away advertising circulars and the leftovers of bill paying that had their names and addresses on them. Only one can had a few ads addressed to Current Resident but nothing more personal.

Not surprising—these particular residents didn't seem to get any mail delivery that was personal. Conall knew, because he'd taken a quick look after the postal carrier came and went each day. He'd half hoped to see that his targets had bought a locking mailbox he'd have had to break into, but no. It would seem snail mail didn't interest them.

Going through someone's garbage was a potentially interesting but invariably odoriferous task. Conall wore latex gloves for that reason.

What he discovered was that the residents were subsisting on frozen food and pizza. Clearly they weren't getting their daily quota of fruits and vegetables. There wasn't so much as a carrot peeling or apple core in the can. The pizza, though, was interesting. Either they were having it delivered, or someone was going into town and picking it up. Either way, it suggested possibilities.

The pizza parlor whose boxes had been smashed flat to fit into the can must be new since Conall's day, but he could find it. Possibly the owner could be induced to cooperate. Say, allow someone to substitute for the delivery driver, or even look the other way while a listening device was inserted in the corrugated cardboard of the box. Right now, Conall would give a great deal to listen in on even one conversation. Maybe more than that, if the box then sat in the garage for up to a week until the next trash pickup.

He put the lid on the can, then ducked down as a car passed on the road, the headlights momentarily blinding him. It kept going; no one had seen him.

Conall jogged up the gravel road, careful to keep to the weedy verge where there were no pot-holes. Breaking his ankle wasn't part of the program.

He wished he'd learned more, but was energized by having any idea at all of how to penetrate the perimeter. He was usually more patient than this; a surveillance could go on for weeks or months, and rushing it could be fatal. But this time he had reason for his impatience. He needed to get the hell away from his hometown, from Duncan and Jane whose eyes were as discerning as Lia's, from Lia herself and Walker and Brendan.

He'd spent his career playing perilous games with cold-blooded killers and rarely felt even a pang of fear. Conall felt one now. He told himself it was stupid to believe he was in any kind of danger, but the way he'd felt earlier, gut clenched and heart hammering, told him he was. He didn't know how or why, and that made the threat all the greater.

As he let himself into the dark house, he remembered that tomorrow was the family reunion there was no way in hell he could avoid it. He winced. Brothers, their sweet wives, a herd of children. And him, in the spotlight.

If ever there was a time he'd needed backup.

CHAPTER SIX

LIA'S GRIP ON the shoulder belt became white-knuckled as the Suburban slowed. "Are you sure they're expecting us, too?"

"I'm sure."

She could tell Conall was trying to sound relaxed. It was absolutely no comfort to her at all that he had failed. He didn't want to be here. She and the kids were camouflage, and she, for one, didn't feel exuberantly leafy.

The boys looked... Lia stole a glance over her shoulder. Surprisingly, although they looked nervous, they were also craning their necks as Conall turned into a driveway. Sorrel was the one who sat stiffly, her expression one of massive indifference that thinly masked anxiety.

As if *she* had anything to fear. Lia, now, felt like a dumb lamb trotting through the chute into the slaughterhouse. Accompanied by a federal law enforcement agent, she was going to a potluck at a cop's house. Where yet another guest was the local police chief.

Way to avoid attention.

Why, oh, why hadn't she said gee, thanks, but no?

At least Stacy had been able to babysit and Lia hadn't had to bring the two obviously Hispanic, Spanish-speaking children. Although she had no doubt Conall had mentioned them.

The house was a white-painted bungalow. The backyard was enclosed by a six-foot board fence, gate closed. The lot was a large one for being in town, and it looked like there might be a smaller house in back.

The Suburban came a stop behind a massive black SUV. Conall set the brake and turned off the engine. Nobody moved. After a minute, Lia turned to look at him. Really look at him. That was the moment when she realized he was even more nervous than she was.

"Have you met your brothers' wives?" she asked.

"Duncan's. Her name is Jane. We said hello the other night."

"But not Niall's."

"No." Staring at the still-closed gate, he looked grim unto death.

"Aren't we getting out?" Walker asked.

Somebody had to move. Lia guessed that would be her.

With a smile over her shoulder, she said, "You bet. You can help carry things." She released her seat belt and got out. The others followed her example. By the time she was distributing covered dishes, the gate had opened, and first kids then adults poured out.

"Oh, let me take that," one of the women exclaimed, relieving Lia of a casserole dish. "My goodness, you didn't have to bring so much." She lifted it closer to her nose and took a whiff. "Although it does smell fabulous."

"Thank you," Lia said, pasting a smile on her mouth. "I wanted to make up for you, well, getting saddled with a bunch of strangers."

The woman's smile was warm. "Don't be silly. We're glad to have you. I should introduce myself, shouldn't I? I'm Jane, Duncan's wife."

"Rowan," the smaller, blonde woman said. A little girl pressed close to her side. A boy, much bolder, had already approached Walker and Brendan.

"Hi. My name's Desmond. This is my house. I'm seven. How old are you?"

"I'm eight," Walker said. "And my brother is ten."

"Oh. You want to come meet my dog? His name's Super Sam."

Super Sam broke the ice. A homely but happy creature with a tail whapping back and forth like a metronome, he licked hands and whined and tried to stick his nose under the napkin covering the dish Brendan carried. One of the men lifted it out of danger in the nick of time.

"Sam! You have to wait for leftovers."

Lia felt herself relaxing. Everyone *looked* friendly. Except she hadn't seen Duncan yet. This man must be Niall, the middle brother. He and Conall bore a close resemblance, but he had short-cropped hair that was a deep auburn.

He gripped Conall's shoulder. "Good to see you."

"And you." Conall produced one of his charming smiles for the women. "Jane. And you must be Rowan."

Introductions followed. The little girl's name was Anna. Conall drew Sorrel out and coaxed her into saying hello. Eventually they all moved into the big backyard with a huge apple tree, a small cottage at the rear of the property, and a smoking barbecue grill being tended by the other brother, whose gaze moved swiftly but thoroughly over all of them before he nodded a greeting. He was the harshest-looking of the three men, she thought, until his eyes rested briefly on his wife and his face softened.

"I heard a few squalls from the house," he said.

Jane sighed. "Thinking she'd nap while I ate was too good to be true."

"We'll take turns," he said.

"A baby?" Lia accompanied the other two women into the house, leaving Sorrel standing beside Conall. Her arms were crossed tightly over her chest, but her hands kept twitching as if she didn't know where to put them.

"I'm sorry we don't have one her age," Rowan murmured, setting Lia's bean salad on the counter and nodding toward the teenager.

Lia laughed. "That's asking a bit much. Sorrel is good with babies, if Jane wants to add her to the rotation while she eats."

Jane reappeared with a beautiful, redheaded girl. "Meet Fiona, just shy of six months. And if Sorrel would like to hold her, many blessings on her."

The two women were obviously friends, but they included Lia with such warmth, she had mostly relaxed by the time they went back outside.

The first hamburgers and hotdogs were ready for buns and condiments. Rowan told everyone to grab plates and go into the kitchen to dish up.

"After," she said, grabbing her son as he started dashing by, "washing hands." She leveled a look at Lia's two foster sons. "You, too."

They both looked alarmed but nodded.

"And you, pumpkin," she said more quietly, shooing her daughter after the boys.

Conall had one foot on the picnic table bench and a beer in his hand. Niall sat across from him, and Duncan stood with a spatula and a beer only a couple of feet away. They were an extraordinary group of men, Lia couldn't help noticing. Not exactly handsome. Their faces were too craggy, too…lived-in to qualify for *GQ*. But they were all broad-shouldered, well-built and very, very sexy. And all three had some quality that she guessed was cop. A watchfulness, a sense that they were aware of their surroundings in a way most people weren't.

Jane carried Fiona over to Conall. "Your niece," she said simply.

He studied the little girl, who studied him right back. "With Niall's hair," he said, a smile in his voice. He tossed a grin at his oldest brother. "Bet that took you by surprise."

"Dad was a redhead."

That wiped out Conall's smile. After a moment he said, "Yeah, I guess he was." To Fiona, he said, "Hey, little one."

Her eyes narrowed in suspicion, and he laughed.

But Lia's heart ached, because she didn't believe any of those smiles or laughs. She knew she was right not to when his eyes met hers and for a moment she glimpsed desperation.

There wasn't anything she could do for him but make conversation and give him pockets of time when he didn't have to try so hard, so that's what she did. When she and Sorrel went to dish up, he came with them, sticking so close his arm brushed Lia's a few times. He sat with the two of them, too, but she was intrigued to see that he also kept an eye out for the boys, not seeming satisfied until they had settled at the second picnic table with Desmond and Anna.

Jane gently questioned Sorrel and volunteered the fact that she owned a dance shop. "I so wanted to dance when I was a girl," she said, "but I never had the chance. My father didn't approve. So I've been making up for it ever since. I take classes— although it's been hard getting my body back into shape since I had Fiona," she added ruefully.

Her husband's mouth quirked. "Her store is filled with everything pink and sparkly."

She grinned at him. "We sell black leotards, too. But I do a good business in costumes for dance recitals."

Rowan talked about her desire to go back to school to get her teaching certificate, and Lia admitted that she had a certificate but had never used it. She'd been a social worker before inheriting her great-aunt's house.

"I wanted to focus on a few kids at a time," she said. "Sorrel's been a huge help with the boys, and even more with the two little kids I have temporarily."

"I guess you couldn't bring them, could you?" Jane said. "You'd have needed a school bus."

"This is nap time for them, anyway."

"Like it *should* be for my darling daughter." Jane pretended to frown at Fiona, who was currently on her dad's lap, being fed bites of baby food in between his bites of potato salad and hamburger.

Lia became increasingly aware of Conall's big body so close to her. Their thighs touched, their shoulders bumped. She could see the individual bristles on his chin when she was unwary enough to glance at him. He leaned his head close once and said, "Can I get you seconds of anything?" and took her plate when she asked for some of the fruit salad. It felt…odd, the two of them in the position of being a couple when she really hardly knew him.

Except that that wasn't true, of course. You couldn't help getting to know someone you lived with. She knew that he often forgot and left the toilet seat up, which presumably meant that he didn't live full-time with a woman. He was neat; he'd been careful to clean his whiskers from the sink when he shaved, and he was generous about doing other laundry besides his when he ran a load and about helping clean the kitchen after meals. It was funny, really, because he was more helpful than Jeff, whose wife, Lia had come to suspect, must wait on him hand and foot.

Conall was unfailingly courteous, and he was as wary as any foster child she'd ever taken in. And yet he was amazing with the kids. When Niall suggested a game of horseshoes, Conall accompanied

Walker and Brendan and she saw him bending over, showing them how to throw, guiding their hands, until she got a lump in her throat. After a minute he called Sorrel over and had her playing, too. All three men supervised, Niall carrying Anna piggyback, Duncan bouncing his daughter against his shoulder.

Lia stayed where she was, watching. Across the table from her, Rowan said softly, "He's as good with them as Niall was with Desmond and Anna."

Without taking her eyes from him, Lia said, "I don't think he realizes he is."

"Niall didn't want to care about my kids." Rowan waited until Lia looked at her, startled. "They didn't have a very good childhood, you know."

"I'm not..." Oh, boy, was this awkward. "I think you've misunderstood our relationship. Conall and I aren't... Well, anything, really. He's staying at my house because of his job." She couldn't tell if Rowan understood what she was saying. "I suspect he asked us to come today so he could lose himself in the crowd, so to speak.'

Jane had joined them, and now both women laughed. "We guessed," Jane said. "But he doesn't treat you like a casual acquaintance, either. Or—" her head turned toward the horseshoe pit "—the kids."

"I think," Lia said softly, "he sees himself in the boys."

They wanted to know Walker and Brendan's history, which she shared. She was grateful when they continued to ask questions about fostering children instead of quizzing her about Conall.

The men wandered over eventually, and conversation became general. Lia found herself laughing often, her cheeks flushed with pleasure at the company…and with her awareness of the man who once again sat close enough to touch when either of them shifted on the bench. Despite her enjoyment, Lia became aware of a deep ache of what she finally, disconcerted, decided was envy.

She had always wanted a family like this. She loved her parents, of course, but she would have given almost anything for siblings. Being an only child was lonely, especially given the lack of extended family nearby.

Mama had sisters and brothers in Mexico, of course, and they had children, Lia's cousins. She remembered them distantly from the year she and Mama had lived down there, when Lia was five. As an adult she had visited their village in Chiapas, but she was a visitor, with her paler skin and odd-colored eyes and American ways more of a curiosity than really family. She'd had the awful feeling that their friendliness had more to do with their hope that she'd help some of the young adults come to the United States than to any closer feelings.

This was the kind of family she wanted. Laughter, affection, people who would love your children if anything ever happened to you. She could tell that much of the relaxed atmosphere came from the two women, and she wished she knew more about them. Had they grown up taking this for granted?

But she couldn't exactly ask them.

The ache stayed, and some of it was for Conall who, on the surface, was comfortable sipping a beer, laughing at his brothers' stories, telling a few of his own, but who was really faking it, Lia suspected. She intercepted a couple of keen glances that made her wonder if Niall and Duncan suspected, too. Jane kept an eye on her husband as if worried about him, and that made Lia wonder if *he* was faking it, too.

The more she became aware of the undercurrents, the more she realized her envy might be misplaced. Maybe nothing was as it appeared.

Except she didn't believe that. The way Niall touched his wife occasionally, as if he needed to reassure himself that she was there and his; the way Duncan's hard mouth softened for Jane, his gentle hands on small, redheaded Fiona. Undercurrents there might be, but there was love here, too.

The ache intensified at the fear she might never find this. Maybe she'd never be anything but a temporary mother.

You made your choices, she reminded herself. She should be glad to know there *were* families like this, given the awful backgrounds so many of her kids came from. If she could give them even a glimpse of what it could be like, hope to hold on to while their own families worked out their problems or they waited for adoptive parents, then she was doing something worthwhile. She didn't usually waste time and heartache being greedy and wishing for everything. Maybe it would have been better if she hadn't come today.

But no. She was no good at resisting when someone needed her, and today Conall had, if only temporarily.

Story of her life.

WELL, THAT WAS DONE, Conall thought. The need to relieve Henderson had been a good excuse for an early departure. He couldn't help noticing how hastily Lia had agreed to head home. Maybe she was worried about Julia and Arturo, or maybe she was bored out of her skull, he didn't know. Sorrel had slipped quietly out of the yard with them and into her seat in the Suburban, but the boys couldn't make such an easy getaway. Desmond wouldn't let them. He followed, chattering and wishing Walker could play soccer, too, cuz there was a spring league, you know, and he was starting swimming lessons pretty soon, too, when school let out. Swim lessons were fun. Maybe Lia would bring Walker and Brendan, too. Did they know how to swim?

Conall swore his mouth was still moving even as the Suburban backed out of the driveway. He had to admit to being mildly amused at Niall stuck living with a motor-mouth. Niall never was much of a talker himself.

The drive was mostly quiet, the kids having all lapsed into silence. Once Conall glanced at Lia and said, "You okay?" and she nodded.

At home, with a hand on her arm he stopped her from getting out with the others. "Thank you for coming."

Her smile was unbelievably sweet. "You're very welcome. We all had a good time, you know. You have a nice family."

"Yeah." The concept was new enough to him to take him aback. "I guess I do."

She touched him this time, a quick squeeze on his bare forearm. "You're lucky," she said, her voice momentarily husky. And then she slipped out, slamming the door and hurrying toward the house.

He was left sitting behind the wheel, staring after her, feeling…hell. Dazed. Normally it took a pretty good punch to make his head swim. Frowning, he tried to figure out what she'd done or said and couldn't put his finger on it.

He heard her talking to the babysitter as he went upstairs, but didn't see her. Later, Brendan brought up a light supper for him and he told himself he was glad he wasn't downstairs with everyone else, including his partner. He'd used up his social quotient for the day. He was irritated that he felt restless rather than relaxing into the pleasure of solitude.

Except for a couple of visits to the john, he didn't leave the attic again until morning. He'd missed breakfast, it seemed, and ate a bowl of cold cereal at the kitchen counter. Muted explosions sounded from the living room, where the TV was already on. Sorrel's bedroom door had been shut when Conall came down; he had no idea whether she was up.

The phone rang, and someone answered elsewhere in the house or outside. A moment later the front door opened and footsteps hurried in. Leaving his bowl in the sink, he stretched and then wandered out of the kitchen to see what was going on.

Lia, carrying Julia, was dashing for the stairs.

"Where's Arturo?" Conall asked.

She spun to face him. "Oh. I left him with the boys. They can watch him for a few minutes. That was Julia and Arturo's caseworker. He's on his way to pick them up, so I need to hurry and pack their things."

He loved the way her cheeks flushed. Lia wasn't a very good liar. Her voice had hitched on the word *caseworker*, not so as most people would have noticed, but reading people's motives and intentions and honesty was a life or death skill for him.

"Need help?" he asked.

"No." She took a couple more steps, then stopped. "Unless..."

Even before she turned, he knew what she had in mind. Damn, he'd had to open his mouth.

The next thing he knew, he was left with an armful of baby girl while Lia dashed upstairs. What was he supposed to *do* with her?

She looked at him with equal alarm. When her face started to redden, he jiggled her. "Uh...what say we go back outside? You like it outside, don't you?"

She was withholding judgment. The day was nice, he discovered the minute they stepped out. A hint of spring crispness in the air, a promise of warmth by midday. Conall thought of sitting down on the rocker, but the little girl's suspicious stare convinced him she required greater distraction. Cows, he decided. Or maybe horses. Yeah, the pony was right beside the fence.

He carried Julia down the steps and jogged across the lawn. "Horsie," he said. "No, *el caballo.* Actually, *caballito. Sí?*"

She didn't care what the pony was called. Babbling happily but unintelligibly, she twisted in his arms and tried to lunge for the fat little beast, managing to grab a fistful of white mane when the pony stuck his head between fence rails.

"*Bueno.* Pet the pony. See?" He demonstrated, patting the neck.

Julia laughed and pulled hard. One of her hands separated from the mane, taking a few long strands of stiff hair with it. Conall winced and gently pried her other fist from the poor animal. He spread her fingers and ran her hand over the nose, and was surprised by an expression of rapt delight on her round face.

"Yeah," he murmured, "that's more like it. Nice pony. *Caballito.* That's how we pet the pony."

His head came up when he heard a car engine on the road. The vehicle wasn't either the pickup or SUV with tinted windows he and Henderson had seen coming and going from the neighbor house. This one, he could tell even before it turned into Lia's driveway, was aging and needed a tune up.

The car was a big old Buick, almost old enough to beg for restoration if it weren't for the fact that it probably got twelve miles to the gallon. Besides, who'd want it? The door squealed when the driver opened it. Conall wondered what shape the shocks were in and how the car had handled the potholes.

A Hispanic man who might be in his forties stepped out, his dark eyes going right away to Conall who, carrying Julia, strolled over to meet him.

"Lia expecting you?" he asked.

"Yes, I'm Mateo Gonzalez." He had a slight accent. "And you are?"

"Conall MacLachlan. Julia and I were visiting *el caballito*." He grinned at the little girl, who grinned back.

"I'm here to pick Julia and her brother up. Her, er, aunt has arrived to get the kids."

"Has she," Conall said blandly. "And here I thought Lia said their mother would be back for them. When she could make it."

The guy was sweating. Conall knew he shouldn't toy with him, but he couldn't seem to help himself.

Lia burst out the front door, and both men's gazes swung to her. "Mateo. You've met Conall? I've got their stuff, but I'll have to go back for Arturo. Oh, and their car seats are still in the Subaru."

"Right. I'll go get them," Conall said.

Julia indignantly declined to go into Mateo's arms. Accordingly, Conall carried her to the barn where the Subaru was parked, handing the other man one of the child seats while Conall grabbed the second one with his free hand. Mateo had buckled both into the back of his Buick by the time Lia returned, breathless, with Arturo. While Mateo loaded their limited possessions into the trunk and slammed it, Conall watched as Lia settled Arturo into his car seat and said her goodbyes. Her eyes were glazed with tears as she took Julia from him and circled the car to put her in, too. Then she and Mateo talked quietly, giving a couple of quick glances at Conall, before Mateo got in and drove away. Lia watched it go with one hand pressed to her mouth.

"How long have you had them?"

"Only…uh, three weeks." She gave a tiny, resigned sniff. "I know I'm being silly, but I hate to say goodbye."

"But you do it all the time."

She nodded.

"It must be a hell of a lot harder when you've had the kids for months."

"Yes."

"Why? Why foster if it kills you every time they leave?" He didn't begin to get it.

Her eyes were still shiny when they touched on his, then slid away. "It's…complicated."

Complicated. What did *that* mean? And why did it matter to him?

He shook his head. "You need to learn not to get attached."

Lia's laugh was small and broken. "You're kidding, right?"

"Why would I be kidding?"

"How can I make them feel safe and loved if I don't get attached?"

"Pretend," he said, with a shrug. "Say the right things, cook for 'em, rock them to sleep if you have to, but don't let yourself feel anything."

Her eyes searched his. "So easy."

He shifted, not liking the pity he saw on her face. "It has to be when you do my job."

After a minute Lia said, "I suppose you're right. But you know, it's a lot easier to pretend with adults than it is with kids."

Conall guessed that might be true. Maybe that's why kids usually made him uneasy. The way they'd stare so openly, laying their emotions out there as foolishly as a wild animal that didn't guard its scent from predators.

When he didn't say anything, Lia started for the house. "I need to check on the boys."

To her back, he said, "Lia."

She stopped without turning.

He made his voice hard. "Tell me Matteo doesn't know who I am and why I'm here."

Her shoulders stiffened. At last, slowly, she faced him. "He won't say anything."

"Goddamn it!" he roared. "The one and only thing I asked of you."

Her eyes widened in outrage. "The one and only?" She stalked to him and stabbed his chest with her index finger. "Along with breakfast, lunch and dinner? Sharing my bathroom with two men?" Her voice kept rising. "Making excuses every time anyone I know wants to visit? Scaring me now that I know I have drug dealers living next door?"

Would it help to argue that he was doing most of his and Jeff's laundry and helping clean the kitchen? Seeing her expression, he guessed probably not.

"I needed him to know how important—" She screeched on the brakes, likely remembering exactly why she had *needed* the kids gone.

Did she really think he'd turn her in? Her lack of trust stung for no good reason. He'd only been here a week. She didn't know him that well.

Conall sighed. "I won't turn you in, Lia."

Could her eyes get any wider? "Turn me in for… what?" she whispered.

"I know those kids are illegal."

"How…?" She really was scared now, panting for her next breath. "What?"

"It's all right," he said quietly. "I promise you."

"Oh, God." She backed away.

Conall held both hands up, palms out. *No harm.*

"Lia, I mean it. I know you think you're doing a good thing..."

That fired some anger on top of her panic. "Think?"

"Will you tell me why you do it?"

She was beautiful scared and mad. The green seemed intensified in her eyes. Lashes clumped together from her earlier tears. She almost vibrated from the force of her emotions.

No, she was always beautiful. He admired her bustling in the kitchen, he liked her shy, maybe most of all he was stirred by her tenderness with the children. He had yet to see a moment when he didn't think she was beautiful.

"Why do you want to know?" she asked, her voice constrained.

"I want to understand."

"Why?" she said again.

He scrubbed both hands over his face. "I don't know."

Lia blew out a breath, her eyes closing momentarily so that those thick lashes fanned above her cheeks. When she opened them, he saw resignation again, deeper and more hurtful than what she'd felt at saying goodbye to two small children. Conall felt a kick in his chest.

"I really do need to check on Walker and Brendan."

He nodded.

She hurried away. He couldn't help appreciating the view from behind of her graceful gait and subtle curves. The braid, fat and black, swinging gently, seemed to emphasize the slenderness of her rib cage and waist, the feathery tip pointing to her perfect ass.

God, he was a bastard.

When the screen door slammed behind her, Conall walked over to pet the pony again. This time the horse came to the fence, too, both noses nudging him hopefully.

"I'll bring you a carrot next time," he told them. He hadn't had much to do with horses, but they did like carrots, didn't they? He'd met more burros in his time, still popular as a beast of burden for the poor in Mexico.

He heard the screen door again, but waited where he was for her. When she joined him at the fence, he turned and leaned his back against a post.

"I haven't seen Sorrel this morning," he said, trying to lessen the tension.

Lia went along with it. "She's eating breakfast right now. I think she stayed up late online last night."

"Does she have friends there?"

"I think so. And a Facebook page, of course." At his expression, she said, "I'm keeping an eye on it. She hasn't said anything about you or Jeff there.

And nobody who has posted has commented. I really do think she understands why it's important that she keep quiet."

She was thirteen. A mass of hormones. Conall only shook his head, hoping.

Stroking the shaggy pony's ears, Lia didn't look at him. "How did you know?"

"About Arturo and Julia?"

She nodded.

"You're not a very good liar," he said gently. "And I could see that you were worried." He hesitated. "Duncan told me he'd heard something."

That brought her terrified gaze to his. "Your brother?"

"He told me he didn't know if it was true or not, but he wasn't going to do anything about it. The local P.D. stays out of immigration issues. People have to trust them, be willing to talk to them when a crime has been committed. If they're afraid of being asked to prove their citizenship, they won't talk to cops."

"But there's been talk." This was said so softly, he had to tilt his head to hear her.

"Maybe not that much." Watching her, he said, "Do you want me to ask him?"

"I...don't know." Lia turned blindly back to the animals, leaning her face against the horse's neck.

"The kids are gone. You have nothing to fear right now."

She laughed, but not happily. "Right now."

"You could quit."

"It's…important to me."

"Make me understand," he said again.

Her eyes lifted to his, and he couldn't have looked away to save his life. "Do I have a choice?"

He felt again as if the horse had somehow planted one of those hooves smack in the middle of his chest, maybe denting a few ribs. Conall hadn't felt anything like this since he was a kid.

Back off, he told himself. *I don't need to understand. I don't need anything from her.*

But now he was lying to himself.

He swallowed. "Yes." His voice roughened. "I meant it when I said I won't tell anyone. Talking to me is optional."

Still she looked at him, her eyes searching, intense. He couldn't remember the last time he'd taken a breath.

Abruptly he was freed; she was stroking the horse, gazing out across the pasture. "I guess it doesn't matter now. You're right. Julia and Arturo are gone. If you really want to know…"

"I want." Hell, now he sounded hoarse. He wanted her in a hundred ways.

Foolish, and dangerous.

Lia only nodded. "Okay."

She laughed, but not happily. "Right now,
You could quit.
"It's important to me.
"Make me understand," he said again.
He eyed... wouldn't have
looked away to save his life. "Do I have a choice?"
He felt again as if the horse had somehow

CHAPTER SEVEN

LIA CLIMBED THROUGH the fence rails, wanting a
barrier of some kind between her and Conall. As
if it would do her any good at all.

After hopeful and unfruitful nudges at her
empty jeans pockets, horse and pony wandered
a few feet away and began to graze. She crossed
her forearms on the fence.

"My mother was here illegally." She grimaced.
"I told you that, didn't I?"

He rested one booted foot on the lowest rail
and nodded.

"Mom came here with two of her brothers. I
guess they stayed in the L.A. area for a bit, then
gradually headed north. None of them wanted to
work in agriculture. My uncle Guillermo is a me-
chanic and Uncle Jorge mostly did construction,
I think. Mom found jobs as a maid." This wasn't
the painful part of the story for her. Very aware
of Conall's keen gray eyes, she continued.

"Mom met my dad when she was cleaning of-
fices. Dad is an electrical contractor. They had a
thing, she got pregnant, but they didn't get mar-

ried at first. Maybe he was embarrassed by her, I don't know."

"Why would he be embarrassed?"

"She was uneducated, a maid. I doubt she'd picked up more than broken English by then. She still has a really strong accent."

"Is she as beautiful as you are?"

That made her cheeks heat. "I— Mom is pretty. But she's darker-skinned, of course." Dad and Mom hadn't done much socializing, and by her teenage years Lia had suspected he was still embarrassed by his obviously Hispanic wife. Lia had never been sure; her father wasn't exactly the warm and fuzzy kind, so maybe he simply hadn't made friends.

"But he did marry her."

"Not at first. We lived with him, but…it was more like she was his housekeeper. Mostly I remember Mom yelling a lot and him getting stony-faced and slamming his study door." She shrugged as if it didn't matter. "When I was five, Mom and I were deported."

Shock showed on Conall's face. "What?"

"She was cleaning rooms at a hotel and she'd taken me to work with her that day. There was a raid, and we were rounded up with a bunch of other maids and, I don't know, I think a gardener and a maintenance guy—all illegal. Of course Mom didn't have my birth certificate with her, and I doubt it would have made any difference if she had had it." Lia toed a rough clump of grass, focusing on it. "I remember being scared. They weren't very nice to us. It was like we were cattle. We got taken to some kind of processing place where there were a couple hundred other people they'd rounded up. We slept on pallets and then they flew us to Mexico."

"Was your mother able to contact your father?"

"I don't think they gave her the chance. She did later, once we were in her home village, and that's when he decided to marry her. But getting papers for us even after they were married wasn't easy. We stayed there for a year and a half." She swallowed and said with quiet force, "I hated it."

"Mexico?"

"Yes…no. It was being transplanted like that. I had nightmares for a long time about being rounded up. I think I got separated from Mom once. At least in my nightmares I always did." She hadn't had that one in a long time, but it had made occasional appearances even when she was in her twenties. "These men were laughing and grabbing at me…" Her throat closed at the memory. "Probably they were trying to help, but they scared me. Even once we got there and Mom's family took us in, I never fit in the village even though I spoke Spanish." She laughed a little. "Honestly, I was probably a spoiled little princess. It was really primitive compared to what I was used to. I became painfully shy and I clung to Mom but I was mad at her, too, because she didn't take me home."

"Thus Arturo and Julia." The understanding in his eyes twisted something in her.

"Yes. Maybe for kids like them it would be less traumatic to have stayed with their mom, but I'm not convinced. I'd like to think the process isn't as brutal now as it was when it happened to Mom and me, but I've heard some awful stories. And also…" She hesitated. "Well, obviously the kids weren't with their mother when she was arrested. If she'd told immigration agents where to find her children, she'd have been ratting on a bunch of other people who probably didn't have papers, either. If they'd been family, they probably would have taken care of Arturo and Julia, but they weren't. There's this sort of, um, underground network for making sure the children stay safe when that kind of thing happens. Sometimes when the kids leave me they do go back to Mexico or the Dominican Republic or wherever their parents are. Sometimes another family member eventually comes for them. And sometimes…" She flicked a glance at him.

"Sometimes Mom or Dad sneaks across the border and comes to pick up their own kids."

"Yes. I never meet them. Matteo is my main

contact." She narrowed her eyes at Conall. "Will you report him?"

He shook his head. "I said I wouldn't get you in trouble, Lia. As far as I'm concerned, Matteo was never here. I didn't meet him. Some caseworker picked up the kids. Why would I pay attention?"

"Thank you," she made herself say.

"You don't have to thank me, Lia." His voice was like a soft touch, one that raised goose bumps on her arms. He sounded…tender, a word she immediately tried to reject. She had to be imagining it.

"Yes, I do." She stiffened. "Does Jeff know, too?"

"I don't think so. He hasn't said anything and neither have I. I don't get the feeling he's all that observant."

Lia didn't, either. "But he's a DEA agent."

"He's good for this kind of job, but I don't think he's done much undercover work. He hasn't learned to watch everyone, always."

"How can you do that? Doesn't the stress kill you?"

"It becomes habit. Everybody has an intuitive awareness of their surroundings. It's a survival skill. Most people deliberately tamp it down. They convince themselves it's unnecessary. For me it is."

That simple. He was matter-of-fact about it. He did a dangerous job and needed to be preternaturally aware of everyone and everything around him. She'd never had a hope of avoiding his sharp eye, Lia realized. She was lucky, that's all, because he'd deemed what she did harmless enough not to weigh against her usefulness. He was being practical, that's all. For him, the mystery was solved. For her…well, she either had to trust him or to say no the next time—and every time—Matteo called.

"Will you ask your brother who he heard the rumor from?"

"Yes." He paused. "Are you close to your parents?"

Lia gave a choked laugh. "You noticed, huh? I talk to Mom regularly. Dad only when he happens to answer the phone. He's a really distant guy. I love him, but I'm not sure I like him very much. He and Mom still have kind of a strange relationship. She waits on him, he takes her for granted." She laughed again. "Okay, maybe not so strange. There are probably lots of marriages like that."

"No sisters or brothers?"

"Mom got pregnant once after me, while we were down in Mexico. She started hemorrhaging and ended up not only miscarrying but having to have a hysterectomy. It was…really awful." Another shadow on her memory of that time.

"You relate well to the kids who come to you because you know what it feels like to be abruptly transplanted."

"I suppose so."

"You really do care about them all." His tone was odd and she looked at him in surprise.

"Of course I do." Understanding, she tilted her head to one side. "You thought I did it for the money."

"Do you blame me for wondering?"

Lia spread her arms out. "Do I look like someone who is very interested in money?"

Conall sighed. "No. Call me a cynic. I've never had occasion to meet anyone prepared to give their all to someone else's kids."

Or their own? His parents apparently hadn't given much of anything to their sons.

"No, I don't blame you for being a cynic. And I can't deny there are people who *do* foster for the money. That's not the end of the world if they're reasonably kind. They still give refuge to kids who need it. And really, no matter how much we love our jobs, we expect to be paid, right? For me, though, fostering children is more of a vocation."

"Yes." He studied her then with minute attention to detail, as if she was a curiosity he never expected to encounter again and wanted to remember. Lia was uncomfortable but withstood it.

After a minute she said, "I had the impression your brother Niall loves his stepchildren. He was really good with them."

"I noticed. He said *our children*."

"Desmond is quite a character."

"Yeah." Conall smiled. "Not what you'd call shy."

Relaxing finally, Lia giggled. "Definitely not shy. Walker and Brendan didn't know what had hit them."

"What do you think about those swimming lessons? Will they be here with you long enough?"

"I don't know. I hope so."

"Does the state fund stuff like that?"

"When they don't, I do. I treat the children I have as much as if they were really mine as I can."

"And then you let them go." The understanding in his eyes shattered her.

Her voice a little thick, Lia said, "Yes. I have to."

"Are you ever tempted…?"

"Of course I am." She tried to smile. "Most of the time, my keeping them isn't even a possibility. They're here while their own families work out their problems. It's unusual for me to have kids who have been released for adoption."

"Like Walker and Brendan."

"Yes." Part of her hoped they were taken away soon. If they stayed too long, saying goodbye might kill her. She wanted so much to see them happy again. She straightened her shoulders. "Speaking of which, I'd better go in."

"Yeah, I should probably relieve Jeff or try to get some more sleep."

"You keep weird hours," she observed, as she ducked through the fence.

He fell in at her side when she started for the house. "You get used to that. Bad guys tend to be nocturnal."

"I suppose it makes sense that they like to operate under the cover of night." She glanced at him. "Are you nocturnal?"

"I...adapt." His face gave nothing away. "I'm good at adapting."

Why did that make her sad? Because she wondered how much of himself he held on to, beneath the ever-changing protective coloration? Would she even recognize him in a different role? Would he be as...kind, if he had become someone else entirely?

I will always recognize him, an inner voice whispered. The set of his shoulders, the long lazy stride, the way his mouth tightened or shadows crossed his eyes. The flicker of his smile, the rough texture of his wavy, too-shaggy hair.

Shocked, Lia kept her gaze fixed on the house. She was halfway to falling in love with a man who she really, truly didn't know. Who was so not a settling down kind of guy.

A picture of him running through the sprinkler, laughing at Arturo, coaxing Brendan and Walker to dip their toes back into life, passed through her mind and so did a wistful belief. *He could be.*

Dream on, she thought wryly. He was sexy, he was nice to the boys, and here she was having fantasies about him transforming into a family man. A guy who'd obviously rather be in a gunfight than spend a sunny spring afternoon with the family he did have.

Yes, but...

Forget it, Lia told herself firmly. If she ever had a real relationship, it would be with a man who could love each and every child she took in as much as she did. And face it, guys like that were thin on the ground. Maybe nonexistent.

Conall might be attracted to her, too—not *might be, was*—but he hadn't even tried to kiss her. *He* knew how ill-suited they were.

She should be glad. He was temporary. She'd really like not to have to cry when he left.

CONALL'S INSTINCT WAS to sneak past the living room, where the boys were, once again, watching... He paused to hear a line of dialogue from the movie. Yeah, what else, *The Transformers*. One, two or three, he wasn't sure. Only that this could not possibly be healthy for them.

He stifled a groan. Lia was out weeding her vegetable garden. He'd seen her from the window, watched hungrily for several minutes as she looked up to watch a robin, a smile lighting her face with joy he could see even from a distance.

Damn it, she should have dragged the boys out with her whether they wanted to go or not.

Stepping into the doorway, he said, "Hey."

They both glanced away from the TV, which was progress from the first time he'd met them.

"It's a nice day. Why are you in here? I'll bet Lia could use some help outside."

"We don't want to weed. She said we didn't have to."

Well, okay. He guessed that forcing foster children to provide free labor might get her into trouble. Or maybe she thought they shouldn't have to do chores yet. She was wrong, but that was her business.

He hesitated. He had told her he'd try to spend some time with the boys, and it wasn't as if he had anything important to do right now. He'd slept for close to six hours—enough for him—and had eaten lunch.

"Let's do something fun," he suggested. "We can throw the ball a little." If there was a baseball to throw. Or mitts to catch with, come to think of it. "Let me check with Lia and see what she has."

They studied him then looked at each other. It was Brendan who finally said, "Okay." He didn't exactly sound excited, but willing was good enough.

Lia was on her knees in the middle of a row of…something. The label at the end said carrots.

Did carrots from your own garden taste any better than ones from the grocery store?

His speculation was mere distraction from the woman. She wore faded overalls that would probably be sacky were she standing...but she wasn't. The denim pulled taut over a tight, firm ass that had already been fueling his dreams. Only one shoulder strap was fastened; the other hung down her back beside that fat, glossy braid. She wore only a thin tank top beneath the overalls, exposing her shoulders and arms, both tanned to a pale gold. He wanted desperately to drop to his knees behind her, shift her braid aside and explore her neck with his mouth while feeling her rump against his groin.

He gritted his teeth and managed to ask his question with only a slight huskiness in his voice to betray him.

She turned in surprise, blinking up at him. "Baseball mitts? Sure, there's a whole bin full of sports equipment out in the barn. It's on the left side, made out of plywood, with a lid that lifts."

"Right." He remembered seeing it.

"Watch out for spiders."

"Good thought," he muttered.

"Thank you," she said, which left him irritated.

"Damn it, would you quit that? I live here with you, I have time on my hands and I'm decent enough to spend time with the kids. That doesn't make me a saint, and it's sure as hell no reason for you to be grateful." He stalked away without giving her a chance to respond.

Decent. Was he really? He'd been standing there with a damned hard-on imagining taking her from behind, and she was apparently oblivious and probably eager to get back to pulling weeds.

Conall growled a few obscenities under his breath, just to get them out of his way, then commandeered the boys and dragged them out to the barn with him.

There were spiders in the bin, but he brushed them off. Grinning at the boys who'd leaped back in obvious horror, Conall said, "These are nothing. You ever see a tarantula?"

"My third grade teacher had one," Brendan said cautiously. "He brought it to school a couple of times. In an aquarium."

"They're all over in Mexico and farther south. I was taking a shower one time and when I reached for my towel my hand brushed this black, hairy tarantula. Had to be this big." He made a circle with his hands. "Scared the…uh, crap out of me."

They giggled.

"Like I said, these itty-bitty spiders are nothing."

Walker broke into a sing-song. "The itsy bitsy spider went up the waterspout…"

They all laughed.

Conall found mitts that fit their hands pretty well, and one for himself, too. Lia had baseballs, softballs and a variety of bats. Not to mention soccer balls in a couple of sizes, ditto basketballs, even what looked like, when he partially untangled it, a net for badminton. Hey, that might be fun. He hadn't played it since he was a little kid. Yeah, when he dug deeper there were rackets and shuttlecocks buried at the bottom. He dragged them out and set them aside.

Then he and the boys threw the ball for a while, with him making a few suggestions and watching their aim and velocity improve. Brendan, it developed, had played Little League for a couple of years, Walker T-ball when he was really young.

"Lots of the kids at school are playing Little League right now," Walker said, sounding envious.

"Next year, I bet you can, too," Conall said. "In the meantime, we'll work on your skills. What do you say?"

They thought that sounded fine. When their arms started to get tired, he brought out the bats and created a makeshift home plate from a piece of plywood he found in the barn. Lia had damn near everything in there, although some order might make it easier to find things. Maybe while he was here he'd offer to put up some racks for tools, clean up a little. Make himself useful. The boys could help. Helping would be good for them, and learning some basic construction skills wouldn't hurt, either.

Brendan had a good eye, and popped up some nice fly balls and one line drive that got by Conall, to the boys' delight. Conall began to wonder whether Walker was seeing the ball very well, but he didn't say anything.

"We'll try you out as pitchers tomorrow," he suggested. "Nope, not today. We don't want to wear out your shoulders. Come on, why don't you help me set up that badminton net? I'll bet Sorrel would like to play, too."

They decided to set it up at the side of the house, so as not to get in the way of their baseball field in front. Lia came to see what they were doing and helped.

"I think I hear the school bus," she said. "Girls against the boys."

Conall mostly coached from the sidelines, but a few times he got talked into substituting for one of the boys. Lia played with vigor if not a lot of skill. She got pink-cheeked and sweaty and stubborn, refusing to lose. Lucky for her, Sorrel was good with the racket.

"We play in P.E. sometimes," she admitted. "I like to win."

"Me, too," her partner declared.

Conall was in at match point. He blasted the shuttlecock over the net and laughed aloud at the sight of Lia diving for it. Somehow she scooped it up and it fluttered weakly over the net where he was waiting to slam it back at her. He hadn't paid enough attention to Sorrel, though. She blocked it and dumped it over the net and to the ground on the guy's side before either Walker or Conall could get to it.

Jumping up and down, Sorrel yelled, "Yes, yes, yes!" Lia hugged her and did some jumping up and down, too.

Conall grinned and bent to put his mouth closer to Walker's ear. "They're not what you'd call gracious winners, are they?"

Brendan had come over and heard him. "We'll beat their pants off tomorrow."

Conall really wanted to see Lia with her pants off. He wanted that more than he'd wanted anything in a long time. But if it happened—when it happened—it would be a private event.

"Darned straight," he told the boys, his eyes meeting Lia's laughing, triumphant gaze.

IT WAS A GOOD WEEK.

Except for the job, that is. The surveillance was going nowhere fast. Duncan had talked to the owner of the pizza place, but next thing Conall knew there were pizza boxes from a couple of different restaurants in the trash. No interesting mail. No more late-night visitors. Two men came and went a few times, during the day. Henderson followed them once and came back reporting that they'd grocery shopped and filled the pickup with gas. He'd gotten close enough in the grocery store to see that they were buying mostly frozen food and packaged cookies, plus some magazines and the Sunday *Seattle Times*. Neither of the two were familiar to either Conall or Henderson. They took pictures and sent them off to see if a match could be made. Conall waited semi-patiently for the late-night visitors to return, but it didn't happen.

He marveled at how little he minded. He should be getting irritable by now. Two weeks, and no breaks. That wasn't unusual, but he preferred action of almost any kind to these long, wait-and-see-what-happens gigs. This time…okay, this time he was enjoying himself. He decided he would think of it as a vacation. He didn't often do those, but this could be a good, if unlikely, substitute.

He mentioned to Lia his observation about Walker, and she made an appointment to take him to an ophthalmologist for an eye exam. The kid came home wearing glasses. He looked surprisingly cute in them, and he kept saying in amazement, "Wow. I never noticed before." He spent a lot of time staring at blades of grass or spiderwebs in the barn and even faces. Heck, *The Transformers* would probably seem new to him.

They played baseball every day, the boys noticeably gaining strength and skill until they were keeping Conall on his toes. Neither had ever played soccer, so he taught them that sport, too.

"You must have played when you were a kid," Lia said at dinner one evening, but he shook his head.

"Little League, but not soccer. These past few years I've spent a lot of time in Latin America. Everyone plays. Well, the boys and men play," he amended, grinning at the way Lia's eyes narrowed.

"The village where I lived had a soccer field," she said. "Not really a field because it was bare dirt, but that's where they played."

"Most of them are bare dirt. Not only in Mexico. South Africa, Greece…" He shrugged. "Any place with a dry climate where they can't afford to water a field that isn't productive."

Brendan wanted to know what he meant about productive, and he explained, "Where they grow food. Or grass to feed animals that provide food."

"Oh. Like Lia waters her garden."

"Right." They were eating the first green beans from her garden tonight, and they were really good. Jeff and Conall alternated nights at the dinner table, although Jeff had mostly conceded him the days downstairs.

"Those boys freak me out," he'd said. "They're like zombies. I don't know what to say to them."

"You were supposed to be the expert on kids."

"I guess I'm not that good with them. My own are— They're *normal*. You know?"

"Because their father didn't walk out on them and their mother hasn't died."

He'd flushed, and Conall regretted his harsh tone. Henderson was an okay guy, but he'd grown up in a *normal* family himself and then found himself a nice wife. He wasn't what you'd call imaginative. Conall found himself spending more and more waking hours downstairs with Lia and the kids. He felt a little guilty about that, but Jeff bored him.

Conall should be bored with eight- and ten-year-old boys, too, but he wasn't. These two were really growing on him. He liked less and less thinking about what their future held. They could be happy here with Lia, couldn't they? Why shouldn't she keep them?

Conall knew they'd been curious about what was happening in the attic, so when Brendan asked to come upstairs and see the equipment the men were using to spy on the house next door, Conall agreed. Lia looked a little more doubtful, but finally said, "Well, I guess."

Maybe he shouldn't be sharing so much with the kids, but he couldn't see how they'd be a risk. They never went anywhere or talked to anyone outside the household. Sorrel was a different story; Conall still worried about her opening her mouth at the wrong time or place. But what was the harm in giving Walker and Brendan something new to think about?

Walker almost immediately became distracted by the other wonders the attic held. He bounced on the bed and said wistfully, "It would be fun if *we* could sleep up here." The naked mannequin was a source of great fascination for him.

Conall, grinning, asked, "Haven't you ever seen a girl naked before? Or your mom?"

Walker's eyes got wide and he shook his head so hard he had to grab for his new glasses. "My *mom*? I barely even saw her in a bathing suit. Right, Bren? And I never saw a girl without her clothes on." He sounded aghast but simultaneously intrigued by the idea, which amused Conall. Brendan didn't say anything, but his cheeks colored some.

Jeff let him look through the scopes and the binoculars and see what the digital video looked like when they ran it back. He asked if they could hear what the people over there said, and Conall explained why they couldn't but how listening devices worked when it was possible either to get close enough to utilize them, or for a bug to be inserted.

"You've seen on TV shows how the cops use a van that's filled with computers? That works in a city where no one notices an extra van with darkened windows parked down the block, but not so well here in the country."

The boy nodded, his forehead furrowed.

"If we could set up a sort of satellite dish listening device close to the house—say, right at the fence line—we could probably hear what they say when they're outside, but that's not practical. The dogs would hear us if we got that close, for one thing, and the men would come to investigate. Our cover would be blown."

"Would they shoot you, like on TV?"

Conall hesitated, wondering how Lia would want him to handle a question like that. "That depends what they're up to. If they're dealing marijuana, they might not even have guns, and they sure wouldn't take a chance on shooting a law enforcement officer. If they're doing something really bad, they might think it was a risk worth taking."

"So how would you get one of these bugs in their house?" Brendan asked.

Out of the corner of his eye, Conall watched Walker who had begun cracking open boxes and peering at the contents. He wasn't dumping things out, though.

"Depends," Conall said. "Sneak over there, maybe, or get really clever." He explained about the pizza box idea and why it had been a no-go so far. He also explained a little about laws and warrants and what he and Jeff had to do to make sure any evidence they gathered would be admissible in court, and why illegally acquired evidence wouldn't be.

The kid listened solemnly, soaking it all in. Conall was afraid he had become the object of a minor case of hero worship. Still, what had it hurt to indulge Brendan's curiosity?

Walker materialized at his side. "Can we go outside? I want to practice batting now that I can see."

"Why not?" Conall gripped his shoulder. "Let's be careful not to break those new glasses, though. Lia wouldn't be happy with us."

"She bought insurance," Walker told him happily. "She said she expects I will break them."

"Sensible woman. Bren, you up to doing some pitching?"

The older boy looked up from the array of small listening devices he'd been examining. "Huh? Oh, sure. Yeah." Politely he turned to Jeff. "Thank you for showing everything to me."

Smiling, Henderson said, "My pleasure."

"Remember," Conall cautioned as he escorted the boys downstairs, "the attic is still off-limits. Okay?"

"I wish we could have a sleepover." Walker looked up at him hopefully. "I'd really like that."

"Nope." Conall made sure he sounded firm. "When we're up there, we have to concentrate.

What we're doing isn't fun and games. We're trying to catch some criminals. That's an important job. Do you understand that?"

They both nodded.

"Cuz you're the good guys," Walker said, "and they're the bad guys."

Conall tugged his hair affectionately. "You got it."

"Can I bat first?"

"If it's okay with your brother."

Brendan rolled his eyes. "I'd rather pitch anyway."

"That makes me the catcher."

"I bet Lia would play outfielder. Do you think she would?"

Lia hated playing outfielder. But Conall laughed. "Never hurts to ask, does it?"

CHAPTER EIGHT

SO FAR JEFF had continued to sleep in the attic, while Conall had taken over the small room with the childish twin bed. He came downstairs sometime between 3:00 and 5:00 a.m., whenever Henderson relieved him. The house would be completely silent, the boys' and Sorrel's bedroom doors closed, Lia's open a few inches, presumably so she could hear a child in distress if need be. Some nights Conall found himself hesitating a few feet from her door, imagining that she was awake and watching for him.

Did she feel any of the frustration that wracked him? The hunger for a kiss, a taste? He wouldn't say he avoided her daytimes; how could he? But unless it had to do with the kids, he wasn't seeking her out, either, because he wanted her and he knew damn well he shouldn't have her.

He wondered what she slept in. She presumably wore a gown or pajamas of some kind, because of the kids. Sexy? Probably not, he had thought wryly, and made himself keep going, first to the bathroom, then the twin bed where his feet would hang off the end.

But at least he had the privacy of his own room. He hoped Lia didn't accept another foster child until he was gone.

Tonight there had been a modest stirring of activity next door. A car had come and gone, the driver alone. He'd gone into the house and stayed for a good hour. This guy wasn't one of the two who'd brought the crates or any of the three who seemed to be living in the house. But his face, too, was familiar.

Conall was still thinking about it as he came downstairs and quietly closed the attic door. This familiar was different. He'd met the man from the pickup truck, had seen him move, speak. He knew it, even though he hadn't been able to nail down when or where. The wondering stuck with him like an itch.

He was confident he'd recognized this new visitor only from a photo. Depending on the operation, he looked at a hell of a lot of images. Face recognition software would find a match, he was willing to bet. His preoccupation took him safely past Lia's bedroom door.

Nights weren't hot yet, except in the attic where the air remained stuffy. He'd have liked a shower, but the noise of it running might wake someone. Instead, after brushing his teeth he stripped off his shirt and stuck his head under the faucet, scrubbed his underarms and ran the wet washcloth over his chest and as much of his back as he could reach, then toweled himself dry.

This time his feet came to a stop in the hall, refusing to carry him on to his bedroom. He stared at that dark opening.

Did Lia sleep with her hair braided or loose? Because of the way he and Henderson had broken down their shifts, Conall had yet to see her first thing in the morning. He had the stupid thought that right now he'd be satisfied if he could only get a look at her. Find out whether she slept with abandon or curled into a defensive ball. Wore a long-sleeved, floor-length flannel gown or a T-shirt that ended at mid-thigh. But he knew damn well he was lying to himself. His fantasies would grow more vivid once he could picture her accurately in bed.

He rasped a hand over his jaw, sighed and prodded himself into motion…at the exact moment her door opened silently and she stepped into the hall. He stopped but not quite in time. Lia walked right into him.

She gave a startled gasp. Conall gripped her shoulders—almost bare, oh damn, they felt delicate—and said quietly, "Shh, it's me, Lia. Conall."

Her "Oh" came out in a shocked exhalation. "What are you doing…?"

He bent his head so his mouth wasn't far from her ear. "On my way to bed."

"Oh," she whispered again.

His hands, all on their own, slid up and down her arms. Bare arms. He was gently kneading, arousal having slammed into him. He'd been half-way already, thinking about her. Now her hair was tickling his face. It was braided, but strands had slipped loose. The scent was tart, lemon or lime. He'd seen her shampoo in the shower, imagined her naked with the water pouring over her body and her arms raised as she washed her hair.

His hands cupped the balls of her shoulders. A shiver ran over her. Her collarbones were fragile, the skin unbelievably soft. Only a camisole with tiny straps kept him from sliding his hands down to cover her breasts. God, he wanted to strip it off her. She stood very still, as if paralyzed. He could hear her breathing, quick, hard pants. He nuzzled her cheek and murmured, "Lia."

"What…what are you doing?"

"Touching you," he whispered. On impulse he dropped his hands to hers and lifted them to his own chest. "Touch me," he said, near soundlessly. She jerked, and he realized she hadn't known in the dark that his torso was bare. He pressed her hands flat against his chest and almost groaned from the pleasure.

He removed his hands from hers. For an instant

she didn't move at all and he was afraid she would back away. Then she stroked him, almost shyly, a timid exploration that made a groan rumble in his throat.

He wrapped one of his hands around her nape, beneath that heavy braid. The other he slipped under her camisole to feel more of her soft skin. Her fingertips found his nipples and paused with interest, then skated upward as if she were discovering how his muscles lay. Once her fingers curled into his chest hair. He thought about the kneading of a small cat. His own hands had mostly stilled; he was frozen in wonder at the sensations she was awakening. Conall had never had a more sensual experience. He couldn't make out her face, any more than she would be able to see his. The darkness was near complete with no windows opening into the hall. It was all touch, and the tiniest of sounds. The hitch of a breath, a whimper, another groan he couldn't stop.

He wanted desperately to haul her against him, to shove his hips against hers. He wanted to rip that camisole off and feel her breasts against his bare chest. He wanted to find her mouth in the dark, swallow her small, helpless sounds, dig his fingers into the richness of her hair as he angled her head.

Instead, he stood completely still and experienced more pleasure than he'd had from a woman in…forever. It was torture, and it was exquisite.

She stroked his belly. The muscles tightened and quivered beneath her palm. She traced the line of hair to the open snap of his jeans, hesitated and then stopped.

Recoiling, she remained in place only by his hold. "No!" she whispered furiously. "I can't."

"Lia." Now he bent his head and tried to find her mouth, but she evaded him, stiff, her entire body trying to pull away.

"Stop. Please stop."

His brain was hazed by desire, but from force of will he let her go. She jumped back two feet and collided with the door frame. Her "Ow" was muffled.

He'd blown it. Upset her.

But she'd touched him, and damn it, she'd enjoyed it.

Conall realized with shock that he was shaking. There wasn't anything he could do but say in a low voice, "I'm sorry. Good night, Lia," and retreat.

She had hurried to the bathroom and closed the door behind her with a decisive click before he reached his bedroom.

Conall stripped and got into bed, then lay staring at the ceiling, his body ready to bury itself in hers, a hundred emotions he didn't understand brushing against each other and rattling like a not very melodic wind chime.

THE NEXT DAY was Saturday. Lia took all three kids swimming. She didn't wait until Conall appeared, having no desire to invite him. Not, she realized belatedly, that he likely would have come anyway, since he was trying not to be noticed.

They had fun, but she knew they would have had more fun if he'd been with them. Especially the boys, who'd latched onto him with a fervor that had taken her by surprise.

Conall MacLachlan was temporary, she brooded. She hated the fact that she had to keep reminding herself of that. Maybe she'd made a mistake encouraging him to spend time with Walker and Brendan. Yes, he'd been good for them— but what would happen when he and his partner packed up their equipment and went away, never to be seen again? The brothers' mother had died, and now they'd let themselves care about someone else who wasn't in it for the long haul. Did they understand that?

Lia didn't even know why she was upset. No, mad. The boys were attached to her, too. Lots of the kids she took in got attached to her. She offered herself up to them, even though she knew she would be hurt later, when they left to go home. But this felt different, as though Conall shouldn't be promising something he had never intended to give.

He said he'd spend time with them. That's all he ever promised.

With words. That's all he'd promised with words. But with smiles and affectionate touches and his amazing patience, he'd given them so much more than time. Didn't he *know* what he was doing? she raged. He was being the father they'd never had. The father no other man would ever match.

Lia was astonished at the pain clutching her heart into a fist. Pain that wasn't even hers.

Conscious of shock, she sat poolside and watched the two boys halfheartedly splashing each other.

Was she angry at Conall because *she,* too, wanted to believe he'd never go away? Was she that foolish?

She squeezed her eyes shut. *Dear God, yes. Yes, I am.*

Closing her eyes had been a mistake, because it cast her into an instant flashback. Dark hallway, realizing it was his body with which she'd collided. Those big, callused hands moving with such delicious care over her. It had been ages since anyone had really touched her, and no one ever had quite like that. Savoring instead of demanding. He wasn't here now, but she could still smell him, soap and something muskier. Man. Aroused man. She'd known almost instantly that he was without ever feeling his erection.

But she'd wanted to. Oh, she'd wanted to.

Lia told herself surprise explained why she hadn't stepped back immediately, excused herself and gone on to the bathroom. Why she'd stood there letting him grope her.

Surprise didn't explain why she'd been unable to resist temptation when he'd pressed her hands to his hard, muscled chest. But how could she resist, after seeing him several times shirtless when he roughhoused with the boys, after watching him walk with that long, smooth, purely masculine stride? She hadn't been able to stop herself from watching him, sometimes surreptitiously, drinking in every detail of his lean, strong body, the flash of gray eyes, the occasional lightning surprise of a laugh.

Lust. Only lust, she told herself desperately, and knew she was lying. Maybe if she'd never seen him with the boys, she wouldn't have fallen in love, but she had.

And he would disappear from her life as completely as he would from Walker's and Brendan's, with as little warning.

It was all she could do to smile when one of the boys called out to her.

They arrived home to find Conall on the porch,

talking on his cell phone. When she reached him, he said, "Let me call you back," and slid the telephone closed. His gaze flicked over all of them. "You went swimming?"

"Yeah! Lia said we shouldn't wake you up. And you probably wouldn't go anyway," Walker said. "But I wished you had."

"She's probably right, I couldn't have gone. I shouldn't be away from the house for long."

"In case something happens." Brendan nodded solemnly.

"Right." He ruffled the boys' hair and smiled at Sorrel. "Have fun?"

"It was okay." She scuttled past, head down, and vanished into the house.

Conall looked after her with surprise Lia shared. Had Sorrel felt shy because she hadn't put a top on over her bathing suit? She sometimes seemed so normal—interested in boys, insecure about her appeal, giggly. But Lia couldn't forget that she was also a child who had been sexually abused by a man she should have been able to trust. She had a long road ahead of her before she could feel secure in a romantic relationship. If she ever would be able to. Conall was blatantly male. The real surprise was that Sorrel could ever relax with him.

"Lunchtime," Lia told the boys. "Why don't you go get changed?" When they'd gone in, she said, "Sorry if we interrupted your call."

"You didn't." He hesitated. "Lia…"

"If this is about last night, don't worry. Nothing happened."

His dark eyebrows rose. "Nothing?"

"Nothing important," she said firmly.

He absorbed that, his eyes flickering. "You know I'm attracted to you."

"And I know it's not a good idea to go anywhere with it. I have children in this house. It's important that I set a good example for Sorrel especially." She was pleased at how brisk she sounded. "Besides, I don't do one-night stands, or two-week stands. My emotions have to be involved."

Idiot that she was, Lia desperately wanted him to say, *Don't you feel anything for me? Because I do for you. Can't we find out where it takes us?*

Instead, muscles flexed in his jaw as he stared at her. After an appalling length of time, he nodded. "I hadn't actually suggested anything like that."

"But you would have, wouldn't you?"

His face was particularly devoid of emotion. "Maybe."

"Well, then." She reached for the screen door handle.

"Wait." Was that a thread of desperation in *his* voice?

Slowly she turned back.

"That was Niall on the phone. My brother?"

As if she wouldn't remember. Lia nodded.

"He wants us all to get together again. He said Desmond really enjoyed the boys."

"Are you asking for my permission to take them somewhere?" How should she feel about that?

"No." He took a deep breath. "I'm actually wondering how you'd feel about having them all out here. I know that's asking a lot of you, but I imagine Rowan and Jane would bring some of the food and you've got a good place for it." He was talking faster than usual. "I thought it might be easier than packing up our crew again."

Our crew? Her heart pinched. She wished he wouldn't say things like that. It hurt.

"Wouldn't that be kind of conspicuous? I thought you were trying to keep your presence quiet."

A rueful smile lifted one corner of his mouth. "I'm spending half my time outside with the boys. If our neighbors have had any reason to come looking, they'll have seen me already."

She suddenly had the creeps. It was all she could do not to turn her head and stare at the woods separating her house from the neighbor's. "What do you mean, come looking?"

"They haven't," he said quickly. "We'd have seen them. But they may have heard me talking to the boys. We get kind of noisy out here sometimes." Seeing her expression, he added, "It's okay, Lia. They have no reason to think I'm anything but a friend. Maybe a boyfriend. Why would that worry them?"

"A boyfriend." It hadn't occurred to her what this would look like. Alarm quickened her pulse. "I could lose my license."

He was shaking his head before she finished. "We'll explain if we have to."

"It never even occurred to me."

"I'll take care of it," he repeated.

She marshaled her thoughts. "I guess the neighbors wouldn't have any reason to think anything of me having a bunch of friends over for a barbecue."

"Nope."

She'd *liked* his sisters-in-law. Staying friends with them probably wasn't an option, given the fact that their husbands were in law enforcement and she regularly broke the law, but she could enjoy them now, couldn't she?

"A party sounds fun. It'll be good for the kids. If they're free, why don't we do it tomorrow? Otherwise it'll have to wait until next weekend."

She could tell he'd be just as glad to put off further family interactions for another week, but with a sigh he slid open his phone. His eyes were warm on her face when he said, "Thanks, Lia."

She waited until he had spoken briefly to his brother and confirmed that yes, Niall and family at the very least thought tomorrow sounded great. Niall would call Duncan and let Conall know whether he, Jane and Fiona would join them. Lia immediately revised her afternoon plans to include a trip to the grocery store.

"Great," Conall growled. "One more thing to look forward to."

"You should be glad to have family," she told him crisply, and went inside.

So SHE THOUGHT he was an ungrateful bastard. No news there. He was.

Conall's irritation eventually wore off, leaving him with the memory of Lia's expression.

Fostering children was a vocation, she'd said. Because she wanted a family, the kind she hadn't had. The kind she didn't think she ever would have. No, Lia *hadn't* said any of that, but Conall was good at reading between the lines.

She couldn't understand why he had rejected his brothers, and along with them lost the chance to have more family: their wives and children. She was maybe even a little angry at him for not appreciating something she hungered for.

She hadn't said that, either, but he could tell.

The hell of it was, Conall knew she was right. He'd lost a great deal. No, not lost—thrown away.

From his adult perspective, he was having trouble remembering why. All he knew was that, for years, anger had simmered inside him. It was one of the few emotions he felt. Most of the time, he

was barely conscious of it. He'd always believed
it was directed at Duncan, the oppressor.

Tonight, sitting at the attic window watching
a dark house, he knew differently. Maybe he'd
felt safe to channel all that rage and hurt on the
brother who had refused, no matter the cost to
him, no matter what they did, to turn his back on
Conall or Niall.

Conall's attention was momentarily caught by
movement. After verifying that it was only one
of the Dobermans trotting across the yard, Conall
thought, *I locked away everything I felt for Mom
and Dad. I convinced myself I felt nothing.*

I lied.

Asked at any time in the past fifteen years, he
would have sworn he was self-aware. Live and
learn.

The necessity of keeping watch freed his
thoughts. He played back a hundred reels of his
childhood and teenage years. College graduation,
with Duncan in the audience even though Conall
hadn't invited him.

Maybe the damage had been done early, when
Conall had wished for so much more than he ever
got from his brothers, and especially Duncan, the
big brother he'd worshipped. He couldn't help
wincing as he thought about how young Duncan
had been. *I resented a fourteen-year-old for not
wanting to spend time with his shrimpy eight-year-*

old brother. Of course he hadn't wanted to. He'd been kind enough, but six years was a big age spread then. Too big for them to have been the kind of friends Conall had yearned to be.

Had he been angry because when Duncan turned into a father figure, it erased all possibility for them ever to be simply friends and brothers? Thinking about their couple of meetings these past weeks, Conall had a minor revelation.

Not all possibility *had* been erased. It wasn't too late. Duncan was still willing, God knows why considering what a jackass Conall had been.

Because we are *brothers.*

Maybe because Duncan had always understood more than Conall had realized.

Conall had another uncomfortable realization. Despite what he'd said to Lia, he wasn't dreading tomorrow. He was actually looking forward to spending time with his brothers and their families.

His family.

And one reason he felt that way was because he felt secure here, as though they were coming onto his territory.

Apprehension stabbed between his ribs, stiletto sharp. This wasn't his home. Lia wasn't his woman, Walker and Brendan weren't his kids. It scared the crap out of him to realize that he felt like they were.

He stared at the dark house, willing a light to

come on, the garage door to open, the sound of an engine to cut through the night, and thought, *Goddamn you, make a move. Make a mistake.*

He needed this operation to be done. To get back to his life before he started wondering whether that was what he wanted at all.

NIALL PITCHED THE BALL over the plate. Brendan swung hard, and connected. *Crack*. The ball soared and the batter tore for first base.

"Home run! Home run!" Walker chanted. Conall indulged in a few catcalls as the ball passed over Jane's glove and rolled beneath the fence into the pasture, ending up with a splat in a cow patty.

As Brendan triumphantly rounded the make-shift bases, Jane stopped at the fence and said, "Ew. Someone else come and get it."

Even Duncan laughed at her. "Can't be any worse than Fiona's diaper."

Conall and Brendan exchanged high fives as the boy smacked both feet on home plate for emphasis. The pitcher called, "Replacement ball."

Jane returned carrying the now greenish-brown-tinged baseball between two fingers. "What kind of baseball field is this?" she asked.

Duncan kissed her on the cheek and declined to take the ball. It was Lia, still giggling, who led her to the outdoor faucet where they rinsed and re-rinsed the ball, then dropped it and went into the house to scrub hands.

"Seventh-inning stretch," Niall declared. "We've lost our outfielder. I could use a beer anyway."

"You just want to quit because you're losing," Conall said amiably. His team—Walker, Brendan, Lia and himself—was trouncing Niall's, which consisted of Desmond, Niall, Jane and Anna alternating with Duncan. Rowan had been declared ineligible to play ball because no one wanted to be responsible for sending a line drive into her pregnant belly. Niall was operating with a disability; he'd had to tackle a suspect that week and his left side was a mass of bruises and knotted muscles. His pitching wasn't too bad, but his batting sucked. Des was decent for his age, Jane had turned out to be athletic, and Anna had managed to make it to first base on a bunt, but Conall and the boys had been doing some serious practicing.

"You've got a weenie for a wife," Conall told Duncan as he delved into the cooler for a beer.

He'd never seen his big brother more relaxed. Duncan was currently lounging on one of the Adirondack chairs Lia had brought out onto the lawn. "Weak stomach," he said easily. "You should have seen her the first few months she was pregnant. She could hardly keep anything down. We ate the blandest diet you've ever seen for a while there."

"Killed his sex life, too," their brother said, joining them. Trailed by Rowan, the kids had all run over to pet the pony through the fence. The men were left momentarily alone.

Duncan shot him a look. "Didn't sound like yours was any too hot for a few months there, either."

Amused, Conall wondered what their wives would think of this discussion. He could imagine what Lia would say if he…

Goddamn it. There he went again, thinking of her as *his*.

Duncan continued, "But when that crazy son of a bitch tried to slit Jane's throat, she had a spine of steel."

"That's true," Niall admitted. "Jane's a gutsy woman."

"Looks like you both got lucky," Conall said after a minute.

"Oh, yeah," Niall said softly.

Duncan grunted agreement. Gaze resting on Conall, he said, "You've never been tempted?"

Words rose automatically to his tongue. *Not happening.* That's what he'd always said, wasn't it? But those familiar words remained unspoken. It was scary as hell, but for the first time in his life, he could feel the pull. He understood why a man might want only one woman. Kids.

"Hasn't happened yet," he finally said, then

almost cursed at the way his head turned when he heard the screen door opening. Lia had never looked more beautiful to him than she did today, wearing cut-offs, tank top and athletic shoes, a sheen of sweat making her glow. She emerged, followed by Jane, and he quickly turned back, but too late. Heat ran across his cheeks when he met his brothers' interested gazes.

"She's a beautiful woman," Duncan observed, voice pitched to be sure it didn't reach the women.

Conall muttered without meaning to be heard.

"What's that?" Niall asked, leaning forward.

"Stuff it."

"She involved with anyone?" Duncan asked quietly.

Conall hadn't asked her. Hadn't dared. But he thought she would have said. She wasn't the kind of woman who'd have explored his bare chest with such curiosity and hunger if she had a lover.

"No." He frowned slightly, hardly aware he'd turned his head enough to watch her and Jane descend the steps and start across the grass toward the children. "I get the feeling she thinks no guy would want her as long as she's determined to keep fostering." He glanced at Niall. "She admired the way you've taken on Rowan's two kids. She seemed…surprised." Interesting; he hadn't realized at the time that she was, but he knew now that's what he'd seen on her face.

Seems the two of them had something in common: a lack of faith in their fellow man. Or woman.

Same cause, of course. Some wounds never healed.

Conall frowned. Desmond had lost his father, but he would grow up secure, knowing he was loved. So would Anna and Fiona. Rowan and Niall's baby, when it came along. Conall identified one of those strange emotions that had been pressing against his breastbone as if making a place for itself, even though he still didn't know what to call it. Faith? Belief? Not in God, but in a truly loving family. The one thing he'd been most cynical about. Probably it shouldn't have surprised him that Duncan the perfect had been able to form a family like that. After all, he was the man who would never fail anyone who depended on him. But Niall had managed the trick as well.

And then there was Lia, giving her all to frightened kids who had no one else.

He moved restlessly, not wanting to think about this.

Neither of his brothers had said anything, but both were watching him.

"We going to finish this game or not?" he asked, his edgy mood coming out in his voice.

Niall rose from his chair, whacked Conall on the back and called, "Hey, team! Let's get back on that field and prove what the MacLachlans are made of."

A sharp cramp of envy disconcerted Conall. *He* was the only MacLachlan on his team. And, damn it, for a split second he wanted to change that.

He laughed and raised his voice. "Come on, gang, let's keep kicking their butts. Seems to me I'm up to bat."

Duncan snorted and said, "Guess I'd better step in as catcher so Niall could put some heat on those pitches."

Conall snorted. "Does he have any?"

The boys had gotten close enough to hear the exchange. They hooted, and Desmond stuck his chin out. "My dad's a good pitcher."

Niall pulled him close for a one-armed hug.

More of that funny feeling Conall didn't want to think about. He grabbed a bat and called, "Better get ready to visit the cow pasture again, Jane."

Everyone got into position. Conall took a few practice swings then stepped up to the plate, cocky, ready for his brother's first pitch.

CHAPTER NINE

CONALL HAD NEVER been obsessed with a woman before. He thought about Lia as he was waiting for sleep, and first thing in the morning. He could hardly wait to see her. The sound of her voice coming from another room was as tactile as a touch. Every other day, when it was Jeff's turn to eat dinner downstairs, Conall felt resentful and sulky, banished to the attic.

It was ridiculous and embarrassing. So, okay, he wanted her. There had been women he'd wanted and not had. Maybe not one he had to share quarters with for weeks on end, but he could have avoided her more than he did. *He* was the idiot who'd taken to playing house with a beautiful woman and a couple of boys who reminded him uncomfortably of himself at their ages, not to mention a pretty, sometimes shy teenage girl who also, if he wasn't mistaken, was suppressing a whole lot of anger and anxiety.

What he should do was start spending more time in the attic and less downstairs. He could do it gradually, so as not to hurt the boys' feelings.

Conall couldn't make himself do what he should do. Damn it, he was having fun with Walker and Brendan. What's more, he was good for them. They were blossoming by the day. Truth was, he'd miss them when he left.

And Lia. Damn it, he'd miss Lia. He'd never missed a woman before, either. Not even his mother.

He relived the scene in the dark hall a hundred times, but in his imagination his mouth caught hers. He found out what she tasted like, what sounds she'd make, whether her mouth would soften, how she'd feel pressed up to him. Unfortunately, his fantasies weren't healthy for a man trying to fall asleep. They weren't great when he was spending so much time around a bunch of kids, either. He was willing to talk about almost anything with them, but would prefer not to include sex as one of those topics.

Today, he was pouring his usual late-morning bowl of cereal when he heard footsteps coming into the kitchen. Conall stiffened slightly, bracing himself for his reaction to Lia when he turned around. It was the boys, though, not her, and he relaxed. "Hey."

"We're bored," Walker announced.

Some mornings Conall found them watching *The Transformers,* or occasionally something that was on TV, but increasingly they were lying in wait for him. He found it really hard to say, *No, I can't do anything with you, I need to go back upstairs.*

He waved a spoon. "I'm game for something after I eat."

The younger boy's face brightened. "Cool."

He pulled out a chair and sat, crunching away on his too-sweet cereal. They sat, too. Walker drummed his heels on the chair legs and watched Conall eat. Brendan looked withdrawn, more as he had when Conall first came. He stared at the tabletop.

Conall got up to pour his coffee. "Have trouble sleeping last night, Bren?"

He looked up, his eyes haunted. "Kind of." He went quiet then said in a sudden burst, "I keep thinking about Mom. Does she...does she still *look* like Mom?"

Oh, damn, Conall thought. Maybe he would rather talk about sex.

"Um...that depends."

They both fixed their eyes on him with unnerving intensity. "On what?" Brendan asked.

"Well..." Did parents normally have these kinds of conversations with their kids? "She wasn't cremated, was she?"

"What's cremated?" Walker asked.

"Ah...burning the body. So you're left with only ashes."

The horror on their faces made his first swallow of coffee go down wrong. He coughed and finally had to wipe his face with the back of his hand.

Walker looked at his brother. "They didn't do that to Mommy, did they?"

"I don't think so," Brendan said uncertainly. "There was a coffin. If they do that, is there still a coffin?"

Conall was glad to be able to shake his head. "No. She wasn't cremated then. Um, did you see her after she died?"

"Right after. She looked like she was asleep." Brendan hesitated. "Kind of."

Conall knew what he meant. People sometimes said that—*Oh, he looked like he was sleeping*—but really, he hadn't. Conall wasn't a spiritual man, which was probably just as well given his profession and the fact that he'd killed a few people along the way. But there was no question something left the body at the moment of death. A dead person didn't look peaceful, he looked *dead*.

Keeping his voice matter-of-fact, he said, "Your mom was probably embalmed, which means chemicals were used that will keep her from decomposing." He could see from their expressions that they didn't know the word. Well, crap. "Rotting," he admitted. "Normally, living things rot after they die. If a raccoon dies in the woods, its body eventually enriches the soil that helps plants grow that will feed that raccoon's kits—that's their babies—and *their* kits and so on."

Lia walked into the kitchen right then. Conall was fiercely glad to see her, and not only for the usual reason. She gave them a general smile that didn't linger on him any more than on the boys. "What are you talking about? What kind of kits?"

"We're talking about what happens to dead people," Brendan said.

Her gaze flew to Conall's. He grimaced.

"And…what does this have to do with kits?"

Brendan explained about how raccoons died like people did, and how their bodies helped make berries and stuff like that grow better to feed baby coons. "And they're called kits. Right, Conall?"

"Right."

She blinked. "Okay. Um, do you mind if I join you? I might have a cup of coffee."

He noticed belatedly that she was grubby. She'd been working in the garden, then. Actually, the boys were pretty dirty, too, especially beneath the fingernails. He tilted his head to one side and saw that the knees of their jeans were filthy. So she'd succeeded in putting them to work this morning. No wonder they were desperate for new entertainment.

"Do you know anyone who's dead?" Brendan asked her.

"Not well," she admitted. "I mean, my great-aunt died a few years ago, but the funeral wasn't open-casket."

They turned aghast looks on her and she hastily explained how sometimes at funeral services the casket was open so mourners could view the body.

After which they'd all murmur that he or she looked so *peaceful,* Conall thought cynically.

More horror showed on the two young faces.

Lia stood, went around the table and gave each of them a hug. "Your mom would want you to re-member her alive. Smiling at you, playing with you. She can keep living in your memories."

They thought about that as she returned to her chair. She'd obviously plopped down on her butt between rows in the garden. She must have no idea how enticingly the circle of dirt emphasized one of Conall's favorite parts of her body.

Having thought about their mother alive—or not—the boys turned as one to Conall. "Have *you* ever seen anyone who's dead?"

He opened his mouth and then closed it. Lia's eyes had widened in alarm. He was momentarily distracted by the way they seemed to deepen in color. Sunlight, oddly enough, brought out the brown, making the color rich and warm and earthy. Indoors like this, the green predominated, making him think of the mysterious, green light in old-growth forests.

God.

He dragged his focus back to the subject. He wasn't enthusiastic about remembering the faces of men he'd shot. They had not looked peaceful when he was done with them. "Yeah," he admitted. "I have."

"Did you go to any of their funerals?"

"Once." He'd been under deep that time, for over a year, with a Central American crime cartel. He hadn't lost himself, exactly, but by the end he'd been grimly holding on to memories of what life for a normal American was like. He'd needed desperately to think of a man mowing the lawn, the scent of newly cut grass sharp in the air; people texting on their fancy phones as they stood in line at a Starbucks to order a Cinnamon Dolce Frappuccino, kids throwing wadded up paper balls at each other on the school bus. People who weren't ruthlessly killing to achieve their ends and satisfy their egos. He'd been caught somewhere he shouldn't have been and had had to knife a man, and, yeah, four days later he attended the solemn church service for that vile excuse for humanity. He hadn't wasted time contemplating the dearly departed's soul. Instead, Conall had sat there wondering how much humanity *he* still clung to.

There was no part of that he wanted to share with two boys who were still grieving a mother who had actually loved them.

"He was Catholic," he told them. "The priest

droned on and on. The service was in Spanish," he added. Yeah, that was the way to go; throw a bunch of irrelevant details at them and maybe they could talk about what the difference between a Catholic and a Protestant was, or why a priest talked so long, or—

"Did he die because he was sick, like Mom?" asked Walker.

Conall's eyes met Lia's again.

No, he died because I stuck a big honking knife blade into his body right beneath his rib cage and then I thrust upward until blood gushed and his eyes went sightless and his knees sagged.

"It was…an accident." He thought he'd done well in keeping his voice free of any inflection whatsoever, but she heard or saw too much.

"That's enough talk about death and dying," she said, sounding sharp. "Why aren't you kicking a soccer ball instead?"

"Because I haven't finished my morning cup of coffee?" he said mildly.

"Well, why don't you?" Lia suggested.

"*We're* almost hungry for lunch. Is it time for lunch?" Brendan asked.

"Nope. Why don't you each have an apple or a banana? Or there are some baby carrots already peeled in the crisper."

Walker turned big eyes on her. "Can we have a cookie if we have an apple first?"

"We have dessert after some meals. *Not* after snacks." Lia stood. "*I'm* going back to my weeding."

Her coffee, Conall saw, was almost untouched. That wasn't really why she'd come in. She'd been checking on the boys.

Maybe she wanted to see me. It was a wisp of hope that felt embarrassingly juvenile. He felt thirteen years old again, like poor Sorrel, slumped at his desk in Language Arts as Mrs. Barnes talked about organizing information into a coherent piece of writing. He was wondering for a fleeting, agonizingly sweet second whether Kayla Czernek had flipped her hair to get *his* attention, before he saw her peek beneath her eyelashes at Guy Hedman and he knew that, of course, she didn't even know Conall MacLachlan existed.

For a second almost as fleeting he felt ashamed, the way he had that day, and even angry. Then he got a grip. There was nothing wrong with the boys being Lia's priority. And also…he knew damn well she was as aware of him as he was of her. She could pretend all she wanted, but she looked for him, too. She couldn't help herself any more than he could.

And yeah, he'd hurt her if she let herself get involved with him. He wasn't her type. He wouldn't stay around. She needed a guy cut out to be a husband and father, not an emotionally scarred man who had no problem conjuring the faces of the dead, because he'd killed them.

He took his dishes to the sink. "So what's it going to be, soccer or baseball?"

He let the boys squabble over which sport they'd play as he ushered them outside, wondering why he was so content spending half his days playing daddy when he didn't actually want to be one.

LIA WAS IN TURMOIL when she returned to the incessant weeding and watering a huge garden required. She wished the two men would go away.

No, I don't.

Yes, she did.

For one thing, the whole time she was out here she remained aware that Jeff was upstairs at the attic window, able to watch her if he felt inclined. She didn't know if he did; she hadn't gotten any sexual vibes from him, but that didn't mean he wasn't bored enough to keep an eye on her anyway.

She was also aware of the voices on the other side of the house. Mostly the boys' carried, high-pitched and excited. Occasionally she'd catch the deeper bass note of Conall's reply.

How was it possible he could be so blasted good with two unhappy boys? She didn't get it. Lia examined the possibility that she was jealous because Brendan and Walker were clearly more attached to Conall than they were to her. But she really thought she was being honest with herself when she concluded that didn't bother her. She was *glad* they had him.

What upset her was that he was such an enigma. A man who, she sensed, didn't let himself feel much attachment to other people. He had the murkiest depths of anyone she'd ever met, and that was saying something. Her own were less than crystalline.

She brooded as she thinned the new shoots of lettuce. *Just listen to him out there,* Lia thought indignantly. Being kind and funny and caring and domesticated. And yet he'd chosen a job that was exceedingly dangerous, undoubtedly violent and took him away from home—assuming he actually had one—for months at a time.

Did he die because he was sick, like Mom?

She heard Walker asking the question in all innocence and saw again the way Conall's face had frozen. He was very, very good at wiping his expression clean, but not so good she hadn't seen something, however fleeting, that had shocked her. He'd killed, she knew it. Probably ruthlessly, but not without conscience, or he wouldn't be haunted by faces he didn't want to remember.

Her hands went still and she frowned toward the fence, not really seeing it. He'd said a few things about being undercover. A person would

have to be something of a chameleon to do that—
to immerse himself in a role night and day with
no weekends or holidays to shed the new skin.
Appalled, she wondered if that was all he was
doing here: assuming a suitable personality, sliding deftly into the role that would allow him to fit
in the best. Dad.

Did he want her only because if he was dad,
well, she was mom? The thought made her feel
sick to her stomach.

"No," she said aloud. "I don't believe it."

How could she be falling in love with him, when
there was so much about him she didn't know?

A strange, choked sound broke from her throat.
A near sob. Her eyes were dry, but anguish
clutched her.

*Please let this be lust, curiosity... Anything but
love.* Conall didn't only have a dangerous job. *He*
was dangerous.

And *he* could entertain himself with the boys
today. She would do her damnedest to avoid him.

LIA SUCCEEDED IN HAVING very little to do with
either of her unwanted houseguests for a good
part of a week. She absented herself for most of
one day doing errands: bank, hardware store,
grocery store, post office and farm co-op. Conall
had agreed to keep an eye on Walker and Brendan.

My DEA agent babysitter, Lia thought semi-hysterically.

She took the boys on a couple more outings that didn't include Conall. Once, she said, "I'm sure you'll enjoy some peace and quiet" as she swept them out the door, and didn't let herself look back in case he felt abandoned rather than pleased not to have a pair of boys trailing him everywhere.

She picked and froze blueberries. She made everyone help her pick the raspberries and made enough jam to see her household through the year. She tried not to be touched that Conall had insisted on helping pick. Instead, she was careful to stay a row or two away from him at all times. And she somewhat sharply declined any assistance in the kitchen.

She cleaned the bathroom upstairs when he was downstairs talking to the boys. When midmorning came, his usual time for getting up, she made sure she was washing windows or outside fertilizing annuals.

The awful thing was, she remained painfully conscious of him. She'd turn her head and see him striding past the window, head thrown back as he laughed at something one of the boys said. At the dinner table she'd fixate on his hands as he reached for a dish or wielded knife and fork. It was stupid that his hands in particular made her shiver inside, but they did. They were so purely masculine: broad across the palm, long-fingered, strong. She knew he had calluses. She could close her eyes and remember the feel of those hands sliding up and down her arms.

His voice was low and calm, but she always heard it like the thump of bass in another car at a stoplight, deep enough to rattle her bones. And she tried but couldn't always prevent herself from meeting his eyes, gray and invariably thoughtful.

Oh, yes, he'd noticed she was avoiding him and hadn't said anything, but he was thinking about it, and her, and… Lia didn't know what, only that something was going on in his head when he looked at her. And, damn it, he looked at her a lot. Even when she thought she was alone, she'd feel a prickle and glance up to discover he was passing in the hall or standing on the porch, his eyes resting on her.

It had gotten so she was having trouble sleeping.

Conall took over for Jeff in the early evening. Lia was secretly a little relieved that Jeff had chosen to sleep in the attic so far rather than in the bedroom across the hall from hers. She still met him coming and going to the bathroom sometimes and they'd exchange greetings, but she didn't feel anything except, sometimes, mild startlement because who was that strange man coming out of her bathroom? The truth was, she could forget his existence for hours on end, while she couldn't seem to forget Conall's for a single moment.

Thank goodness Conall was in the attic in the evenings. Daytimes were difficult enough. At least in the evening she could read and sew or do some mending or spend time with the kids without him being there, too. This week she'd started the boys on some schoolwork, an hour in the mornings before Conall appeared, another hour or two in the evening. The boys and she would *all* have been distracted if he'd been around.

And she could brush her teeth and wash her face and move back and forth between bathroom and bedroom without worrying about running into him.

Which did not prevent her from picturing him the minute she was in bed with her eyes closed. How could he sit up there for hours on end the way he did? Wasn't he bored to death? Or was he like any predator, endlessly patient?

Lia knew he always carried that big, black gun. She wasn't sure the boys had noticed. She hoped not. She didn't want them to become curious about it. Conall would have the sense not to show it to them if they asked, wouldn't he?

Most nights she eventually dropped off, but she also often woke when he came downstairs at three or four in the morning. As a foster mom, she'd become super sensitized to any sound in the night;

she mostly woke if one of the boys or Sorrel got up to use the bathroom, too. The plumbing in the house wasn't quite antique, but it was old enough to be noisy, which didn't help. The thing was, she heard Conall from the moment the attic door quietly opened and closed. He moved soundlessly down the hall, but she knew where he was every second, knew he sometimes paused outside her bedroom. She would lie rigid in bed, aching for him to push the door wider and come in. One night, when he stood out there for a particularly long time, she had to bite the back of her hand to keep from whispering his name.

Then there would be the equally quiet click of the bathroom door, water running, the toilet flushing. Sometimes he'd hesitate outside her room again. And at last his door would close. Silence would last for a couple of minutes, during which she imagined him stripping. Then the bed would creak as he lay down.

By that time—she couldn't help herself—she'd be so turned on she could hardly bear the weight of the covers. She could feel the dampness between her legs, the need clenching in her belly. Staying still nearly killed her, but if she so much as moved restlessly, *her* bed would creak and he would hear and he might know that she was lying awake thinking about him.

Wednesday she had less success than usual

avoiding him. It was drizzling, which meant all of them except Sorrel, who'd gone to school, were stuck inside. Lia pretended to be busy with housework for an hour, but really the house had never been cleaner, thanks to days of evasive maneuvers. Then she insisted on an hour sitting at the kitchen table with the boys working on a math chapter from their respective textbooks. Finally she succumbed and agreed to play Monopoly with Conall and the boys.

They let her be the banker. Walker turned out to have a ruthless streak almost as deep and long as Conall's, while Brendan didn't get lucky rolls and Lia was—she had to admit—too softhearted. Even so, they all had fun. Her heart ached at the boys' giggles and whoops and Conall's lazy grins, many directed at her. So much fun, she was sorry when she had to admit to bankruptcy and left the two remaining real estate moguls to duke it out while she started dinner. By that time, Sorrel was home and happily ensconced on the sofa behind Walker to root him on.

"Why him? Why not me?" Conall was complaining when Lia left the room.

The good mood lasted through dinner but was killed when Conall's cell phone buzzed before he'd finished dessert. He glanced at it, said, "Jeff needs me," and disappeared with startling haste.

Was the indefinable *something* finally happening? The something that would mean she could have her house back? She made the evening as normal as she could for the kids while living with a clutch of anxiety in her chest so big and dense, she suspected it would form a dark shadow on an X-ray.

Sleep was more elusive than ever. Didn't Conall know they would all worry? Would it have killed him to pop down and say, "False alarm?" Or "I've got what I need to get a warrant, and we'll be out of your hair in no time?"

She woke abruptly and lay rigid, knowing she'd heard…a whimper? Or was that part of a dream? No, there was another muffled cry, and she jumped from bed and hurried to the hall, where she had to stand still until the next sad sound came. Sorrel's room, not the boys'.

Lia pushed open the door. "Sorrel? Honey?"

The teenager moved restlessly. "No." A gasp. "No, please! Please! No."

Lia went to the bed and sat, laying a gentle hand on her foster daughter's back. "Wake up, honey. It's a bad dream. Only a dream."

"Mommy?" Sorrel whispered.

"It's Lia." She moved her hand in a soothing circle, murmuring, "Shh, you were having a nightmare."

She kept talking for a couple of minutes in a near sing-song, keeping her voice barely above a whisper. Gradually Sorrel's body relaxed beneath Lia's hands, and finally her breathing deepened. Lia kept sitting there, waiting, but the girl's sleep was peaceful now.

Lia slipped out of the room and eased the door shut.

A deep, low voice asked, "Is she all right?"

Lia squeaked in alarm and swung around.

Conall's big hands gripped her arms. "Hey, it's me. I'm sorry, I thought you'd heard me."

"No." Her heart was slamming.

"What's wrong with Sorrel?"

"A nightmare. She kept saying, 'No, no, please.'"

"You don't know her history?"

Lia hesitated. "Let's get away from her door."

He let go of one of her arms but maintained his hold on the other. It was only a few steps to her bedroom door, and once they reached it Conall steered her inside.

"Let me turn on the light," she said. The memory of their other encounter in the dark hall was too vivid. He let her go, and she went to her bedside to switch on the lamp.

She felt a shock when she saw Conall wearing only jeans, zipped but unsnapped. He must have left his T-shirt in the bathroom laundry hamper. His bare chest was all male—hard muscles and dark hair in a triangle like a kite with a tail that disappeared inside the denim of his jeans. He took her breath away.

His darkened eyes swept over her, making her painfully aware of her skimpy attire, only flannel boxer shorts and a well-worn tank top. She'd never thought of them as sexy before.

"Sorrel?" he asked hoarsely.

"Oh, um." Her mind was astonishingly blank. Remembering who Sorrel was took an embarrassing moment. "She was sexually molested."

He went very still, but his expression didn't change. "Yeah," he said after a minute. "I thought it was something like that."

"I shouldn't tell you more than that. I really need to keep the kids' problems confidential."

"That's okay." His voice was a gentle rumble. "I understand."

"She hasn't had a nightmare in weeks that I'm aware of. She had a counseling session yesterday." He nodded; she'd left the boys with him when she went to pick Sorrel up. "Maybe whatever they talked about triggered this."

Conall took a long stride closer to her. Lia crossed her arms in self-defense and he stopped.

"Lia?"

Oh, dear Lord, don't let me do something stupid.

She was breathing in quick gusts. She couldn't look away from Conall. Those eyes, so dark a charcoal right now they might have been black.

His hair, coarse and ruffled and wavy, droplets of water clinging here and there. The shadow of a beard on his jaw, the hollow at the base of his throat, his utter self-containment. His whole, big body had remained still, waiting, rigid with tension.

It seemed the Lord wasn't listening right now, or the temptation was too great. Lia wanted this man more than she'd wanted anything in her whole life.

She let her hands drop to her sides. Took a step herself and saw him break.

The next second he'd crushed her in his arms and his mouth devoured hers.

CHAPTER TEN

LIA HAD NEVER felt anything like this. All patience deserted her, replaced by urgency so huge and overwhelming, she was ready for him *now*. She kissed him with fervor that was probably clumsy, it had been so long since she'd done even this much with a man. She rose on tiptoe and strained against him. Her arms locked around his neck, and she had the heady pleasure of plunging her fingers into his hair, finally feeling the springy coarse-textured silk.

There was no tenderness in this kiss, only need. His tongue established a hard, driving rhythm interrupted only by sharp nips on her lower lip. She returned them, and followed his tongue into his mouth with her own.

She was trying to climb him, she should have been embarrassed to realize, but any ability to feel shame had been supplanted by this all-consuming *want*.

When the back of her legs hit the bed, she realized Conall had walked her the few steps. "Yes," she whispered, and moved her open mouth over his jaw and down his throat.

He groaned and peeled off her tank top then looked at her. Dark color ran over his cheekbones and he made a sound deep in his throat.

"You're beautiful. So beautiful."

Lia slid her hands over his strong chest. "You are, too," she whispered.

With something like a laugh, he lifted her and dropped her on the bed, coming down over her with one knee planted between her thighs. His mouth settled on her breast. As when he'd kissed her, he didn't bother with preliminaries. He suckled her deep and hard, and she gripped his head to keep him where he was. He had to fight briefly to switch to her other breast. Lia pushed her hips up, almost but not quite satisfied to press against the powerful thigh she straddled.

Eventually that wasn't enough. She moved her hand over the hard bulge beneath his jeans, loving the growl that escaped him. The zipper was stubborn; while she worked it lower he sucked in his belly and lifted his head to look at her face.

His was transformed by passion. It was as if the skin had tightened over the angular bone structure, erasing some of the care-worn lines, deepening others. His mouth was sensual, hard, his eyes lit by a molten glow that matched how he made her feel inside.

He jerked when, at last, she was able to lay her hand on his erection, stroking, gripping, savoring the astonishing pleasure of finally touching him.

She was shocked when he wrenched himself back.

"Don't move," he said in a low, harsh voice. "I've got to go get a condom. Unless you have some…?"

Lia shook her head.

"Stay."

He muttered under his breath when he left her bedroom, swearing, she thought. Oh, heavens—he was trying to pull up his zipper. Lia was giggling when he returned, which earned her a dark look.

Conall shut the door, which was when she realized it had been standing open the entire time they were kissing and stripping each other. Would she have even heard one of the kids getting up?

He hadn't quite managed the zipper, she saw when her gaze lowered. Conall glanced down, his expression momentarily rueful. "I'll keep some of these in your bedroom from now on," he muttered, dropping a handful of packets on her bedside table.

From now on? Splayed wantonly on her bed, Lia knew that he meant to come to her bed every night, and she was glad. Fiercely glad.

Every night until he had to leave.

I won't regret this. I won't.

"You have amazing legs," he whispered. "I watch you all the time, you know."

She nodded. "I know."

Conall wrapped his hands around her feet and gently squeezed, then worked his way upward, stroking and kneading. Lia whimpered.

"Can we...not go slow? This time?"

He didn't answer with words. Instead he tore her shorts off and wrenched his zipper down. He stepped out of his jeans even as he reached for one of the packets.

She was staring, wanting to touch him, but he said in a guttural voice, "No touching. Not now."

Another time she might like to put the condom on for him, but at this moment she was only glad of his speed. He came down on top of her, some of his weight on his elbows, thrusting even as she lifted her legs to accommodate him.

Her body arched and a keening sound slipped out. Conall swallowed it with his mouth. He took her at her word—the rhythm he set was hard and fast and had her frantic within seconds. They grappled and plunged. The headboard whapped against the wall and Conall flipped so that she rode him. Even if she'd wanted to slow the pace, he didn't let her, his powerful hands gripping her hips and lifting and lowering her even as he drove upward.

Release came shockingly soon, rolling over her in intense waves that were barely subsiding when Conall arched, bared his teeth in ecstasy and came. The cords in his neck stood out, and the sound he bit back was raw. It was a long moment before his hands first relaxed on her, then finally slid up her back to pull her onto him.

She lay there, limp and replete, feeling glorious so long as she didn't let herself think. Thinking would open her to worries and fears.

Then I won't.

"How the hell did we manage to hold out until now?" he muttered.

Lia smiled against his throat. "I don't know."

"Do you have any idea how many nights I've stood out there in the damn hall wondering what you'd do if I got into bed with you?"

"Mmm-hmm."

He bent his head. "Mmm-hmm, what? *You knew?*"

Lia couldn't help a soft laugh at his outrage. "Of course I do. I hear you every night, you know. I always wake up when you come downstairs."

"It's been killing me."

"Me, too," she admitted with a sigh. She kissed his neck right where it joined his shoulder. He tasted salty. She licked him for another sample. Who would have ever thought sweaty male could be so delicious?

"I've got to take this damn condom off." He groaned, lifted her off him, and heaved himself out of bed. Her lamp was still on; she was able to drink in the sight of his broad back, lean hips and long legs as he left her room naked.

That gave her a moment of concern—what if one of the kids got up?—but it didn't last long. For all she knew, he slept naked every night and chanced running into someone when he got up to use the bathroom. He was back before she had a chance to wonder whether he'd return. He was also semi-aroused, she saw.

She smiled when he reached the bedside. "May I touch this time, Agent MacLachlan?"

A grin flashed across his face, lightning quick and very sexy. "Certainly, Ms. Woods. To your heart's content."

Her heart would not be content for a very long time, she thought, speared by the pain that would be so much worse when he packed his bags and left.

But he wasn't going yet, and she'd made her choice. For a second, sadness wanted to smother her. Was this the closest to true love she'd ever find? Perhaps it was inevitable that she'd fall in love with a man who would only be in her life for a short time.

So be it.

She reached out and cupped him in her hands, watching his face, learning what he liked.

CONALL DIDN'T LET HIMSELF fall asleep in her bed, even though he desperately wanted to. Lia had conked out after they made love a second time. Once the pressure cooker had been released the first time, they managed slow and tender, and, God help him, he'd never had sex like this.

Asleep, Lia was slight in his arms, her bones delicate when he moved his hands over her. Fulfilling a fantasy, he'd taken her hair from the braid and it now fanned over the both of them, a thick silken blanket. He gently lifted a handful at a time and let it run through his fingers.

She hadn't told him to go. But he knew she wouldn't want the kids to discover him in here, or to see him emerging from here later in the morning.

So at last he separated himself from her, kissed her softly when she mumbled protests, and tucked her in before picking up his jeans from the floor, turning off the lamp and slipping out of her room. He left her door ajar, exactly as she always did— and he'd memorized it down to a fraction of an inch—then took himself to the bathroom to discard the second condom and wash.

When he was done he braced his hands on the sink and looked at himself in the mirror. He'd never bothered before, after sex, to look deep. Well, not since the first time, when he was an exhilarated sixteen-year-old on a high from what he'd done with Autumn Hiatt who was short, probably on her way to being plump but possessing huge tits. Sex otherwise was great, one of life's pleasures. But the partners he'd had that sex with had never mattered all that much. He was shaken to find out how much different it was when the woman did matter.

When he had the really bad feeling no other woman ever *would* matter the same way. And that maybe sex wasn't going to be so good in the future, either, when it wasn't Lia's gorgeous mouth he was kissing, her slick, heavy hair he'd buried his fingers in, her slim body beneath his, her green-brown eyes, glazed with passion but widening with amazement...

"Oh, hell," he groaned, and let his head fall.

Tonight he and Henderson had finally caught a break. The men in the pickup had come back with another load, and before dark. They were getting cocky, it seemed. Given a good look, Conall had placed that familiar face, and they'd gotten some decent photos of two of the three residents of the house as well as the visitors.

The bastard Conall knew was a gunrunner. Gordy Costello been peripheral to an operation Conall had worked in Southern California and had escaped the net before arrests were made. He wasn't important enough then for them to bother pursuing aggressively. A confirmation of his identity now, though, would help justify a warrant that might bring this case to a close.

And then he'd pack his duffel bag, toss it in the Suburban, say goodbye to Walker, Brendan and Lia and drive away.

He swore again, low and ragged.

He was good at moving on. A regular champion at it. Increasingly, he'd gotten bored with whatever he was working; he wanted nothing more than to move on to a new challenge, something that might engage him. It was ridiculous to think he was so happy living the bucolic life he didn't want to leave. He pictured the damn cows chewing their cud and everything in him rose in outrage. No! This wasn't him. It was…an interlude. That's all. Pretty damn amazing sex, sure. Nice kids. He should be glad he'd been entertained while he was stuck here, because he would have gone out of his flipping mind otherwise.

He ran both hands over his face, turned off the light and made his way to the bedroom and twin bed he currently called his. Where he lay awake entirely too long, his gut roiling with some unnamed anxiety as the same scene kept playing through his head: him saying goodbye to those two boys then turning to do the same to Lia, knowing this was it. Moving on.

BY AFTERNOON CONALL WAS getting emails giving him names to go with faces. Lia's neighbors were, of all damn things, survivalists. White supremacists. The group with whom these three were affiliated was small. A couple of members had recently bought a chunk of acreage in rural Idaho, triggering some interest but no action. They hadn't taken out a loan, but nobody within the organization had ever held the kind of job that would have brought in money like that. Whatever was going on next door to Lia was the answer, or part of it.

Conall hadn't seen any evidence yet that they were moving drugs, although he hadn't ruled out the possibility. It was a tried-and-true method of raising big bucks, after all. Maybe Gordy Costello had switched his trade from weapons to white powder. Anything was possible. Conall kind of doubted it, though. He thought the neighbors were buying guns, but whether for resale or to arm themselves was another question. They wouldn't be the first nuts with an us-against-the-world mentality. When they gathered on their Idaho enclave, they were likely to embrace a paranoid lifestyle, certain the FBI was watching through long-range binoculars.

He smiled grimly at that. Little did the fools imagine they were already being watched by federal agents.

Henderson, it developed, had worked an operation involving white supremacists who cultivated high-quality marijuana to support the war they envisioned coming between their kind and the U.S. government in its too-liberal, multi-ethnic arrogance.

Telling Conall about it, Jeff had shaken his head. "Despite the quantity they were growing and dealing, the sentences handed out were pathetic. They probably bought a new piece of property and went right back to farming the minute they got out. The profit was worth the risk."

Yeah, wasn't that always the case?

It occurred to Conall that his frustration with outcomes had been fueling his growing dissatisfaction with his job. Was he accomplishing anything meaningful? He'd begun to doubt it. Sometimes he wanted to do something where he could see a measurable impact. Maybe not a big one, but the faces of people he'd helped. The victims of the drug wars were mainly faceless to him. He spent his life immersed in the underworld of users and dealers. Too often decisions made and handed down from above were tainted with politics.

Maybe that was why these weeks had felt so *clean* to him. Why he half envied his brothers, who protected the townsfolk they considered their own.

He shook his head over the idiocy. Niall and Duncan arrested their townsfolk, too, some of whom were scum not that different from the men

Conall put behind bars. Their crimes were committed on a smaller scale, that's all.

Part of his mood, he admitted, had to do with the fact that here it was mid-afternoon and he was working instead of hanging out with Walker and Brendan. Lia had taken them somewhere a couple of hours ago; he'd heard the engine and from one of the attic windows seen her Subaru going out the driveway. He'd gone downstairs, ostensibly to use the john, but hoping to find a note. There was nothing. All he could tell was that the house was empty.

Later, Henderson had gone down and made a sandwich. He sat eating it now while he idly watched the house across the pasture.

Laptop open, Conall sprawled in the big easy chair Jeff had been enterprising enough to find behind a towering pile of boxes up here in the attic. No new email. He knew his restlessness had more to do with listening for the Subaru than because of anything he should be focusing on.

"I haven't been pulling my weight," Conall heard himself say.

Henderson turned to look at him in surprise. "You're pulling your shifts."

"Shorter ones than yours."

"Not much. You're doing most of the night."

"And playing all day."

"I'm okay up here. I don't mind surveillance."

He hesitated. "I call my wife and we talk for a while every day."

"No reason not to." Uncomfortable, Conall wondered why he'd initiated this conversation.

"I wouldn't have made friends downstairs like you have." Weirdly, the other man was the one looking squirrely. "I'd have probably been sitting up here reading anyway." He hesitated. "I told you once. The kids here...I don't know what to say to them."

"They're regular kids." *Like I'd know.*

Henderson was shaking his head. "No, they're not. The girl is...I guess I don't know any teenage girls, but she's...sometimes the way she looks at me." He stopped. "And those boys, if they talk at all, they ask weird questions."

Well, that was true enough. Curiosity stirring, though, Conall asked, "Like what?"

"Since I go to church, can I tell them what happens to souls when people die. Or whether it's true that fingernails keep growing after you're dead."

Conall's mouth crooked into a smile. "Those sound like pretty normal questions for kids who've had a parent die to ask. And, okay, where souls go is hard to answer without sounding glib, but the fingernail question is easy enough."

"Easy?" His partner stared at him as though he was crazy. "I'm supposed to talk about gruesome stuff like that to an eight-year-old kid? I asked where he'd heard that and all he did was mumble, 'Dunno.' So I said no, it's not true, and he said how do you know? Had I ever looked at anyone when they first died and then a week later to *see* if the fingernails and hair and stuff had grown."

"They're thinking about death a lot," Conall repeated. "I think maybe they have to have answers, or they'll keep wondering. Answers let them, I don't know, process their grief."

"How do you know that?"

He shrugged, uneasy but not wanting to give that away. He said abruptly, "It makes sense, that's all."

He'd had a lot of questions about prison the first time his dad was sent away, too. The Washington State Correctional Institute was a great unknown to him, maybe not so different than death. Dad was just…gone.

Mom had shut Conall down every time he asked questions. In those days, he hadn't had the internet to look up answers. He'd found a couple of books at the library and secretly studied them, but they were about correctional institutes in general and not the one his father was at in particular. He hadn't been very satisfied with them. In retrospect he realized the books had been dated and he'd known that without putting his finger on what was wrong.

He hadn't thought about any of this in a long

time. He hadn't remembered, either, that it was Duncan who'd finally told him what he knew. Mom had dragged Duncan, the oldest, on a couple of visits to Dad. Duncan told Conall he was lucky he hadn't had to go. That it was scary going into that place with buzzers going off and heavy doors closing with muffled thuds behind Mom and him as they worked their way through security. That knowing they were locked in, too, made Duncan want to run out screaming.

Duncan scared. Conall had marveled at the concept. Hell, he *still* marveled at the concept. Didn't Duncan face life square on? Had he ever once in his life flinched?

Feeling that streak of bitterness surprised Conall, and for the first time ever, he was ashamed of it. Yeah, Duncan was all about duty and doing the right thing, but that didn't mean he was never scared or uncertain or furious at fate. He *had* to have been furious when Mom ditched them all.

I've held a grudge all these years over nothing, Conall realized. He *should* be ashamed. It seemed like every time he dredged up memories, Duncan was at the heart of them. It wasn't his fault that Conall had felt inadequate in comparison. It was probably even natural, given the age difference between them. How did a kid that much younger ever equal the big brother whose achievements loomed so large?

Conall had known all this intellectually. Even known that if their family hadn't been so screwed up and Duncan had gone away to college, Conall would have been grateful when his big brother called or noticed him during school breaks. They might have grown into friendship later, as the years passed. But as things had been, even before Mom walked out, their relationship was doomed. Conall could close his eyes and recall what an explosive mass of anger he'd been. Duncan had saved him. The fact that he resented being saved had never made sense.

But that crawling sense of shame gave him a clue. Until then he'd been able to pretend he was keeping his head out of the water on his own. From the instant Duncan sat him down to say, "Mom's left us," Conall had known the truth. He was drowning, and his only chance of survival was the brother he admired so much, the one who was having to ruin his own life because he had to rescue Conall—the pathetic, scrawny, excuse-for-a-MacLachlan youngest boy. He'd known Duncan despised him even as he felt obligated.

That was what he couldn't bear knowing. He'd wanted to hate someone else instead of himself.

He eventually heard the Subaru and couldn't stop himself from going to the window to watch Lia, the boys and Sorrel troop across the yard. He could see their mouths moving but couldn't hear a word. They were all carrying bags that looked like they held clothes and shoe boxes. So she'd taken them shopping, even picked up Sorrel from school so she could join them at the mall. The sight made Conall feel disgruntled. He took himself and his bad mood back to the other side of the attic.

Tonight was Jeff's turn to eat downstairs. Conall didn't get a chance to see anyone but Sorrel, who delivered his dinner tray. Her face was brighter and happier than usual.

"Hey," he said. "Good day?"

She nodded vigorously. "Lia said we needed some summer clothes so she took us to the discount mall. I got some really cool sandals and shorts and—" She eyed him and said, "I guess you don't care about clothes, do you?"

Conall looked down at himself and laughed. "I guess I don't." It was stuffy up here, and he wore sacky cargo shorts and a faded T-shirt. A clothes horse he was not.

"Dinner smells really good," she told him cheerily and left him alone.

Dinner *was* good. Lia had used veggies from her garden in a stir-fry on rice. Just like one of the kids, he got a big glass of milk and two home-baked cookies, thick and chewy. He ate without the pleasure he would have felt if he were sitting at the table with everyone else.

He wondered what Walker and Brendan were

asking Jeff tonight. Had they started speculating about sex yet? Conall kind of thought that by age ten he had been. Were they worrying about what would happen to them, or were they still too caught up in their mother's death for it to occur to them how uncertain their futures were? He'd have to ask Lia.

When Jeff came up, Conall said in frustration, "We're wasting our time sitting here staring at that damned house. It's not quite time for the utility district meter reader to make the rounds, but would those guys know the difference?"

Jeff pushed out his lower lip while he thought about it. "Maybe not."

"Could we get their electricity knocked out and use that as a guise to go visiting?"

Knocking out phone service was a handy dandy excuse, but these guys had never signed up for a landline. In fact, it appeared any telephone communications they had with others were made using throwaway cell phones. No major service listed them as customers.

"Hell," he said irritably, on a sudden realization, "I figured out why they were so unfriendly to Lia. Her skin probably isn't lily-white enough to suit them."

"She looks more Caucasian than Hispanic."

"Not with that hair," he argued.

"No suggestion they've been real chummy with any of the other neighbors, either," Jeff said mildly.

Conall grunted and kept his mouth shut. Behind him came the rustles and thumps that indicated Jeff was disrobing and stretching out in bed. Dusk was settling, plunging the never-bright-and-sunny attic into purple-gray gloom. They didn't turn on lights up here, which might catch someone's attention. Maybe the hours sitting in semi to complete darkness were getting to him.

The fact that everything he believed about himself was now floating around like the sparkling bits in a snow globe, likely to form an unfamiliar landscape when they settled, was completely irrelevant.

HE CAME TO HER BED, as Lia had expected he would. She'd tensed the moment she heard the quiet click of the attic door. Even so, Conall took her by surprise, slipping into her room like a ghost. The mattress sank from his weight, and then he had her in his arms and was kissing her with intensity and need that found an instant response in her. It seemed like forever since she'd seen him. This morning when she awakened alone, she'd been both grateful and disappointed. To not see him all day was almost more than she could bear.

Ridiculous, but, oh, she needed him.

If anything, their lovemaking was more powerful than last night's. Maybe it was the anticipation, the fact that they now knew each other's trigger points. But Lia thought there was something about the way Conall touched her tonight, as though he'd missed her, too. Needed her.

When it was over, he rolled to one side pulling her with him, so that her head rested where it was meant to be, in the hollow formed by his shoulder. His hand kept sliding up and down her back, his fingertips testing each vertebrae, the curve of her waist, the sharpness of her shoulder blades. Happiness mixed with a kind of desperation filled her chest. It was like holding her breath underwater. The moment would inevitably come when she had to let it all out and she'd be left hollow inside.

"Why aren't you married, Lia?" Conall's voice was a rumble that vibrated beneath her cheek. "Why don't you have your own kids?"

Surprised, she tilted her head but, of course, couldn't see his face. She took a minute to formulate a reply.

"I didn't want a marriage like my parents'. It's so…unequal. I saw friends' families, of course, but I never felt that close to any of their parents. I always had this feeling of separateness, I wasn't like any of them."

"Because of getting deported."

"Maybe. Probably. It made me feel dirty, like I didn't belong here. But I didn't belong there, either.

Dad and Mom are so different from each other, I guess I've always felt split down the middle." She didn't remember ever saying any of this before, even though she'd figured it out a long time ago. Maybe it was the darkness and the comfort of Conall's embrace that made speaking now so easy.

"You've had boyfriends."

She was glad he didn't ask if she'd ever been in love. He wouldn't want to hear her say, *Until now, you mean?*

"Only a couple that were semi-serious. One in college. That was the closest call to anything permanent. Emilio's parents were migrant workers, but legal. He was warm and funny and we had something in common."

There was a small silence. "But?"

"But it turned out he was also really traditional. He assumed we'd get married and there wouldn't be any reason for me to go to grad school, would there, although it would be okay if I worked for a couple of years until he was making enough to buy a house and start a family. I panicked."

He chuckled. That vibration felt so nice, Lia kissed his chest. Muscles flexed and his arms tightened.

"What about you?" she asked. "Your brothers are both married. Is it your job?"

At first she didn't think he was going to answer

at all. "No," he said finally. "Although it would be tough, doing the kind of work I do."

Lia had no trouble imagining how awful it could be—him disappearing for weeks or months on end, her having no real idea where he was or what he was doing, knowing only that he was probably in danger. Yes, that would be hard on a relationship.

"Jeff's married, though. You knew that."

She nodded.

"I know other guys who are. A couple of female agents, too." Again he was quiet and she had the sense of him collecting himself. "I vowed years ago I was never going there."

The heaviness in her chest felt a lot less like happiness now.

"My parents weren't a shining example. Dad wasn't abusive, nothing like that. I picture him now and I can see that he was handsome, maybe charming. He was good at making people laugh. He didn't really like working for a living, though. Mom and he fought bitterly. It got physical sometimes, which scared the crap out of all of us. They'd break stuff, put holes in the walls." He was silent for a moment. "She ended up doing everything around the house and holding down a job, too. Sometimes we'd suddenly have money. Later I realized it was when he was dealing. Mom kept making him swear to go straight, and he'd try, but it didn't last long. He wasn't…reliable."

"He must have loved her, to try."

"Maybe." The way his muscles twitched felt involuntary. "I didn't see anything that looked like love."

His voice never gave much away, but she couldn't possibly mistake this kind of searing pain. Lia lifted her head, wishing she could see him. She would have sat up and reached for the lamp switch except that she guessed he, too, was talking more freely because the darkness hid so much. In a way, she hoped he didn't realize how much he'd revealed.

"But you…" she whispered. "They must have loved the three of you."

His laugh hurt to hear. "I was nine years old when I heard my parents fighting. My father called me a pathetic excuse for a boy and said I was Mom's fault. They were screaming at each other. She said she'd never wanted me, that Dad was the one who'd insisted they have another kid."

Lia listened in horror. She didn't move even the tiniest bit, even though she wanted to throw herself on top of him and hold him and tell him that his parents were idiots, that he was lovable. So lovable she hadn't had a prayer of resisting him.

But his body was utterly rigid. She could tell that he was talking to the ceiling, maybe hardly aware she was there. She doubted that he'd ever told this story to anyone.

"Dad said I didn't have the makings of any kind of man. He asked whether I was even his." He gave another ugly laugh. "Mom started throwing things. I shut myself into my room. It wasn't a good day, anyway. I got in a lot of fights, and I'd just had the crap beat out of me. My eyes were swollen shut." His voice had noticeably relaxed; he was okay with telling her about this part. But then that quiet tension reintroduced itself. "It was seeing me that set them off. I didn't exactly make them proud."

"Oh, Conall." She couldn't stand it another second. She climbed on top of him and squeezed him with both arms. She burrowed her face against his neck. "They didn't deserve you. I want to *hurt* them. I swear I'll never say anything bad about my parents again. Even Dad loves me, I know he does. How did you turn into such a good man?"

"Hey, hey!" His arms had closed tightly around her, too, but he was laughing. Only then he said, "Are you crying? Lia?"

Damn it, she was. She never cried.

"Oh, hell. For me? Lia, that was a lot of years ago. It's water under the bridge. I shouldn't have told you."

"No," she cried. "I'm glad you did. And it does matter. When I think of you not having anyone—"

"Shh," he said against her head. "Shh, Lia, you'll wake up one of the kids."

"I don't care."

"Yes, you do." He was smiling, she could hear it. His hands moved over her, soothing, kneading, calming her. "And I did have someone. I had Duncan." There was the smallest of pauses. "I had both my brothers."

Lia went still. "Then why…?"

His pauses were hard to interpret but deep and dark with the things he chose not to say.

At last his shoulders jerked. "That's the complicated part. I'll say this much, though. That day, Duncan found me in my room. He brought me an ice pack and he talked to me. He was…there."

"I may have to hug him the next time I see him." She rubbed her wet cheeks on his shoulder and sniffed. Maybe she should feel foolish, but she didn't. Mostly, she was mad.

"All I ask is that you don't kiss him." He was joking, she could tell. "Keep the kisses for me," he said, and he didn't sound humorous anymore. He sounded like he meant it, and her heart squeezed.

No wonder he was so damaged. Too damaged, maybe, to ever love a woman—her—the way she wished he could. Although she'd never really felt violent, Lia wanted to kill his parents, two selfish people who never should have had children.

"I shouldn't have told you," Conall said again, softly.

"I'm glad you did," she repeated. And then they were kissing, first with astonishing tenderness, then with some of the earlier ferocity. They made love, and she wished he wouldn't slip out of the room when they were done, that she'd wake to find him beside her come morning. But she knew that wouldn't be, and that the kids weren't the only reason.

Which hurt.

CHAPTER ELEVEN

THE SCREEN DOOR slammed and Conall looked up. Sorrel.

"Hi," she said.

Had she known he was out here? Conall smiled lazily at her. It was good timing; he'd had in mind to catch her alone and impress on her for the eighty-ninth time that she could not mention him and Jeff at school, online or anywhere else. Truthfully, he wasn't worrying that much, not the way he had at the beginning. The targets were pretty anti-social; Henderson had noted that even when they were grocery shopping and the like, they didn't make conversation with locals. Conall couldn't imagine them prowling a teenager's Facebook page. Still, it would be better if Sorrel kept quiet in the first place.

He couldn't claim to understand her the way he did Walker and Brendan, which made him nervous. She was different than girls he'd known—mostly in a Biblical sense—when he was a teenager. Sometimes she acted no older than the boys, then a minute later would eye him in a way that suggested she was on the cusp of being a woman. The girl part he could handle; the woman, not so much.

"Hey," he said. He sat on the top porch step, his plate of potato salad balanced on his knee, a sandwich in his hand, a can of soda next to him.

Sorrel settled carefully a few feet away. That was something he'd noticed about her; she held herself in tight. None of a teenager's usual expansive, dramatic body language.

"What's up?"

"My caseworker called." Her voice was tight, too. "She says I have to go to counseling with my parents."

He'd heard the phone ring a few minutes ago and could tell somebody had grabbed it. Sorrel didn't seem to get many calls, he'd noticed, unlike the typical teenager. Partly, he supposed, because she'd gone to school here for only a couple of months.

Conall knew little about her background except that she'd been sexually molested and had run away from home repeatedly. He'd as soon not learn the details. "You don't sound very enthusiastic."

She hunched over, her arms held to her body. "They just want me to say I was lying."

Oh, man. Already they were out of his depth. But he didn't feel like he could blow her off, either. "Lying about what?" he asked cautiously, although he knew.

"Everything. They don't *want* to know the truth."

They. That surprised him. "You kept running away. That's what Lia said."

She nodded.

He cleared his throat. "Was it your dad…?"

Sorrel's eyes widened. "You think my *dad* would…?" Shock sounded in every word.

"It happens."

She closed right up. Body, expression, everything. Curled in on herself. Then she mumbled something he couldn't hear.

"What?"

She mumbled it again.

"Tell me, Sorrel."

She lifted her head and yelled, "It wasn't him! Okay? It wasn't him!"

Slowly Conall moved his plate to the porch behind him and swiveled to face her. It was all he could do to keep his voice calm. "Who was it?"

Her hair swung as she shook her head.

"I'll believe you," he told her, voice hard.

They stared at each other. Tears flooded her eyes. "It doesn't matter anymore. Not even if Mom and Dad decide to believe me. I did stuff—" She shuddered.

Conall wished like hell he was somewhere else. Why had she cast *him* in the role of confidant? He couldn't think of anyone more ill-qualified. The boys were one thing, she was another.

But he couldn't bring himself to hurt her. She'd chosen to talk to him, for whatever reason.

After a moment, he said, "You mean when you were on the run."

She nodded.

He was afraid he knew what she meant. "Did you turn tricks, Sorrel?"

She was back to staring at him. "How did you know?" she whispered.

"There aren't too many ways to get enough to eat when you're twelve or thirteen and living on the street," he said, wearily. "You steal, or you sell yourself."

"Did you ever…?"

There but for the grace of God, he thought. Or Duncan.

"No, but I know people. I see kids all the time in Miami, where I live now."

"Oh." She began to rock herself. "I can't tell my parents. I can't!"

"Who was it?" Conall asked. He knew how to interrogate, when to let his voice harden. When to make it plain the game playing was done.

"My uncle." She rocked a little faster. "I tried to tell them, but they wouldn't listen. Mom slapped me!"

What in God's name should he say? *Pick some-*

thing. Don't let this silence deepen her wounds. No, it had to be right.

"It could be they're ready to listen now. Does your caseworker know what happened to you?"

She bobbed her head.

"Does she believe you?"

She shrugged.

"What about Lia?"

The teenager was quiet for a minute. "Maybe."

"So why are you telling me, Sorrel?"

"I like that you're here." Face flushed, she straightened. "I like living here. I don't want to have to go home. I thought maybe… Sometimes I wish…"

Instinctively Conall recoiled from finding out what she wished. He cast a brief look of longing toward the screen door, through which he could see the empty entryway. This would be a really great time for someone to interrupt.

No one did.

He made himself ask. "What do you wish?"

Color flamed in her cheeks now. She kicked up her chin. "I wish that you would…you know. You wouldn't have to pay me or anything. I like *you*."

Oh, shit, oh, shit. It took everything he had not to leap to his feet and back away. This pretty, curvaceous *girl* was gazing at him with yearning in her eyes.

In an act of will, he stayed where he was. Long

practice kept his posture relaxed. "I'm old enough to be your father, you know, Sorrel."

"Yeah, so?" She inched her butt a little bit closer.

Another *shit*. The men who'd bought her, a desperate runaway girl, had probably been his age. Or older. Lots older.

He unclenched his jaw. "I'm thirty-three years old. Twenty years older than you. You're a nice girl, Sorrel, but you should be flirting with boys your age."

She wrinkled her nose and he laughed.

"Yeah, I know, middle school boys haven't exactly hit their stride yet, have they?"

She gave a tiny giggle that heartened him. Had her hectic flush subsided, too?

"You'll be in high school next year, won't you?"

She shook her head. "The middle school here is grades six through nine."

"Really? It wasn't when I went here."

"Wow. I can't imagine you in middle school."

His laugh was genuine. "Trust me, you wouldn't have looked twice at me, not a girl as pretty as you. I was really short until I hit…oh, sixteen, seventeen. I was scrawny and wild." He smiled at her. "Some of the boys your age are going to turn out okay. Some of them, more than okay."

"Mostly thinking about boys freaks me out," she admitted, so softly he had to strain to hear her.

"But you're different. And—and I know there's no reason you'd want me—"

"Whoa. Let me say this. You're right. I don't. No man my age *should* respond sexually to a girl your age. It's wrong. And I'm betting you've been thinking about me that way because you know I'm safe. You're afraid of the boys at school because they probably *are* checking you out. You really are pretty. And after your uncle and the creeps who paid you for sex you're not so sure about men, but you've gotten to know me and—"

"I wish a guy like you did like me," she mumbled, hiding her face again.

He took the risk of laying a hand on her back and rubbing gently. "Someday one will," he said. "When the right time comes. In the meantime, I think what you're doing is looking for, I don't know, a role model, I guess."

She gave an audible sniff. Her cheeks were wet when she lifted her head to look at him. To his dismay, she flung herself at him and wrapped her arms tight around him. Conall froze, unsure what to do. At a flicker of movement, he looked over her head to see Lia standing on the other side of the screen watching them. He hoped like hell she'd been there long enough to hear at least part of the conversation. After the longest hesitation, he enclosed the girl in his arms and hugged her, then carefully set her away from him.

"This counseling thing. I think you should give it another chance. Your parents might have decided to listen."

"I don't care."

"I know you're mad at them. I don't blame you. But holding grudges..." He hesitated. "I'm here to tell you how much you miss, cutting people who love you out of your life." Conall didn't even know if he meant it; the words coming out of his mouth surprised him. But he thought it was what she needed to hear, and that's what he was good at telling people.

"I don't know," she whispered.

The screen door squeaked as it opened. "Was that your caseworker on the phone?" Lia asked.

Tears flooded Sorrel's eyes. "Yes."

"Oh, honey." Crouching, Lia gathered the girl into her arms. "It's okay. You can tell me what *you* want to do."

"I don't know," she wailed.

"Then we'll think about it, as long as you want. And if you have to talk to your parents or anyone else and you want me to be there, I'll go with you. Okay?"

Sorrel went still and tilted her head back. "You promise?"

Lia kissed her forehead then began to rock her gently. "I promise. Cross my heart."

The thirteen-year-old laid her face against her

foster mom's shoulder and gave way to heartbroken sobs.

Conall grabbed his plate and soda and stood. "Later," he mouthed, and Lia nodded. Her smile was shaky but real.

"Thank you," she whispered, and he fled. No, beat a sensible retreat.

She caught up with him an hour later. The boys had decided to go "riding," which meant Walker sat on the pony's back and Brendan's on the horse's. With no bridles or saddles, the animals had continued to placidly graze, but the boys were clutching the manes and talking excitedly, seemingly feeling like knights of yore or some such thing. Since Lia's one rule regarding the animals was that they couldn't go into the pasture or get onto the horse or pony without an adult present, Conall had accompanied them. Now, he leaned his back against the fence and watched Lia cross the lawn to him. He loved the way she moved, her stride long and lithe, and he really loved the way her shorts bared her amazing legs.

"She okay?" he asked when Lia got close enough.

She sighed and propped her forearms on the top rail beside him. "Yeah. Telling you about it seems to have helped."

"Me? Why?"

She laughed at his expression. "You obviously went into the wrong profession, Conall. You should be a therapist. Tell me, do all the crooks confess all whether you want to hear it or not?"

He grimaced. "If only it could be so easy."

"She came on to you, didn't she?"

He shuddered. "Yeah."

"It sounds like you handled it amazingly well. That's been one of her problems, you know. In her other school, she cornered a male teacher alone in his classroom and started to strip. She got lucky, like she did today, because he handled it appropriately and also because nobody walked in on them at the wrong moment. She swings wildly between scared little girl and promiscuous teenager."

"Is it true that her parents didn't believe her?" he asked in a hard voice.

"Yes. It sounds like her mother was positive Sorrel was lying. It was the mom's younger brother who molested Sorrel."

He nodded.

"My impression is that the dad was less sure. He admitted to the guardian ad litem that there were a few times he'd been uncomfortable with the way his brother-in-law watched Sorrel or hugged her. That kind of thing. But apparently he was too spineless to stand up to his wife and say, 'We should listen to her.' No surprise, Sorrel ran away. She got picked up by the police and returned home, at which point she was angrier than ever and things deteriorated. Gee, you think? The cycle continued until the parents and caseworker agreed she had to live somewhere else temporarily."

"And she got lucky enough to come here."

Lia's smile was slightly shy. "A compliment. Thank you."

"You know I mean it."

She studied him for a moment, those extraordinary eyes seeing things he probably didn't know about himself. After a moment she nodded. "I do believe you're honest."

Conall gave a bark of laughter. "Why do you sound so surprised?"

Creases formed between her eyebrows. "Because you work undercover. You must lie all the time."

Put that on my tombstone, he thought dryly. *I'm a hell of a liar.*

"I prefer to think of it as acting," he told her. "And when I do it I'm not Conall MacLachlan. I'm someone else."

Again she looked at him, her eyes searching, and again she nodded.

"So what's her conclusion?" he asked. "Is she willing to give her parents another chance?"

"I think so." Lia made a face. "I wish I had a guarantee that they *are* willing to believe her."

"You don't have any doubt."

"Do you?"

He shook his head.

"Her behavior is classic. Somebody molested her, no question."

"It wasn't only, er, touching, then."

Her glance speared him. *"Only?"*

"You know what I meant."

Lia let out a breath that had her shoulders sagging. "I'm sorry. And no, when her mother marched her to the doctor, it was clear she'd had nonconsensual sex. Her mother didn't take it that way, though. She was positive her daughter had gotten in over her head with some boy, chickened out but didn't want to take responsibility for her own behavior."

"What a winner," he muttered.

"The trouble was, Sorrel and she were already going at it, fang and nail. Puberty had struck. You know what thirteen-year-old girls are like." Her gaze slid sidelong. "Well, maybe not."

He grinned. "Got to say, I haven't so much as carried on a conversation with a thirteen-year-old girl since I was that age."

"If it's any consolation, she threw herself at you because she trusts you."

"I did get that."

"Ditto the teacher. She's really wary with men she doesn't trust. Trouble is, well, the behavior is inappropriate no matter what. She seems to feel it's all she has to offer. It isn't only men, though.

She's conflicted with women, too. After her mother's rejection, she doesn't believe she has anything at all to offer a woman."

"But she seems to trust you."

"We're getting there." After a moment she sighed again, then smiled at him. "Thrills and chills, constant drama. And you thought you'd be bored here."

"I'm bored as hell sitting up in that damn attic," he admitted. He glanced over his shoulder to check on the boys even though he knew Lia was watching them, too. Brendan had dismounted and was trying to convince Pepito the pony to move without notable success. Pepito snatched a mouthful of grass even as Walker kicked his sides. Mouth curving, Conall said, "Do you keep your horses doped up?"

Lia chuckled. "I don't have to. They're infinitely patient, and completely uninterested in any speed above an amble." She turned to look more directly at him. "So what's your job like? Weeks of tedium interrupted by moments of terror?"

He laughed. "Something like that. Not terror, though. Most cops enjoy the rush of adrenaline, you know."

"Do you?"

A year or two ago, he'd have told her he lived for it. Lately, he'd been trying to believe it was still true, that he simply needed assignments that offered more action, more risk. Appalled, he thought he'd been like a drug addict, hooked but finding the same quantity of his drug of choice no longer gave him the rush it once had. Solution: shoot up more.

"I…always have." He knew she was scrutinizing him again, but he didn't meet her eyes. God forbid she see the cascade of doubt that was making him sweat. Now, *that* was terror. *Oh, hell, oh, hell, oh, hell. If I don't have that, what's left?*

"I think there's more to you than you believe," Lia said softly, then pushed away from the fence. "You'll keep an eye on the boys?"

"Yeah, sure," he said automatically.

She nodded and left him.

His head was spinning. The snow globe had been given another bone-rattling shake.

AFTER DINNER, CONALL CALLED Duncan, who agreed to try to sell the local public utility administration on allowing the DEA to borrow a truck, uniform and equipment.

"They'll have to show you how to read the meter," he said. "Your targets will wonder if they don't get a bill."

"Appears the bills go to the home-owner, not the residents, so maybe not. But you're right, we don't want to wave a red flag."

There was a pause. "You going to do it?" Duncan asked, sounding a little too casual.

"No, my partner." The idea made him itchy; Conall wasn't the sit at home and wait on events kind of guy. But for him, showing up next door in a uniform was a no-go. "I've been too visible. I don't know if they've seen me or not, but other neighbors have. These guys might have heard my voice when I was talking to the kids outside. Jeff has stayed out of sight. He's got one of those forgettable faces, too."

"Good." Duncan sounded relieved. He'd met Henderson briefly. "I hate to say it, but you look a little too much like me, in case your neighbors pay attention to local news."

"I hadn't thought of that." *And don't want to think about how much I resemble my big brother.*

"You ever pass as Hispanic?"

"No. I'm fluent enough, but even if I wore colored contacts, my hair and skin aren't dark enough. I'm always a crooked *gringo*."

"Good to know," Duncan said with a laugh.

They talked for a few minutes, Conall asking how Jane and baby Fiona were, Duncan in return wanting to know about the kids here at the house.

"I hear Des thinks Walker is his new best friend," he said.

"I kind of get the feeling Des makes a lot of friends."

"He's definitely a glass half full kid," Duncan agreed. "Something none of us ever were."

Conall stiffened at the offhanded remark about their shared past. He waited for the old feelings to grab him by the throat, but they stayed absent. Finally he said cautiously, "I would have said you were. I always thought of you as the golden boy. Popular, good at everything, most likely to succeed."

"Desperate to get the hell out of Dodge, you mean."

"Really? That's what you were thinking all that time?"

"That's what I was thinking," Duncan said flatly. "Early on, I figured out that Mom and Dad wouldn't be paying my way through college. If I was going, I had to do it on my own. Grades or an athletic scholarship were my way out."

"You worked all those years for something you had to throw away."

"I got my college degree and the career I wanted." Duncan paused. "When I was a kid, I didn't let myself think about what would happen to you and Niall. I won't say I wasn't shocked by what Mom did or by what it meant to me, but whether you think I'm spouting a line of bull or not, the truth is I'm glad things fell the way they did. I didn't have to spend the rest of my life with you two on my conscience."

Stunned, Conall took a minute before he said, with what he intended to be his usual mockery, "Saint Duncan."

He had the feeling his brother was smiling when he said, "I don't hear any bitterness. Don't tell me the years are finally mellowing you."

Was it true? Well, hell. "I guess maybe they are," he admitted. "Or something else is."

"Maybe someone."

"Maybe." His voice sounded thick.

They both backed off after that, but, like every time he saw or spoke to Duncan lately, Conall was left shaken by how much everything had changed. His perception of the past had shifted. It was as if two different artists had painted the same scene, interpreting it with completely different sensibilities. Maybe neither was the truth, but both were true.

Go figure.

He made a point of seeking out Sorrel before dinner, finding her in her bedroom with the laptop open. "You okay?" he asked.

Color swept over her face. "Um, yeah."

He smiled. "You going to talk to your parents?"

Her shoulders jerked. "I kind of have to, don't I?"

"Probably. One of those parts of being a kid that sucks."

She gave a tiny giggle, but her gaze still shied from his. "I'm, well, I'm sorry for…you know."

He stayed relaxed in the doorway, shoulder propped against the frame. "Yeah, I know, and don't worry about it."

Sorrel nodded.

"You know what I'd like? I'd like to see your uncle arrested. Behind bars where he belongs."

"Lia says she bets there've been other girls. Or there will be."

"Unfortunately, that's true. It stinks that he has to hurt more than one girl before anyone takes it seriously."

"Yeah." She sounded militant. Then, the next instant, pathetically young. "I wish I hadn't let him—"

"Let him?" That pissed Conall off. "He had the power, Sorrel, not you. Every single thing that happened is on him. You are not responsible. Don't ever even *think* that again."

"Okay." Her teeth closed on her lower lip. Then she said softly, "I'll try not to."

He made an effort to hide his anger for fear she'd misunderstand it. "Good girl."

"Is it time for dinner?"

"Lia hasn't called us yet. I'm going upstairs to check in with Jeff. Knock when it's time, okay?"

She nodded, smiled, a shy blooming of beauty to come. "Thank you."

He wasn't going to say you're welcome, because she didn't owe him for a thing. It enraged Conall to think of her so vulnerable, betrayed by someone she should have been able to trust. It was worse, so much worse, than the kind of betrayals he took for granted from the scum he dealt with on the job. Would Sorrel ever truly be all right again? He doubted she would; faith in other people, once lost, was probably impossible to recapture.

Except, like him, she'd gotten lucky. Lia would be her refuge until she no longer needed one. One person could make all the difference.

Halfway up the attic stairs, his steps slowed. Was it possible he'd regained his own faith?

I believe that Duncan loved me all that time. It wasn't entirely duty.

And, more shocking, *I believe that Lia will never fail anyone she loves.*

Lucky Sorrel.

CHAPTER TWELVE

CONALL CROUCHED BEHIND a thin screen of black-berries. He was only a few feet on Lia's side of the barbed wire fence that separated her acreage from the neighbor's. Niall crouched beside him, Glock in his hand. Seeing it, Conall had noted the irony that he and his brother had chosen the exact same serve weapon.

Duncan and one of his men, a detective named Sean, were elsewhere along the perimeter, also armed and prepared to move. Conall's intense focus was split between the utility truck bumping along the gravel road, raising a cloud of dust, and the house that lay a few hundred yards across rough pasture. The dogs had given some deep-throated warning barks but were now silent as they raced for the head of the driveway to meet the truck.

"Good thing neither of them wandered this way," Niall muttered.

Conall grunted. He carried a stun gun, not his usual weapon of choice, but he was reluctant to kill the damn dogs if he didn't have to. They were only doing their job.

As the truck rumbled up to the house, the front door opened and a man emerged. The older of the two, Joseph Cufley had thin, graying hair and a body that was going soft. Through his binoculars, Conall tried to tell if he was armed. Henderson parked, then rolled down his window.

His voice came through loud and clear. Good. Wires had been known to fail.

"The dogs gonna bite me?"

"Rufus, Jinx, *heel. Sit,*" Cufley snapped.

The two Dobermans obeyed, but their cropped ears were sharp and their eyes stayed unwaveringly on the intruder.

After displaying understandable hesitancy, Henderson opened his door and got out. "Glad you were home," he said, sounding a little nervous. "PUD. Here to read your meter."

"Sure. Go ahead."

They already knew the meter was on the south side of the house, right beneath the dining room window. It would be natural with the kind of weather they were having for the residents to leave that window open some of the time. Maybe to have some unwary conversations over their pizza or frozen lasagna. Perfect place for a bug.

Primed, Jeff nodded and started around the

house. To Conall's dismay, Cufley followed close behind, the dogs with him.

Niall was swearing softly. Conall lost Henderson visually, but knew Duncan would have picked him up. Jeff was doing a hell of a job, somewhat to Conall's surprise, chatting about the run of sunshine and how those were mighty good looking dogs. "Do you breed Dobermans?" he asked, real friendly but still maybe a little nervous. Who wouldn't be?

The pause was distinct. "No, these are both male." The answer sounded reluctant and not very friendly.

A metallic sound. Jeff had opened the box on the side of the house, Conall guessed. Shit. Was there any way he could plant a listening device right under Cufley's nose? Were these survivalists sophisticated enough to check for a bug after the supposed meter reader had left? Conall's gut was saying, *Don't do it. Bail.* Unless Henderson had a chance on the way to the truck to drop it somewhere else. Too bad there were no foundation plantings.

Conall waited, tense. A moment later, the conversation resumed. Jeff reappeared, Cufley breathing down his neck. There wasn't a damn thing Henderson could do but say, "Have a good day," and leap into the truck. He backed out, turned around and drove away, the dogs racing behind until the boundary of the property.

Conall and Niall were already melting away. The last thing they needed now was for one of the dogs to catch their scent.

Jeff had already turned down Lia's driveway, as would be expected. Conall broke into a trot. Jeff was waiting for them when they ducked between the fence rails. He shook his head.

"Not a prayer."

"Shit."

"You think I should have—"

"No. He was suspicious. You did the right thing."

The real meter reader, wide-eyed at the excitement, reclaimed her truck and departed. The men stayed where they were, by Duncan's now not-so-shiny SUV.

"You think he's afraid they're being watched?" Niall suggested.

"In a general way, yeah," Conall said. "Specifically, no. Our neighbor's whole worldview is paranoid. He hates and fears anyone even slightly different from him. Government protects minorities, which means it's out to get him. Public utility districts are government entities, right?"

"So why didn't we send in a pizza delivery instead?" Duncan asked behind him.

"Because it turns out our guys always pick up

their pizza. Seems they don't want *anyone* knocking on their door. What's more, they buy randomly from different pizza places, or frozen from the grocery store."

Duncan snorted. "Because variety is the spice of life?"

Conall cracked a smile despite his frustration. "I seriously doubt it. It's probably more paranoia in action. Maybe Cufley thinks too much of the same brand will eat up his stomach lining."

The other men chuckled. Conall sighed and held out a hand to Duncan. "Thanks for backing us up."

"No problem." They shook and then he clapped Conall on the shoulder.

Niall did the same, and Sean nodded. They drove away, leaving Niall and Jeff to walk into the house where the boys and Lia lay in wait.

"Did it work?" Brendan asked eagerly.

Jeff looked startled at how well-informed the kids were. Conall was momentarily disconcerted by how utterly he'd violated standard operating procedure where they were concerned. But he still couldn't see the harm, and said, "No. One of the guys stuck to Jeff like stink on— Er, like glue."

They both cackled, knowing what he'd almost said. Lia rolled her eyes upward. *Boys,* her expression said. *Men,* she might as well have said. Conall knew plenty of adult males who still found bodily odors and human excrement to be the foundation of all humor.

"Now what?" Lia asked worriedly.

"Don't know."

"Tomorrow is garbage day," she reminded him.

The boys both stared at him. "You go through their *garbage?*"

"Fascinating stuff, garbage," he told them, steering both of them toward the kitchen with a hand on each of their shoulders. "You know archaeologists are especially fond of garbage, too. Nothing they like better than discovering an ancient dump."

Walker didn't look as if he knew what an archaeologist was, but Brendan's brow furrowed. "Yeah, but that's really *old* garbage. It doesn't smell."

"A guy's gotta do what a guy's gotta do."

Henderson had an air of bewilderment as he excused himself to go upstairs. Conall had come to the conclusion that the other DEA agent lacked any sense of humor. He was an awfully earnest guy. It didn't bode well for his tolerance of his own kids' screw-ups and foibles, but maybe they were earnest, too. Stood to reason.

He grabbed a cola from the fridge and let Lia debate what the boys could and couldn't have. He drained the drink in a few long swallows. He was beginning to think he was going to have to drug or use the stun gun on the pair of Dobermans so he could sneak close to the house. He hadn't wanted to do that since he wasn't sure how often the men checked on the dogs during the night. If they discovered them unconscious or even groggy, secrecy would be a thing of the past. But this couldn't keep dragging on, either. He needed it to be over, before—

Conall didn't let himself finish the thought. He'd long since learned not to dwell on possible risks and wasn't going to make an exception for a risk that wasn't physical.

Lia finally produced homemade oatmeal raisin cookies all around, and he fell on them with as much enthusiasm as the boys did. She watched in amusement. "*They're* skinny. You look well fed."

He grinned at her, making her cheeks become tinged with pink at the unspoken reminder that she knew every contour of his body. "I usually only get store-bought cookies." He patted his belly. "I'll bet I've put on ten pounds since I came to stay here."

She made a scoffing sound accompanied by Walker's and Brendan's laughter.

"You're not *fat*," Walker said. "You have to run lots to keep up with us."

"You do keep me hopping." He smiled at them, thinking about how long it had been since he'd gotten any real exercise. He didn't want to make himself visible by running daily, as he did whenever his job allowed it, and Lia didn't have a treadmill or exercise bike or weights. She kept slim by caring for house, children, garden and animals instead.

He went out and kicked the soccer ball with the boys for an hour, then elicited their help in doing some work on the barn he'd had in mind. Lia provided gloves for all—she had kid-size ones for her garden. Conall put in some nails to hang yard tools, then laid out smaller tools to determine how large a peg board they'd need. Finally he took the boys with him to the hardware store. Lia kept offering to pay any costs, and he stared her down.

He purchased peg board and hooks as well as lumber and brackets to put up shelves. For once he worked up a good sweat by the time he had to go in and shower before relieving Jeff.

Conall was a little surprised when he emerged from the bathroom to find Brendan lurking in the hall.

"I wish you were having dinner with us," the older boy said.

Conall smiled crookedly. "Me, too."

Brendan shifted from foot to foot. "You really, really need to hear what those guys are talking about, don't you?"

"We'll figure out a way to do that. That's what I get paid to do."

"Do you think they have guns?"

Yeah. He was pretty sure the neighbors had enough guns for a small army, but he wasn't going to say that.

"You afraid they're going to shoot me?"

The kid hung his head and shrugged.

Conall ruffled his hair. "Better men than them have tried. You haven't seen any holes in me, have you?"

Actually, he'd had a few, the ugliest of which had been in his groin and another that left a long scar on his thigh. Lia had discovered both—traced them with featherlight fingertips followed by soft brushes of her lips and moist breath. Who knew having a woman inspect his battle scars could be so erotic?

"No-o. Has anyone ever shot *at* you?"

"Yeah, but most people aren't very good shots. Especially when the target is moving."

Brendan frowned as if concentrating hard and nodded. "So you run really fast, right? And zigzag, like they do on TV?"

Conall laughed. "Something like that. Listen, I need to work, and don't I hear Lia calling you?"

Looking sulky, the ten-year-old said, "How come Jeff doesn't eat upstairs every night? He hardly talks to us anyway."

Conall hid this smile. "I promised I'd let him out of the attic every other day. Otherwise he could sue because the living conditions are inhumane."

Pretending to worry, he said, "Maybe every other day isn't enough, though. Do you think he's forgetting how to talk? His wife won't like that when I send him home."

Brendan eyed him. "You're joking, right?"

On another laugh, Conall headed for the attic door. "I'm joking."

For once, it was Lia who knocked half an hour later to hand over his dinner tray, allowing him to steal a lingering kiss and cop a feel that left him aroused with no way to get relief until three in the morning or so.

Well, hell. Anticipation was supposed to be half the fun, wasn't it? He grimaced. He'd rather have made love with her now *and* later. But he guessed in a houseful of kids that wouldn't have happened anyway. He couldn't blame the job for this particular frustration, uncomfortable though it was.

It felt like a miracle to him that she was awake and waiting eagerly for him every night when he slipped into her room. He had yet to catch her by surprise. Her arms always closed around him with fierce pleasure when he got into bed with her.

Tonight he growled, "God, I need you," before taking her mouth with ravenous hunger. He hadn't been able to get her out of his mind the entire time he kept restless, irritable watch from the window. Ten hours of his body aching for hers.

Lia kissed him as passionately and gripped the

nape of his neck with one strong hand while the other explored the contours of his back. He loved the feel of her fingers sinking into his hair, and he loved having to search beneath the curtain of hers for her breasts and belly. She'd taken to leaving her luxuriant hair loose when she went to bed, knowing the first thing he'd do anyway was free it from the braid.

At one point he tore his mouth from hers to say, "I want to make love to you in the daytime. I want to see sunlight across your body. The way your eyes must change color when you get excited. I want—" He groaned when her hand encircled him. He finished in a rough whisper, "I want everything."

She didn't ask what his *everything* comprised. He couldn't have told her, only that he had begun to resent the fact that he couldn't touch her most of the time, not the way he wanted to. Coming to her in the middle of the night like this had begun to feel furtive. He didn't know why it mattered, but it did.

"I'd like to see you, too," she murmured. "But you know we can't. The kids—"

Much as he liked the kids, he wasn't in any mood to think about them. He licked her nipple instead and then drew it into his mouth to suckle. Her hips rose in involuntary response and she apparently lost interest in talking, too. But for one gasp of surprise, a few moans and one keening cry he had to swallow with a hasty, open-mouthed kiss, tonight's lovemaking was silent after that. Silent but shockingly intense.

Conall was left winded, sated, stunned and apprehensive. How could it keep getting better? How could it be so good? What if it never was again, once their lives diverged?

He didn't know if she was asleep or not when he left her. He only knew he had to get away, that it felt too sweet holding her like this with her head tucked on his shoulder as if it belonged, him inhaling her scent, feeling the cushion of her breast against his side, her breath washing over his chest, her warmth.

It was an addiction, that's all. He'd always been wary of men who claimed they *needed* anything. But tonight...

Tonight he'd come frighteningly close to saying, *I* need *everything*.

LIA DIDN'T KNOW what was wrong, but Conall's mood seemed to darken after that day. She couldn't tell if that had anything to do with the change. He'd seemed relaxed enough afterward, certainly with the boys. When she took his dinner up to him, he was sexy and playful. But when he came to her during the night, she felt his tension. A couple of times, he lost some of the care with which he usually touched her. It was almost as if he was angry, whether at her or something else she didn't know.

It wasn't only a bad mood, because it lasted. He still spent time with the boys, but was more abrupt with them. Less inclined to talk to Lia. He came to her bed every night, but didn't talk at all and silenced her with his mouth when she tried. The cuddle after lovemaking was brief and seemed almost reluctant, as if he longed to be gone. She could feel his muscles taut with the desire to get away.

On day three of his emotional withdrawal, Lia braced herself to talk to him. Not for her sake, she told herself, but for the boys'. She found her moment when he came into the kitchen alone to grab a drink.

"Something's going on with you," she said directly. "What's wrong?"

"Huh?" Conall turned from the refrigerator. "What are you talking about?"

"You've changed."

His face was devoid of any expression. "I'm doing a job. It's past time I paid a little more attention to it."

"And we're not part of the job." Chilled, she began snapping green beans into a bowl, her head bent so she didn't have to look at him again. Humiliation crept over her. She sounded like an out-raged wife. No, not outraged—whiny.

"I really don't know what you're talking about. The boys have been helping me finish up in the barn." His voice softened. "You should come and see what we've done. They feel good about it."

"Later," she managed to say. "Or I'll go out in the morning."

He stepped close to her, close enough she could feel the heat of his body, and said huskily, "Lia…"

She moved aside, evading his hand, pretend-ing she had to run water into a pan. "Let me get dinner on," she said, in some approximation of a normal voice.

There was silence. Finally he left, and she heard the front door open and close a moment later.

Of course he came to her room that night, and of course she could no more resist his lips and his touch and his body than ever. But afterward she lay rigid beside him, not relaxing against him as she'd been doing, and he didn't draw her close, either. Instead, after barely a couple of minutes, he rolled toward her, brushed a gentle kiss on her forehead, murmured, "Sleep tight," and left as si-lently as he'd come.

HE SPENT A GOOD DEAL of the next day up in the attic with Jeff, leaving the boys to their own devices, which meant they followed Lia around and kept saying, "I'm bored." She offered to kick the soccer ball with them, and Brendan mumbled, "You're not very good at it." Finally Lia saddled the horse and pony, something she didn't do very often, and gave the boys a riding lesson. Afterward they were happy to help her comb out tangled manes and tails and learn to brush in the direction the animal's hair lay. She showed them how to check hooves for stones and clean out packed mud and manure, and they were all sweaty and horsey smelling by the time they went in, which meant taking turns in the shower.

She told herself she was relieved that tonight was Jeff's turn to join them for dinner. Brendan took Conall's meal up to him and came back more quickly than usual, his shoulders hunched. He stayed quiet at the table, Lia watching him covertly.

What a jerk, she fumed. Conall must have been brusque with him. *Hurt my feelings,* she thought, *fine. But not the boys'.*

Not until after dinner, when Sorrel disappeared upstairs to spend time on the computer and Walker and Brendan decided to watch TV, did Lia have time to brood.

What had changed? She couldn't figure it out. The boys were upstairs getting ready for bed and Lia was rinsing plates and loading the dishwasher when she thought again about the way Conall was all but leaping out of her bed the minute he was done with her these past few nights. With an icy tingle, she remembered thinking, *As if he longed to be gone.*

Yes, that was it exactly. And it wasn't only the sex. It was everything. He'd had fun here for a while, but he wasn't anymore. Conall was ready to wind this operation up and move on to one that was more exciting. One that might give him a real shot of adrenaline.

She had gone completely still, scarcely conscious of the hot water pouring over her hands. The most awful pain tore through her, a brushfire that seared and blackened all of her as it burned. A small sound escaped her, quiet but raw.

She'd been fooling herself all along. He was using them as a diversion. The boys filled his idle afternoon hours, and she met his sexual needs. Full stop.

Lia felt cheap suddenly, no better than Sorrel probably had after some dirty old man had let her out of his car. Angry at herself, too, because she couldn't even blame Conall. He'd never been anything but honest. He'd wanted to avoid case of terminal boredom while he was here, and she'd offered herself up because…oh, because she was lonely and probably starved for sex or maybe only for tenderness and the illusion that somebody actually loved her.

And because she could love him.

Because I do love him.

In her shame, she wondered if she really knew him at all. She'd speculated once that he was someone different depending on his assignment, but had come to believe that here, he was the real Conall. On no evidence whatsoever.

She was dry-eyed, thank God. Devastated, but too angry to cry. Yes, he was remarkable with the boys and even with Sorrel. He must have a gift for seeing what each person needed then meeting it. The grief-stricken boys. The confused teenage girl. And Lia herself, who tried to make a family out of children who never stayed long enough to really love her.

"I'm pathetic," she whispered to her reflection in the steamy kitchen window. With jerky movements she turned off the water, dried her hands then got the dishwasher running.

Tired and lonelier than she'd ever been in her life, she went upstairs to tuck the kids in. It was a huge relief to escape outside. She sat for a very long time on the porch steps in the dark.

Finally, when she went to bed she did something she hadn't in years—she closed her door and hoped Conall got the message.

CONALL KNEW HE SHOULD have talked to Lia today. He'd been curt with everyone. Grumpy. Of course she'd noticed. What had he expected?

The trouble was, he didn't know what to say. He couldn't tell her how confused he was, how close to panic. He couldn't admit to her how vulnerable he felt, or how much that threw him back to a time he hated to remember, when he was a kid and still let himself get hurt.

No, it was better that he hadn't tried to explain anything to Lia. Whatever he was feeling, he'd get over it. He'd be more careful with her, that's all. He was usually good at hiding what he felt.

For some damn reason, Henderson was snoring tonight. A couple of times Conall actually stalked across the attic to the bed and heaved his partner to his side to shut him up. Usually he could tune out irrelevant noises, but tonight he was on edge. That panic made him jittery, as if he'd had too much caffeine. Nerves shivering beneath the skin.

Everything would be fine tomorrow. Back to normal. There was no reason he couldn't enjoy the rest of his time here.

With an effort of will, he calmed down. Felt the tension leach from his muscles. He started thinking about Lia without the anxiety. He began to count down the minutes until he could get into bed with her. Right now, kissing her was the reassurance he wanted. What kind of idiot was he to develop a case of the cold sweats because the sex with her was *too good?* He grunted at the stupidity of that.

Henderson slept later than usual. About every five minutes, Conall debated whether he should wake him up. But Henderson *was* getting the short end of the stick with this operation, and the least Conall could do was let the poor bastard sleep.

It was 3:43 when Jeff stumbled out of bed, muttered something about pissing, and went downstairs. He didn't always go down; the guy had a hell of a bladder, but this time he must have gone all the way to the kitchen, because he came back with a glass of juice and a big whopping slice of the carrot cake Lia had baked yesterday.

"Go to bed," he said around a bite, and Conall went. Jeff moved more like Big Foot than an undercover agent. Lia would be awake for sure.

The hall was so dark he didn't notice her door until he reached the bathroom and turned on the light. Then he glanced back and saw four closed bedroom doors.

He stood stock-still, suddenly sick to his stomach.

Lia had closed it by accident. She must be awake; pretty soon she'd notice that she was seeing only a faint band of light beneath the door. By the time he came out, she would have opened her door.

Conall brushed his teeth, used the toilet, then hesitated before reaching for the knob. She'd be waiting for him. She wanted him as much as he wanted her. Maybe more, he told himself, trying to feel cocky instead of shaky.

He opened the door and looked down the hall to see…hers still closed. After a moment he shut off the light and walked toward his bedroom, maybe a little less quietly than usual. Thinking…he didn't know what. His feet stopped at her door the way they always did. His lips formed her name. It was a long time before he forced himself to continue to his own room.

CHAPTER THIRTEEN

FOR THE FIRST time since he'd arrived, Conall dreaded going downstairs come morning. From day one, he'd thought about Lia the moment he opened his eyes, anticipating his first sight of her, the first sound of her voice. Today… God. What would she say? What could *he* say?

"I'm sorry" might be a good start.

Annoyed with himself and trying to ignore the unwieldy lump that had taken up residence in his chest, Conall showered and shaved, finally making his way down. The house was quiet—too quiet—and for a minute he had the fear she'd taken the boys and absconded for the day. He couldn't blame her; hadn't he slunk around avoiding her yesterday?

Some major-league groveling was clearly called for. Not his specialty, but he could do it.

The lump in his chest lightened momentarily when he heard her talking to someone in the kitchen. Thank God, she hadn't left.

She was on the phone, he found when he walked in, leaning with one hip against the counter and frowning while she listened. Her glance flicked to him, but he couldn't tell what she was thinking.

"We can do tonight," she agreed. "Please make her parents understand that Sorrel's condition for coming is that I be present." Pause. "Yes, I know it's unusual, you've already said that." More listening. "Okay, seven o'clock."

He'd already put water on for coffee and was pouring his cereal when she ended the call.

"Sorrel's meeting with her parents at last?"

"Yes." Her gust of breath held exasperation. "They're upset about the idea of me sitting in on the session. Why, I have no idea. The counselor was going to be there anyway. I swear, it'll be all I can do not to slap their faces if they start in again trying to get her to admit she accused Uncle Raymond falsely."

He abruptly fixated on Uncle Raymond. "Is that his name?"

"Yes." She leveled a sharp look at him. "You're not thinking—"

"Thinking?" He lifted both eyebrows.

"Oh, shoot him, I don't care," she muttered, and automatically went to pour the boiling water through the coffee filter.

"You okay?" he asked her. He cleared his throat. "I mean…feeling all right?"

"Why wouldn't I be feeling all right?"

"I thought maybe… Since your door was shut last night—"

"That I was sick? Oh." She laughed. "Having my period, you mean. No, as it happens, I'm not due for almost another week."

Should he be nervous, it occurred to Conall, because they'd been having sex during her most fertile time of the month with only condoms for protection? They had a pretty significant rate of failure. His heart picked up the pace a little, but— Oh, God. The image that filled his head of her pregnant was erotic and…something else, but not frightening.

And *that* scared the crap out of him.

"Was I wrong in assuming you were telling me I wasn't welcome?" he asked, voice even.

Her breasts rose and fell with a quick breath. "No."

"You going to tell me why?"

Their eyes met, hers wide and wary.

"I realized this morning that I let myself get a little too melodramatic last night while I brooded about our relationship, such as it is, but I'm not sure my conclusion was wrong." She stayed where she was, a good distance from him at the kitchen table. His cereal was getting soggy, but he didn't care. "You've…changed these past few days," she continued.

"I've been working through some things," Conall admitted, voice rough.

"You've hurt our feelings. The boys' and mine."

"I didn't mean to."

Lia shrugged. "You did it anyway." She raised a hand when he started to speak. "No, let me say this. The truth is, you've been filling your time with us. And that's okay, to a point. You've been good for the boys. It'll be hard for them when you leave, but you've never pretended. They know your job will take you away eventually. You've helped heal them in the meantime. This may be the first time in their lives they've really had the chance to relate to a man."

It was all he could do to sit still when he needed to jump up, pace, pinch the bridge of his nose, clear his throat again. But he only waited.

"I appreciate what you've done for them. But me... Well, I never should have slept with you. I'm not made for casual sex. And that's what this is for you. I'm another convenience here—meals, toilet, shower, sex."

He shot to his feet, his chair scraping back. "That's bull—"

Lia shook her head so vehemently he had to stop, still ten feet away from her. "It's true." Her voice was so soft he could barely hear her. "I'm not mad. You never even hinted at anything else. We were two consenting adults. But I realized I don't want to consent anymore." Her shoulders moved. "That's all."

"You're not a convenience. You were never that." The words pushed their way out of him. "For God's sake, it never occurred to me that sex would be provided along with kitchen privileges." The idea seriously pissed him off. That she'd think for a minute that's all she was to him. "You have to know that you've got me feeling things I didn't know I could feel."

She stared at him. Her hands gripped each other, her knuckles white. "What kind of things?"

Conall shook his head. He hadn't articulated any of this to himself, how could he now to her? Why couldn't she be patient? Why was she pushing him?

After a minute she gave a small, broken laugh. "*Things*. Boy, am I flattered." She shook her head as if to clear it. "If you'll excuse me, I promised myself I was going to wash the windows today."

Before he could figure out what to say, she was gone. He heard her voice—talking to the boys, he diagnosed. Conall looked down at his soggy cereal, his appetite gone. He dumped the mess in the sink, turned on the disposal then put the bowl in the dishwasher.

He had no idea why he felt shell-shocked. This op wasn't never-ending, however it sometimes felt. He'd be packing up and going soon no matter what. Maybe she was right; maybe it was better if they eased out of the relationship instead of going cold turkey. He looked at the coffee and dumped that, too. For the first time he noticed that the sky was overcast. Perfect. Suited his mood.

CONALL HAD A COUPLE of ideas for unsticking the pause button on Operation Watch The Grass Grow, which made it seem like good timing to call Duncan and ask if they could get together and talk. It wasn't until Conall pulled into his brother's driveway that he realized he wasn't here to secure local police cooperation. He was here because of all these feelings rattling around inside him.

He swore under his breath, set the emergency brake and killed the engine, then sat there for longer than he should have. Was he really contemplating spilling his gut to the brother he hadn't spoken to for ten-plus years? The brother he'd sworn he hated?

Why hadn't he gone to Niall instead? They at least were friends of a sort.

He didn't have to say anything. He could keep this brisk and business-like.

Conall got out when he realized Duncan had opened the door and was waiting, one shoulder propped on the frame. When Conall got close enough, his brother straightened. "I picked up some food at the deli and started making sandwiches."

Conall nodded. "Thanks." He'd suggested lunch if Duncan could choose someplace out of the way, and wasn't surprised at the decisive answer. "My place."

"Jane at work?" he asked, following his brother through the quiet house. He found himself looking around more this time, liking what he saw. The decor was classy but comfortable, with leather furniture that had a masculine feel, gleaming wood floors, white walls, a river rock fireplace in the living room, bookcases everywhere, and some eye-catching gallery quality wildlife photographs. With books and newspapers lying on end tables and a playpen with a bright mobile in the middle of the living room, it felt like a real home, something the house they'd grown up in never had. He wondered how much represented Duncan's tastes, how much Jane's.

"Yeah." His brother's smile was crooked. "I keep listening for her and Fiona. Funny feeling, after I lived alone for so many years, and now the house isn't right when I'm the only one home."

"You've changed."

"People do."

A container of coleslaw was set out on the table, as were sandwich makings. Good ones—crusty rolls, thick slices of turkey, Swiss cheese, lettuce, tomatoes already cut up and some exotic mustard. Conall smiled, remembering the tasteless, squishy white bread he'd grown up eating, the prepackaged lunch meats, the American cheese that came individually wrapped in plastic. His own tastes had become considerably more sophisticated, too.

Duncan offered a choice of drinks. Conall chose the coffee he hadn't been able to swallow earlier. He was starved, too, he discovered, as he assembled a sandwich. Dinner had been a hell of a long time ago.

They'd both taken a few bites before his brother said, "Something on your mind?"

Too much. So much he didn't know where to start, or even if he wanted to start. The itchy, restless feeling ran under his skin, making him wonder what would happen if someone touched him unexpectedly. God, was he twitching?

"Yeah." With his fork, he poked at the slaw. "Coming home like this has been weird." Okay, that was a place to start.

"How so?" Duncan eyed him curiously.

"I hadn't let myself think much about Mom and Dad. Growing up." His shoulders moved uncomfortably, of their own volition. "Or you."

"Yeah, I kinda noticed that when you ignored my letters."

He found himself, strangely, smiling. "Ignoring your letters was when I did think about you.

Telling yourself you don't give a damn takes some effort, you know."

Duncan laughed heartily. "I'll be sure to write you a lot more often in the future."

Conall met his brother's eyes head-on. "I won't be ignoring your letters anymore."

It was a minute before Duncan nodded. "I'm glad." He sounded hoarse.

"I was a bastard."

"Yeah, you were."

Ridiculous to be smiling again, but he was. Duncan was, too, he saw. They both concentrated on eating for a few minutes, the silence easier now, something important out of the way.

"So you've been thinking about Mom and Dad," Duncan said at last, reflectively.

"No." He frowned. "Yeah, I guess I have. Do you remember—" He grunted with amusement. "Actually, you probably remember a dozen times when I'd gotten the shit beat out of me."

"Two dozen at least."

"There was this once when I was about nine. My eyes were both swollen shut."

"God, yes. Your face looked like raw meat." Duncan leaned back in his chair, contemplating Conall. "I heard Mom sobbing in the kitchen. There were broken dishes all over the floor. I sneaked upstairs and— I don't remember why I even checked your room, but you were huddled in bed."

"That sounds like the time I'm thinking of." Conall took a swallow of coffee, striving for a ruefully reminiscent tone. "They were fighting when I got home. Seeing me tipped them over the edge. I guess they thought I'd stayed upstairs. I heard her yelling at him that she had never wanted me, that he was the one who insisted they have another kid. He bellowed that I had to be her fault, that he didn't believe I was his. He couldn't see himself in me."

Duncan bit off a harsh obscenity. "I knew something worse than usual was wrong." Breathing hard, he bent his head for a moment. "You believed them, didn't you?"

"What wasn't to believe?" There. He'd pulled the tone off perfectly. "I think she did love you. Maybe Niall some. Me, not at all. I always knew that."

"No."

Conall didn't know if he'd ever heard so much anger in one word. "What?"

"It's not true. She did love you early on, before things got so bad with him. She pulled back from all of us after that. Niall, too. Why do you think he started getting in so much trouble?"

Was it true? Not that his mother had loved him—Conall really didn't give a damn anymore—

but that she hadn't picked out him alone to reject? "I didn't think about it," he admitted. "I was a mess."

"I've never seen anyone as angry as you." Duncan sounded troubled. "Later, you got so slick no one saw below the surface. Teachers couldn't say enough about you, you took the baseball team to the only championship they've had before or since—"

Conall laughed at that. "Really?"

They exchanged brief, wry grins.

"Really. Our sports teams suck." Duncan returned to his point. "You had the girls eating out of your hand—"

"And other parts of my body," Conall murmured.

Duncan chuckled, but continued, "I'd look into your eyes and I never saw any real emotion at all. I couldn't tell if you'd tamped all that anger down like gunpowder that was going to catch a spark someday, or whether you were absolutely fine and I was imagining that you were a zombie and not the brother I remembered."

A *zombie?* Was that what he'd been? Conall couldn't decide whether to be amused or disconcerted.

"A zombie." He tried it out on his tongue. "I think it was a little of both," he finally admitted. "I tried like hell to believe I didn't feel anything for anyone. Underneath...I'm pretty sure that kid who didn't have anything but his pride and his anger was alive and kicking."

His brother sighed. "I suspected that."

"Maybe that's where it gets weird. I don't think anything changed until a few weeks ago."

"When you came home."

"Yeah."

Duncan swallowed. "You didn't want to come."

"Hell, no."

"You were still pissed at me."

He grunted his agreement.

"So what happened?"

"I don't know." All those unidentifiable emotions felt like bits of flying grit, abrasive enough to scour glass. "I started seeing you—everyone—differently."

His brother's clear, often cool eyes—so much like his own—had softened with what might be compassion. "My suspicion," he said, "is that the way you thought about me and the past was habit. Nothing else. You got home, looked around and realized somewhere in there you'd grown up and the man you are has only a passing resemblance to the kid who left town carrying his resentment like a backpack he couldn't put down."

Unblinking, Conall stared at him. Was that true? Had he been so damned oblivious he didn't notice how he'd changed? *Had* he changed that much?

"I've been living my life based on vows I made

the day I left home," he heard himself say. "I wasn't going to let anyone close. No wife, no kids, didn't want family. Didn't believe in forgiveness."

Duncan only laughed. "Sounds like a teenager, doesn't it?"

Jarred, Conall thought. God. It did. Melodrama city. "Still not so sure about the family ties," he admitted. "I'd be a hell of a husband or father, with my job."

Duncan made a noncommittal sound. Dished up some coleslaw.

"I'm not thinking about anything like that anyway. It's the good ol' days that have been on my mind."

"Uh-huh."

His eyes narrowed. "What's that supposed to mean?"

"You sound like me when I met Jane."

Conall tensed. "What are you talking about?"

"Lia. Those boys. Seems to me you'd make a fine father, not to mention husband."

He gave an irritable half shrug. "That's ridiculous. You're imagining things."

His brother only looked at him.

"She's— Okay, Lia and I have been—" He couldn't say it. Filling in time having the best sex of his life. Talking. Making the air shiver when they were in the same room. "You know I'm out of here as soon as we wind this up."

The pause was long enough to express Duncan's opinion. To give him credit, though, he finally said only, "You have an idea of how to make that happen?"

They did talk business, then, Duncan reiterating his willingness to provide backup however and whenever Conall wanted it.

"If you're right about them, they're nobody I want living in my town." His voice and expression both were hard. Oh, yeah, this was the brother Conall knew and loved.

"I'd better get home," he said at last, stretching, then heard himself. *Home?* "Home away from home," he amended.

Duncan smiled. "Lia seems good at making a home. That's what she sets out to do for all those kids, isn't it?"

Yeah. Maybe he'd only been caught up in something never meant for him. Vegetables from the garden bursting with flavor, homemade raspberry jam, swaybacked, kind-eyed horse and plump, gentle pony, white-painted fences and deep front porch and a woman who presided over it all with warmth and a firm hand.

He liked that hand a lot, especially when it was on his body. Conall felt himself shiver at a flash of memory.

"You ever find out whether those kids were illegals?" his brother asked idly.

Without hesitation, Conall answered, "No. I had no reason to pursue it." He shrugged. "The kids are gone."

"Makes sense," Duncan said with a trace of amusement. "Like I told you, it wasn't the kind of rumor I pay any attention to."

Appreciating the assurance, Conall insisted on helping clean up and left a few minutes later feeling…disconcerted. Strangely, it wasn't his brother's voice he heard, but Lia's.

I think there's more to you than you believe.

Maybe she was right.

LIA WAS ASHAMED of how quickly she came to regret her decision. All she had to do was lurk by the window that afternoon watching Conall playing baseball with the boys after he got back from town.

He was catcher right now, coaching Walker on his batting and Brendan on his pitching. Every so often he'd rise from his crouch and gently wrap his arms around Walker to adjust his grip on the bat, or he'd walk out to the mound he'd created with a couple of shovelfuls of dirt and talk to Brendan, sometimes demonstrating a better way to hold the ball or something about his shoulder rotation. She didn't have to see his smile to know he *was* smiling, or hear his voice to know it was that low, sexy rumble that held amazing kindness.

Who was he, really? Baffled, she found herself drawn to the window again and again even though all she was doing was torturing herself.

She'd accused him of spending time with the boys as nothing but a way to fill in his time, yet she'd known even when she said it that he was out there coaching Walker and Brendan and teaching them to use tools and answering their questions with sensitivity and honesty because he'd seen that they needed someone. He'd given of himself for them, not because he was bored.

The truth was, she had been afraid for herself, not really for the boys at all. And...she still didn't know whether she'd been right or wrong.

You have to know that you've got me feeling things I didn't know I could feel.

Had she been an incredible fool, closing a door she should have left open?

Guys said things like that, she told herself with would-be derision. He'd cleverly implied he cared without actually saying he did. In fact, he wouldn't answer at all when she prodded.

Depression settled on her. What difference did it make anyway? He'd be gone before she knew it.

But I could have had a few more weeks if I was lucky.

She could say she was sorry. She could leave her door open tonight.

Yes, she could. And then feel cheap tomorrow.

Moving slowly, Lia went to the kitchen and reached into the cupboard for the flour canister. She'd make bread, take out some of her turmoil by pummeling dough.

Just think how light your cooking duties will seem when you're not having to feed two men along with the kids.

That was more like it. Nothing like looking at the bright side.

LIA KEPT DARTING looks at Sorrel during the half-hour drive to Mt. Vernon, where the counseling appointment was to be held. She'd closed down after learning she'd be seeing her parents tonight. She hadn't said a word during dinner, and sat silent with her face averted during the drive.

"You okay, honey?" Lia finally asked.

"Uh-huh."

She considered and discarded half a dozen things she could say, eventually settling for a quick squeeze of Sorrel's hand. The teenager gave one small sniff.

Lia had met the parents once. Sorrel had gotten her looks from her mother, who wasn't much older than Lia—mid- to late-thirties, maybe. She'd kept talking about how *difficult* Sorrel was and how brave Lia must be to take her on.

"You know this all started with her telling a terrible lie, just to get herself out of trouble," she'd said, her agitation revealing itself in jerky movements and flared nostrils and a voice sharp as broken glass.

"I'm good at giving kids a refuge where they can think about their behavior and come to decisions," Lia had murmured. "Please don't worry about her."

She hadn't been sure then that Mom would worry. Sorrel's father, a quiet, thin man, hadn't said much but had seemed distraught. He kept patting his wife, but his eyes had stayed on his daughter who was sitting out in the hall waiting for Lia to take her away from her parents.

Tonight, once Lia parked and locked up the car, she took Sorrel's hand as they started toward the building. Sorrel held on so tight it hurt.

Inside, the receptionist let them down the hall and knocked lightly on the glass inset on Jennifer Riordan's door. It opened immediately. Jennifer smiled first at Sorrel, then at Lia. She was young, probably still in her twenties, and hip enough to make the teenagers with whom she worked comfortable. She wore a diamond stud in her nose and half a dozen gold hoops climbing her ears. Her brown hair was worn short and spiky. So far as Lia was concerned, what counted was the warmth of that smile and the way she listened as attentively to the kids as she did to their parents.

"Come in. Your mom and dad are already here.

Thanks for bringing her," she added with another smile to Lia.

Sorrel's feet seemed to have taken root where they were and she still held Lia's hand in a death grip.

Lia bent her head slightly to whisper in her ear. "What's the worst that can happen?"

Sorrel turned an anguished gaze on her.

"They won't believe you, right?"

This nod of the head seemed dazed.

"It's already happened," Lia reminded her. "Hearing it again will be unpleasant, but you'll say with dignity, 'I'm telling the truth,' and we'll leave. Okay?"

The teenager took in a deep breath and let it shudder out. "Okay." She released Lia's hand, wriggled her fingers as if to restore circulation, then sailed into the room with her head high.

Lia was really proud of her.

The parents were both on their feet, attention riveted on Sorrel the minute she appeared. Lia could have been invisible, and she hoped it would stay that way.

"Pumpkin," Sorrel's dad said roughly, and stepped forward to hug his daughter. She submitted briefly then moved back. At her quiet dignity, his face contorted.

Tears ran down his wife's face. "Your dad made Raymond admit…" She pressed fingers to her mouth. "Oh, God, I'm so sorry. So sorry I didn't believe you. I *loved* him. I mostly raised him, which makes this my fault. I never thought he could do something like this, but I should have listened. Oh, Sorrel, can you ever forgive me?"

Sorrel burst into tears, too, and they all hugged and wept on each other, but finally she withdrew and returned to Lia's side. Lia gently squeezed her shoulder for reassurance. Jennifer handed out tissues so everyone could mop up, then skillfully got all of them to open up about their feelings—the parents' guilt and Sorrel's sense of betrayal.

"We want you home again," her mother said. "Please come home."

"Raymond has been arrested," her father told her. "I don't know whether he'll go to jail or not, but I can promise you'll never have to see him again."

Sorrel lifted her chin. "You know what he did to me."

"Yes. Oh, dear Lord, yes." Her mother's voice cracked.

"I wanted to kill him," her father said. "I never imagined feeling anything like this. I broke his nose."

Sorrel's eyes widened. "You *hit* Uncle Ray?"

"Yes."

"Did—did he hit you?"

He shook his head. "He crumpled. Sobbed and

sniveled and kept saying how sorry he was, that he couldn't help himself. I walked out."

"Oh, Daddy." Sorrel threw herself across the room for another, fierce hug, then resumed to her seat.

"Will you come home?" he asked. "Give us a chance?"

If they imagined forgiveness would come in a heartfelt rush, they were kidding themselves, Lia thought. It would be a slow and painful process that might never be complete. But she also knew that the biggest battle for Sorrel would be over-coming her own sense of shame.

She tensed, stole one scared look at Lia, then said in a small scratchy voice, "When I ran away, it was hard to get enough to eat."

Her mother hastened into speech. "I know, honey. I'm so sorry. But I promise we'll listen and nothing like that has to happen again and—"

"I need you to listen now."

The words dried up. Her parents held hands and stared at her, apprehension on their faces.

"I mostly stayed with other kids. Runaways. You know."

Nobody said anything.

"And…the other girls said there was an easy way to make money."

A horrified sound escaped her father.

"And I thought, well, I've done it before so what

difference does it make?" Sorrel sounded defiant and painfully young. She was trembling. "So I had sex with men for money."

"Oh, no." Her mother was crying again. "Oh, honey. Have you been tested? What if you'd gotten pregnant?"

"I'm not."

"She was tested," Jennifer murmured.

"There were only, like, five or six. And mostly when I said they had to use condoms, they did."

All the adults heard the *mostly*. What kind of monster would not only have sex with a young girl who only wanted enough money to buy something to eat, but would refuse to use a condom?

Uncle Raymond, Lia thought grimly, probably hadn't used one either.

"It was really awful," Sorrel said in that same scratchy voice, "but it wasn't as bad as doing it with *him*."

Her father said, almost calmly, "I would like to kill them all. And I will never forgive myself for letting this happen to you."

Sorrel shrugged and looked down at her hands, knotted together in her lap.

"We love you," her mother said. "I know right now you don't believe that, but it's true. We love you so much."

After a very long wait, Sorrel mumbled, "I love you, too."

Her mother gasped and pressed her face into her husband's shoulder. He wrapped his arms around her and cried.

Lia held Sorrel, who continued to sit stiffly with her head bowed. Finally Jennifer stood.

"I think we've made a real start tonight. But I'm going to suggest that Sorrel go home with Lia and we set up another meeting soon. Perhaps Thursday?"

Lia nodded. After a minute Sorrel's father did, too.

"Healing takes time," Jennifer said softly.

The minute Lia stood, Sorrel did, too. They left her parents and the counselor, walking silently out to the car.

Lia handed her more tissues, and let her cry all the way home.

CHAPTER FOURTEEN

LIA DID NOT leave her door open when she went to bed, no matter how much a part of her wanted to. It took her ages to fall asleep; her mind jumped from the scene between Sorrel and her parents to Lia's own decision regarding Conall and back again. Counting sheep didn't seem to be an option.

But apparently she did eventually sleep, because she woke up with a start. It was a second before she realized someone was yelling her name.

"Lia." It was a roar out in the hall. Conall flung open her door and light flooded in. "Where are the boys?"

"What?" She sat up, her covers falling away as fear rushed over her. "They're in bed." She blinked away the confusion of sleep. "Oh, my God, aren't they in bed?"

"No." His face was tense, unfamiliar. It occurred to her suddenly that *he* was afraid, which ratcheted up her own panic.

She swung her feet to the floor. "Why did you check on them?"

"I saw someone sneaking across the pasture

to the neighbor's. He was using cover well. I had a hard time getting a good look. Then the dogs went ballistic and two of the men came out of the house and grabbed the kid." The muscle in his jaw twitched. "It was a kid, Lia. I think it was Bren."

She raced past him to the door of the boys' bedroom, which already stood open. Their covers were rumpled, the bunk beds undeniably empty. The fear swelled like hydrogen in a balloon. "Why would he do something like that?" She didn't recognize her own voice. "If that was Bren...where's Walker?"

"I don't know." He swore. "Get dressed. I'm going out." He was lifting his cell phone as he turned away, punching in numbers. As she hurried to her bedroom, she heard him say, "Duncan? I've got a situation."

She'd never gotten dressed so fast in her life. She crammed her bare feet in athletic shoes, laced them and tore down the stairs. She reached the front door in time to see Conall running toward the horse pasture. A small dark shape was rolling beneath the lowest rail, crawling then scrambling to its—*his*—feet.

"Conall!" Walker sobbed. "Those men took Brendan. You've gotta save him. You've gotta!"

CONALL SWUNG THE BOY into his arms. Walker wound arms and legs around him, clutching desperately. He was astonishingly light. Conall felt a lurch inside at the realization of how little there was to this boy. Brendan, he thought with horror, while probably six inches taller was every bit as skinny.

As urgent as the need for answers was, Conall let Walker sob out his fear.

"We'll get him back," he murmured. "I promise. Shh. Calm down. It'll be all right." He hoped desperately that he wasn't lying.

Lia had reached him, her breath hitching. "Walker. Oh, honey."

Past her, Conall saw that Sorrel had come out onto the porch in her baby doll pajamas and stood stiffly, hugging herself.

"Okay." Conall started walking to the porch. He said with authority, "Tell me what happened."

"Bren wanted to...to—"

Conall took the half dozen steps and sat on the top one, Walker still holding on for all he was worth. It took a huge effort to keep his voice calm. "Wanted to what?"

"He wanted to do something to help you." Face swollen and wet, glasses crooked, the kid stole a look up at Conall. "He wanted to be brave like you."

Conall felt sick. This was the payback he deserved for being stupid enough to talk to the kids about his work. He'd thought he was doing something good, opening himself to them, giving them something to think about besides the death of their mother and their uncertain future. Instead, he'd apparently encouraged Brendan to try to be heroic.

A ten-year-old kid up against a trio of paranoid, crazy bastards with everything to lose.

Lia had sat so close she pressed against him. He guessed she wanted to snatch Walker away, keep him, at least, safe. But she made no move to do so.

"What did he think he could do?" Conall asked gently.

Walker was breathing like an asthmatic having an attack, his whole body shaking. "He took a couple of those bug things. You know, the ones you said would let you hear what they talked about."

Oh, shit.

"He put some in his pocket that day I showed you our equipment."

Walker's head bobbed.

"They won't work," Conall said hoarsely. "The ones I showed you weren't live."

"You mean— You mean you still won't be able to hear anything?"

He'd come close to dying half a dozen times or more, and he'd never felt this kind of fear before. "No," he said. "No, we still won't be able to hear."

Walker's teeth chattered.

"Oh, sweetheart." Lia reached out then, and Conall let her take the boy. Her terrified eyes met his over Walker's head. "What if the men see what he's got?"

Brendan was dead, that's what.

Their best hope was that Brendan had kept his head and lied for all he was worth. Kids did stupid things. They sneaked out at night. God help him if the neighbors found the sophisticated electronic bugs in the boy's pocket.

Conall glanced over his shoulder and saw that Sorrel was crying now.

"All right," he said, pretending he was calm and in control, "here's what we're going to do. Lia, you'll take the kids in the house."

Her eyes widened and her mouth opened to argue.

He shook his head. "Duncan is on his way with a couple of his people. They'll be parking out at the main road and coming in on foot."

She nodded.

"I'm going over there and knocking on the front door. Walker got scared and told me he'd dared Brendan to sneak over to the house and back without the dogs noticing. But he didn't come back, and Walker heard the dogs bark, so he woke me up. I'm there because I'm afraid one of the dogs has attacked Brendan. I'm scared. I'm begging for them to call their dogs in and help me find my kid."

"Your kid?" she said so quietly he had to read her lips.

His throat closed. He was a moment before he could say, "My kid."

"Are you waiting for Duncan?" Lia asked.

Conall didn't want to wait for anything. His body was primed to move. Every second that passed felt like an aeon. But he had to have more backup than Jeff in case things got really ugly.

"Yeah."

"Is Jeff?"

"If he sees anything, he'll call me." He patted the cell phone hooked on his waistband. Jeff could use the night-vision scope and keep an eye from above.

He saw Lia's shudder and hoped Walker hadn't felt it. She stood then and said, "Okay, kids, you heard Conall. Into the house." Her voice was admirably steady.

The wait felt interminable, but was no more than another five minutes.

Conall wasn't surprised that Niall had come with Duncan along with the same detective who'd been here before. They decided that once Conall started up the Suburban, Duncan would use the cover of engine noise to get his SUV and bring it in close. Conall would make the first approach.

As they conferred on the porch, Conall was aware of Lia standing just inside the screen door, listening. Her fingers were pressed to her lips as if that was the only way she could contain a sob or a scream or a plea. He looked directly at her once, nodded meaninglessly and went.

He drove the way a frantic father might, skidding as he made the turn from dirt onto gravel, gunning the engine and sliding to a halt with his bumper inches from the neighbor's garage door.

He took the steps to the front door two at a time, jammed the heel of his hand on the doorbell and held it, listening to the peal inside repeating itself shrilly. It had to be a minute before the door swung open.

"Who the hell—" Cufley said. He wore rumpled khaki pants, and an unbuttoned plaid shirt. The kind of thing a man might yank on when the doorbell rang in the middle of the night. One hand gripped the door, while his other arm stayed stiffly at his side, that hand hidden by the angle of his body.

Conall's adrenaline surged, but he didn't let his awareness that this creep had a weapon in hand affect his own performance. He knew his hair was disheveled and he looked distraught.

Maybe because he was.

"Listen, buddy, I'm sorry if I woke you up, but didn't you hear your dogs barking? One of our kids sneaked onto your property." He ran a hand over his face. "His little brother woke me up. He'd dared Brendan to sneak over here, touch the house and make it back without alerting the dogs. God!" Frantic slid seamlessly into threat. "If they've hurt that kid— Those aren't attack dogs, are they?"

"They are trained to be guard dogs, but I imagine if you go home, you'll find your kid." His eyes narrowed. "I thought that lady ran some kind of foster home."

"She does. We're getting married and adopting the boys. Their mother died—" He broke off. "It doesn't matter. I've got to find him. Can you call the dogs in?"

"The kid's not here," Cufley insisted, trying to sound irritated but not a good enough actor to disguise his nervousness. "I heard the dogs, that's why I'm dressed. I went out and nobody was there. If you go home, you'll probably find the boy already there."

"He's not there," Conall said stubbornly. "You're lying."

The guy's face flushed. "What is your problem, buddy? I'm going to call the cops if you don't—"

"Yeah, why don't we do that?" Conall said softly. The guy started closing the door and Conall shot his foot into the opening. He said loudly, "I'm going in," and grabbed his Glock even as he slammed his shoulder against the door and crashed into Cufley. He had the barrel pressed to Cufley's chest before he could get his own gun up.

"Brendan!" Conall yelled. "Where are you?"

He thought he heard a muffled sound coming from downstairs in the split-level house but wasn't positive. Duncan's SUV was sliding to a stop behind his and the three men leaped out, weapons in hand. Conall gestured for one to go each way around the house, while Niall joined him.

Cufley fought and yelled while Niall wrestled him to the ground and cuffed him. Conall pushed Cufley's gun into his own waistband, then nodded for Niall to go up while he went down.

Niall advanced silently up the stairs. Nothing happened. After watching him ghost out of sight, Conall flattened against the wall and exposed a few inches of himself in the stairwell. Gunfire exploded and he jumped back. The sidelight beside the front door smashed outward. Cufley curled into a tight ball.

Niall bounded down the stairs. "Son of a bitch."

"There're two more of them in the house," Conall said softly. "Shit. I can't return fire with Bren down there."

His brother lifted the radio he carried. After conferring briefly he said, "Sean's got one of the garage doors open. He's going in." Pause. "He's going for the interior door. Duncan's ready to go through a window."

"Can he see anything?"

"Quick glimpse, didn't get a good look."

Conall swore. Then he raised his voice. "This is the police. The house is surrounded. We know you have the kid down there. You've already shot at a police officer. We can end this without anyone getting hurt and without you being in any more trouble than you already are. Let the kid go. Put your weapons down and come out."

If they were garden-variety criminals they would have done it. But they weren't. They were crazies, ready in their own damn minds to be martyrs to their beliefs.

He crouched and prodded Cufley with his gun. "Tell them. Order them to let the boy go."

Cufley wanted to be defiant but he must have seen something on Conall's face, because he shrank away. "You won't shoot me."

"See, here's the thing," Conall murmured. "I love that boy. I'd do anything for him. Shooting off your foot might be a good start." He slid the barrel of the Glock down the scrawny body and then shoved it hard against the bottom of Cufley's bare foot. "Tell them," he snapped.

Eyes fixed in horror on his own foot and the gun held in a rock steady hand, the guy called in a voice that quavered, "Let him go."

"Louder."

"Let the kid go," he yelled.

"Bullshit!" someone downstairs snarled. "I'm

going to kill this kid if the cops don't leave the house. *Now.*"

Conall swiveled on his heels. "You're not getting out of this."

"We've got enough firepower to take you all out."

"I told you the house is surrounded. What are you going to do, start World War Three? You'll still die."

"So will the kid."

The radio crackled. "Keep him talking," Niall murmured.

Goddamn it. Conall wanted to see Brendan, know he was alive and unhurt. He had no patience; this terrible urgency gripped him.

My kid.

This was how he'd feel if Brendan was his.

"Use your head," he called down the stairwell. "You haven't done anything that bad yet. If you hurt a ten-year-old boy, you'll get the death penalty even if you survive tonight. I'll see to it."

A salvo of gunfire was his answer. Bits of wallboard and slivers of the studs beneath flew. Niall and Conall both hit the floor. Downstairs there was yelling. Glass shattered. Guns barked and Conall took a chance, rolling toward the head of the stairs.

The guy at the bottom was half turned away from him. Conall yelled, "Drop it!" When he didn't, when he spun back already firing, Conall squeezed the trigger and saw the red bloom in the middle of the bastard's chest. He squeezed again, and again.

Duncan yelled, "I've got Brendan."

Relief exploding inside him, Conall bounded down the stairs, his Glock held at the ready. He flattened against the wall then spun through the first doorway, his gaze sweeping the room.

A man was down. Sean knelt beside him, holstering his gun even as he was pulling handcuffs from the pocket of his windbreaker.

Duncan was talking to Brendan, who was crying in gulps that shook his whole body. His eyes found Conall and the next second they were both moving until the small body slammed into Conall's.

"You came! You came!"

"Of course I came." Conall bent to wrap the boy in his arms and hold him close. "Oh, damn, Bren. This is all my fault. I'm so sorry. God, I was so scared."

Still shaking hard enough to rattle small bones loose, Brendan pulled back enough to look incredulously at Conall's face. "*You* were scared?"

"I've never been so scared in my life," he said truthfully. Hell, *his* hands were shaking. "When I realized that had to be you creeping across the pasture—" He had to stop.

"You saw me?"

"Yeah." Conall let out a ragged breath. "Let me call Lia. She needs to know you're okay."

The boy swiped an arm across his wet face. "Is everyone awake?" His voice was incredibly small.

Conall actually laughed, although there wasn't a lot of amusement in it. "You think anyone slept through discovering you or Walker weren't in your beds? The damn dogs over here howling—" He held Brendan at arm's length, inspecting him. "Did you get bitten?"

"Uh-uh. One of them knocked me down and I curled up and wrapped my arms over my head and then one of the men yelled at the dogs and they came out and…and they grabbed me and brought me in." He finally petered out. "And then they wanted to know what I was doing here." Fresh tears fell. "I couldn't think of a good lie," he wailed.

Conall's eyes stung and he had to blink hard. He gathered the boy back into his arms and laid his head against the top of his head. "Yeah, I know," he said in a low, rough voice. "I know, Bren. You should be proud that you're not a good liar. Most decent men aren't, you know."

"But I bet you are!" Brendan sobbed.

Conall felt his face contort. He was aware of his brother watching them, but he didn't look at Duncan.

"I learned because it's my job," he whispered. "You can be a hero without doing what I do."

Brendan kept crying, and finally Conall straightened, lifting him in his arms where he clung like a monkey. Indeed, he didn't weigh much more than Walker.

"Take him home," Duncan said quietly.

Conall finally met his brother's eyes. "Yeah." He swallowed. "Thanks."

His brother nodded. "We'll clean up here. Why don't you send Jeff over? Lia and the kids need you."

He wasn't used to being needed, but he nodded.

Conall carried Bren out, placed him gently in the passenger seat and fastened the seat belt around him, even though that was dumb as hell for a drive down one driveway and up another.

Brendan's sniffles subsided by the time they reached Lia's house. He swiped at his wet face as Conall got out and came around to him.

"Walker?" he mumbled. "He was hiding and watching me. Is he okay?"

Conall closed a warm hand around the boy's thin shoulder as they walked toward the house. "He came running to get help when he saw them grab you. He's a smart kid, Bren."

"Smarter than me, I guess."

"What you did wasn't smart," Conall said frankly. "But that isn't because *you* aren't smart.

I don't want you ever to think that. This is my fault as much as yours. I put ideas in your head. When I was your age, I might have done the same thing." He let out a gruff laugh. "I know I would have. I was desperate to amount to something. For anyone at all to notice me."

"You?" Face tipped up to Conall, Brendan looked disbelieving. "But you're...you're..."

Conall stopped, even though he was aware of everyone waiting on the porch. "I'm a highly trained federal agent. I've been on the job ten years. When I was your age, I was scrawny, shorter than you are and mad all the time because my family was such a mess. You've got a big step up on me, Brendan. You grew up knowing your mom loved you and believed in you. That's what you need to hold on to. Okay?"

The kid gave a dazed nod. Conall hoped he got it.

After a moment they moved toward the house, but Lia, Walker and Sorrel spilled down the steps to meet them. Walker's face, puffy from earlier sobbing, was incandescent, and tears still ran down Lia's cheeks even as she smiled. Sorrel had been crying, too. He was the only one who hadn't, Conall realized, but he felt as drained and shaken as if he had.

They all enveloped Brendan. Even Sorrel wrapped her arms around him and whispered something in his ear. Conall stood a little back, watching, until Lia withdrew from the group hug and flung herself at him.

"Thank you," she exclaimed. "Thank you, thank you. Oh, Conall."

She didn't have to say, *I was so scared.* He knew.

"Wh-what happened?"

"It was ugly," he said in a low voice. "Brendan saw things he shouldn't have had to. The last damn thing he needed was another trauma right now." His voice went raw. "I'll never forgive myself for this."

She stared at him in astonishment. "It's not your fault. Of course it's not."

"Then whose is it?" He shook his head in disgust. "I knew he hero-worshipped me. I encouraged it because it felt good. I set him up to do something stupid to prove himself. I just didn't *think.*"

"Boys do stupid things."

Of all times to feel a grin tugging at his mouth. It was ludicrous, inappropriate and felt good. "Only boys?"

She laughed, although he heard a note of hysteria. "Girls are always more sensible, didn't you know that?" Then she wiped her cheeks. "Oh, I'm a mess." Her gaze encompassed the kids, now staring at the adults. "We're all a mess. Let's go in, hear the story, have some cookies and milk, and then go to bed."

Cookies and milk sounded about right to Conall. In fact, a vagrant thought came to him: That day so long ago when he'd had his face pounded, that's what he'd wanted from his mommy. An ice pack, a scold, then cookies, milk and sympathy.

He might have envied Brendan, except something that was relief and more was making him feel light, even happy.

Lia didn't blame him. She'd *thanked him*. And a few minutes later, when they all sat at the dining room table and he told the tale of the night's happenings, skimming over the parts that involved blood and death, Lia's face shone with gratitude and the kind of warmth a man wanted to tuck away in a breast pocket for retrieval at future, lonely moments.

It felt like an intrusion when the others started arriving at the house.

"BEDTIME," LIA SAID FIRMLY.

"But it's almost morning!" Walker protested. "See, it's getting light."

They all turned their heads to see that the black outside the window was, indeed, paling to pearly gray.

"Don't care," Lia said.

"Can I stay home from school?" Sorrel begged.

"'Cause otherwise I have to get up in only an hour."

"You may. Come on, everyone." Lia clapped her hands and the kids shuffled toward the stairs.

Conall gave her a lazy smile. "I'm afraid to disobey, but I'm needed next door."

She was proud of the smile she produced. "You're exempt." She hesitated. "But you haven't had any sleep at all."

On a groan, he lifted his arms toward the ceiling and stretched. She heard a few pops and cracks. When he was done, he said, "I'll take a nap, don't worry."

She shook her head and followed the kids.

Upstairs, she went to tuck the boys in and found Walker sitting on the edge of his bed.

"Can I sleep with Bren?"

Brendan lay in bed, but his eyes were wide. "I don't think I can go to sleep. I keep thinking—" A shudder rattled his thin body.

"I'll tell you what." She hugged Walker and smiled at his older brother. "Why don't you both get in bed with me? I'd feel a lot better if I had you snuggled up and knew you were safe and sound."

"Yeah!" Walker exclaimed. Brendan didn't say anything, but he jumped up.

She gave them both soothing back rubs, and even Brendan succumbed at last to exhaustion. Lia lay awake for a long time, worrying about what had really happened next door and what Brendan had seen that he'd never forget. She'd have to get the true story out of Conall.

Even thinking his name made the ball of misery in her tangle into a snarl she'd never tease apart. The DEA operation was finished. Today or tomorrow, Conall would be leaving.

She'd always known he would, but the unspecified future date had made it hazy enough to be only a vague threat. Suddenly, the end was here.

Oh God, can I bear to say goodbye?

Like she had a choice.

She laid her cheek against Brendan's head and told herself to count her blessings. He was safe. Finally, a boy curled up on each side, Lia slept, too.

CHAPTER FIFTEEN

MOST OF THE day had gone by, and Lia had had no chance to talk alone to Conall. He'd been either next door or working on his laptop. Barely glancing up when she asked, he told her, "Reports. The bane of my existence." She was aware of traffic coming and going next door—dark, official looking sedans and SUVs, and a couple of vans.

Having Conall and Jeff both sitting down to dinner with her and the kids was a novelty. Jeff was his usual quiet self until Lia asked if he'd called his wife.

His ordinary face brightened. "She's thrilled. I'm not usually away this long."

"Really?" Lia asked politely. "I thought DEA agents mostly did undercover stuff."

He shook his head. "We're involved in all facets of drug enforcement. For example, are you familiar with the Controlled Substances Act?"

Unseen by him, Conall rolled his eyes. One of the boys suppressed a giggle.

"Um, no," Lia admitted.

He lectured them with unmistakable enthusiasm about DEA responsibility for overseeing the manufacture, distribution and dispensing of legally produced controlled substances, all of which sounded to her as if it had come right out of a pamphlet. "I've become more of an analyst in my office than an active agent, and I'm considering a switch to being an Intelligence Research Specialist," he said. "Not quite as glamorous, but safer. Once you have a family, you know." He shrugged.

Lia couldn't imagine Conall being content as a research specialist. All that energy, contained in an office. He seemed hardly able to stand the several hours at a time he'd had to work on his computer and had admitted to being bored with the lengthy surveillance on this assignment. She remembered, though, his hesitation when she'd asked if he enjoyed the rush of adrenaline. What was it he said?

I always have.

There'd been something strange in his voice, though, as if he wasn't quite sure about what he was saying.

No, she thought bleakly, *don't kid yourself.* He'd said exactly what he meant. *I always have* was unequivocal.

After dinner, he announced that he and the boys would clean the kitchen. Happy as always with anything their hero suggested, Walker and Brendan jumped up and began clearing the table. Lia lingered over coffee, chatting with Jeff for a few minutes, then went out to give the horses their evening grain.

Neither of the men had said anything, but they didn't have to.

They would be leaving tomorrow. Driving away in that gray Suburban and not coming back.

Her grief was growing like a tumor pressing on essential organs. How had she ever been stupid enough to think she could get involved with Conall and keep it light enough *not* to grieve when he left?

What if Sorrel decided next week she was ready to go home? And the boys' caseworker called to announce that she'd found a potential adoptive home for them?

Almost gasping at the pain, Lia somehow wasn't surprised when Conall separated himself from the shadows on the front porch and stood waiting for her.

"I thought we should talk," he said quietly.

"Yes." She sat on the first step, and after a moment's hesitation he came down, leaning against the hand rail instead of sitting. "Tell me what Brendan saw," Lia said.

"No bodies, thank God."

That shook her, even though she'd suspected. "*Were* there bodies?"

"One." He sounded terse. "I shot and killed one of the men."

"Oh."

"Duncan shot the guy that was holding Brendan, but Bren saw Sean cuffing him and knows he isn't dead."

"Does he know—"

"That one of them died?" He shook his head. "He heard the gunfire, but I was evasive. I thought it was better that he didn't know."

"Oh, God." Lia squeezed her eyes shut. "Imagine if he thought he was responsible."

"I've imagined," Conall said, an indefinable something in his voice. "Steer him away from newspapers and TV news for the next couple of weeks if you can. We've managed to keep the kids out of it for now. But you've got to be aware that there's always the chance Brendan will have to testify when it comes to trial."

"Oh, boy."

"I think that's unlikely, to be honest. Brendan was only the catalyst, although they're being charged with kidnapping."

"Did you find drugs?"

He shook his head. She could barely make out his face, since the porch light wasn't on. "No. Illegal possession of weapons. A National Guard Armory worth of weapons." He sounded grim. "Which opens a can of worms, of course. Where did they get the money to buy the weapons? The rumors had to be right. Sure as shooting—sorry, bad pun—someone in their organization is manufacturing meth, growing marijuana… Hell, who knows. Moving drugs one way or another."

"Will it be your job to find out who and how?"

"Not sure yet. I'm hoping not. Chances are I'll get absorbed in some operation back home long before anything active happens on this front. Or because of the weapons the ATF will take it over for now."

The ATF? After a second, Lia translated: Bureau of Alcohol, Tobacco and Firearms. Another arm of federal law enforcement.

Lia analyzed Conall's tone. He sounded neutral. Almost…flat. As if he didn't have strong feelings either way, or as if he was suppressing what he did feel. Did he want to pursue this one to the end and was disappointed about returning to Miami? Or was he glad to be done with this mess and everyone concerned?

"I see," she said.

They sat in silence for seconds that crawled into a minute or more. Finally Conall asked how Brendan was, in her opinion.

"Okay, I think," she said slowly. "He was pretty shaken up last night—well, this morning. But he didn't have any nightmares that I know about. He's on an adrenaline high—" she winced at the reminder of the conversation with Conall "—but, of course, it was scary and exciting, too."

"Exciting?" He sounded incredulous. "I've never been so freaked in my life."

"Really?"

"Don't tell me *you* think it was exciting."

"No. Heavens, no." She wrapped her arms around herself to contain a shudder. "But me, I hate horror films and I don't read anything meant to make me start listening for the creak of a foot-step on the stairs. I'm a coward."

"No." His voice was a caress, astonishingly gentle. "That's the last thing you are, Lia Woods. You have your own kind of courage. Loving these kids and letting them go, over and over." He shook his head. "I don't know how you do it."

Her eyes stung. So softly she wasn't sure he heard, she whispered, "I don't know how I do, either."

There was a long, long pause. "You know we'll be out of your hair tomorrow."

Thank God he wouldn't be able to see the tears that now dripped down her face. "I figured," she said steadily.

"I'll...miss you."

Lia had to swallow several times before she could tell him, "You know we'll all miss you, too." *But me most of all.*

"Yeah, listen. Would you mind if I stayed in touch? Maybe called the boys, sent them post-cards? At least until—" His voice, already hoarse, seemed to break. "Until they've moved on? And, uh, I'd like to hear what happens with Sorrel. You know."

"I know." She couldn't wipe the tears away without him knowing they were falling. "Of course. Of course you can stay in touch. They'd like that."

This silence was appalling. A deep, dark abyss.

"God, Lia!" he said explosively.

Holding in the agony, she said, "Would you— If you wouldn't mind, I think I'll stay out here a little longer."

He pushed himself away from the railing, stared down at her for a moment, then took a few steps across the porch without saying another word.

Until she opened her mouth, Lia hadn't known she was going to do it or what she was going to say. "Conall."

Even without turning she knew he'd stopped.

"My bedroom door will be open tonight."

His exhalation was audible and might even have been painful.

"I get bedroom privileges again along with the bathroom?" he said with unmistakable bitterness, then kept going.

Curled over, face pressed to her knees, Lia discovered that hearts didn't break; they tore.

CONALL LAY IN BED raging at himself, as far from being ready to fall asleep as it was possible to get. How could he have been such an idiot? He'd had a chance to spend another night with Lia. There was nothing in life he wanted more than to make love with her again. And he'd blown it.

He hadn't realized how much he'd been hurt by her accusation that he'd seen her as merely one more convenience to make his stay tolerable. He was still outraged when he remembered. How could she think that? Had he ever treated her in any way to suggest he didn't value her?

God, that sounded anemic. *Like* her? *Want* her? Better, but still inadequate.

The house was quiet. He'd left his own bedroom door partially ajar, painfully aware that Lia's wasn't. He supposed that tomorrow night, once he was gone, she'd resume her usual habits. Tonight, she was sending him a signal.

You had your chance. Jerk.

Or maybe she was thinking something stronger.

Conall should have been tired. He was. His eyes were gritty and his head throbbed. The two-hour nap he'd taken today was the only sleep he'd had since the previous night. Sleep usually came easily for him. He'd learned to take advantage of any opportunity. He could sleep in the heat of the Mexican desert, wedged beneath a rock outcropping, one ear tuned for the rattle of a diamondback. A small boat, ripe with the smell of fish guts? No problem. A room in a hacienda where maintaining his cover was a daily balancing act and discovery would mean a certain and gruesome death? He could close his eyes, picture a velvety black sky studded with stars, and fall asleep as gently and certainly as a baby.

He was good at turning his mind off. What wasn't so easy, he was discovering, was quieting this crackling static of emotions.

The truth was, he wished it wasn't time to go yet. Eventually, sure, but…not yet. A few more weeks would be good. Long enough to see that Brendan was okay, that his misadventure hadn't left any lingering terrors. Conall would have liked to keep working on his pitching technique, too. And Walker… Had Lia noticed that he'd bent his glasses last night? Those glasses had made such a difference to him. Conall still thought baseball wouldn't be his sport; either he still wasn't seeing real well when he was up to bat or he was worried about breaking the glasses. He had the timing down well enough to swing at more or less the right time, and sometimes he connected, but there was still something blind about the way he swung even though his eyes were open. He was better at soccer, a natural.

A couple of times Conall had noticed Walker wasn't wearing the glasses when he should have been. He made a mental note to say something to Lia tomorrow before he left. His initial excitement had become tinged with self-consciousness because he had to wear glasses when Brendan didn't. Walker tried to be as much like his big brother as he could. No surprise, when he didn't have anyone else.

Please God, don't let them be separated.

They'd survived so much. Remembering his first impression of them as ghosts, he wasn't sure they could survive another blow so devastating.

And Lia. He had a suspicion she hadn't meant him to hear when she'd confessed tonight that she didn't know how she endured loving the kids and letting them go, over and over. He hadn't seen her saying goodbye, but he knew there'd be a smile on her face. She would hug them, and be excited for them, and cry when no one could see.

She could keep Brendan and Walker. Unlike most of the kids she cared for, they didn't have a family to be patched back together.

Maybe she didn't want to. Or maybe she'd be denied if she applied to adopt them. A single woman... Conall could imagine some hidebound fool somewhere certain that boys needed a father. Never mind that they'd been raised by a mother alone.

It came to him slowly as he stared into the dark that they *did* need a father. Otherwise why had they latched onto him the way they had? They'd been so hungry for a role model.

So hungry, he thought bitingly, that they hadn't seen what a piss-poor role model he was. He'd almost gotten Brendan killed. Maybe he should have been more brutally frank about it, encouraged the kid to see that Conall MacLachlan was the last man he should want to emulate.

And it was true. He'd spent twenty years or more being reckless, so cold he didn't give a thought to anyone else's needs or feelings, angry when he felt anything at all. *God forbid Brendan should try to be like me.*

He thought for the hundredth time of getting up, crossing the hall and opening Lia's door. Would she turn him away if he walked to the bed and took her in his arms, started kissing her before she could speak a word of protest?

The old Conall would have done exactly that. He wanted her, and why shouldn't he have her one more time?

This was a hell of a moment to make a new discovery about himself. The new Conall, it seemed, had grown a conscience. He'd already hurt her, and making love with her one more time would tear open a wound that had begun, however tentatively, to heal.

Knowing he was a bastard, wishing he was less

of one, he stayed where he was even though it might be the hardest thing he'd ever done.

SAYING GOODBYE was unspeakably awful.

Jeff and Conall carefully packed their equipment in the back of the Suburban then threw in their duffel bags. Maybe with the intent of giving them a minute, Jeff went upstairs to check again that they hadn't left anything behind, leaving Conall to face Lia and the boys.

He'd already said goodbye to Sorrel, even driving her out to the main road to meet her school bus earlier in the morning. Lia had no idea what was said, but he'd come back looking particularly blank, something she'd begun to suspect happened when he was unwilling to express what he really felt.

Now he went to the boys and stood with a hand on each of their shoulders, his head bent as he talked to them and listened to whatever they were saying. Lia stood a distance away, feeling as if she'd frozen up inside. That was a good thing; she'd melt eventually, of course, but for now this was safest. She was storing up the memory of these terrible few minutes, though, unable to look away from the man talking to the two boys. She saw the way he cradled the ball of each boy's shoulder, his big hands careful, affectionate, strong. A lock of his wavy brown hair had fallen over his forehead.

He wasn't smiling. She wondered if he was any more capable of it than she was.

Maybe all he felt was mild regret. But she didn't—couldn't—believe that. How could he *not* have come to love those two boys, who loved him so much?

She saw him drop to his knees and take them into his arms. They clutched him and cried. When he lifted his head, his face was wet and Lia found to her horror that her own meltdown had already begun.

Not yet. Please not yet. Let him be gone first.

She heard the screen door bang behind her. Jeff's heavy footsteps on the steps.

Conall stood, released the boys and was coming toward her. He had hastily swiped a forearm across his cheeks, erasing most of the visible manifestation of emotions he surely didn't want to feel.

"Well," she said.

"I guess this is goodbye."

"Yes."

He closed his eyes for a moment. "Lia…"

"I don't regret anything," she whispered. "But… please go, Conall."

She was so devastated, she couldn't have said what she saw on his face, only that no matter how viciously he'd clamped down on his emotions they were seeping out anyway.

He stepped forward, kissed her cheek without

otherwise touching her, and walked away. Jeff thanked her politely for her hospitality, said he'd miss her cooking and she somehow responded with a "Thank you. Goodbye."

And then—oh, God, then—they were driving away, Conall behind the wheel. The usual dust cloud rose, still hanging in the air after the Suburban had turned at the end of her driveway and disappeared. After she could no longer hear the engine.

A sob rent the silence and she recalled herself to her role in life. The role she'd chosen, eyes open. Lia opened her arms, and both boys flew into them.

CONALL WALKED INTO his condo on one of the cays reached by bridge from Miami and thought with irony, *home sweet home*. It felt like a hotel. A nice one—he'd gotten lucky and was subletting a high-end place in a development populated by young professionals. He probably would have felt more at home in Little Havana or South Miami, primarily Spanish-speaking, but here there was virtually no risk of meeting someone who'd recognize him under one of his many aliases. He was invisible to neighbors who didn't notice when he went away or how long he was gone. He'd liked knowing he was truly alone here, in the midst of people.

He stood in the foyer and realized he hated this condo. He didn't want to be here.

It took a minute before he could force himself to continue into the bedroom, empty his clothes into drawers—Lia had made sure he came home with everything laundered—and replaced his few toiletries in the bathroom with a Corian counter-top and mahogany cabinets. He had no landline, so there were no phone messages he had to deal with. He'd paid all his bills online while he was gone, and what little mail he'd picked up down-stairs in his box was junk.

A workout. Conall seized on the idea. The com-plex had a well-equipped gym, open at all hours. He'd go lift some weights, spend time on the tread-mill. Maybe if he stayed until his muscles groaned and he was blinded by sweat, he'd get over this unfamiliar depression.

Yeah. That was a plan.

Maybe so, but it didn't really work. He discov-ered he'd lost enough conditioning to alarm him, and knew he'd overdone and would regret it to-morrow, but his mood hadn't lifted.

He'd forgotten to tell her to keep an eye out for Walker ditching his glasses when he should be wearing them. He could email Lia. That was enough of an excuse…no, it was a *reason* for con-tacting her immediately, not waiting a few days as he'd intended.

In fact, if he did it right away she might even read it tonight. The West Coast was three hours behind, after all. Yeah, he should get online now, not wait until he'd showered or made himself something for a late dinner.

The task would have been quickly done if he hadn't hesitated for a ludicrous length of time trying to decide how to end the email.

Wish I was there with you.

He scowled.

Is your bedroom door open tonight?

God.

I miss all of you so much, I ache with it.

His throat closed.

So, okay, they'd gotten to him. But he felt sure it wouldn't be a permanent condition. How could it be? He couldn't picture himself as some kind of family man. Pacing the sidelines at soccer games with the other fathers, yelling advice. Well, actually, he could see himself doing that. He'd spent enough time coaching the boys, it would be hard to keep his mouth shut if he knew one of them needed a reminder.

He swore under his breath.

Sitting at the dinner table every night with his wife and kids... God help him, he'd never been happier than he was at Lia's table, eating her home-baked sourdough biscuits and fresh-picked green beans, answering Walker and Brendan's oddball questions, aware all the time of Lia's gentle smile and the tilt of her head as she listened.

It was new and different, that's all. A sort of cultural exchange program. *This is how other people live.*

How he'd dreamed of living when he was a boy.

He wanted that for those two boys. He wanted them to have what he hadn't had.

Something like despair seemed to make the air thin. He was breathing too hard. He wanted to talk to Lia, but not on the phone. He needed to be sitting out on the porch steps with her, the night air cool, the country scent of manure and growing things so familiar he hadn't noticed how much easier he breathed there.

With a harsh sound, he grabbed his cell phone. He couldn't call her, but he could call Duncan. They hadn't really said goodbye. He'd thought about stopping in town this morning, but his mood had been too lousy.

He dialed before he had time for second thoughts. He was a little startled when Jane answered instead of Duncan.

"Conall. I thought you'd gone back to Florida."

"I did. Funny thing, we have cell phone service here, too."

Her laugh was low and husky. "Okay, I admit, I thought once we were out of sight we'd be out of mind. I'm glad you called. Duncan has been prowling around tonight looking out of sorts."

She went off to get her husband. Conall heard a baby crying, a murmur of voices, and finally his brother came on.

"Con?"

"Yeah, it's me." He was the one prowling, too restless to sit. "I just, uh, meant to call before I left. Or stop by the station."

"I hear the owner of the house isn't pleased to find out what his renters were up to."

"Hey, landlord risk. You got to expect to patch a few bullet holes in the drywall."

Duncan laughed. "Maybe in Miami. That's not in the top ten most common repairs here in Stimson."

Conall was smiling, finally. "No. Mom and Dad put a few holes in the wall during their fights, but Dad never liked guns, did he?"

"That was one of his few good features."

"You ever hear from him?" Conall didn't even know what made him ask. Niall would have said, surely, if their father had made any appearances.

"Not since the once." Duncan was the only one to see Dad when he stopped by the house after his release from the correctional institute. "Niall told me he half expects Dad to walk up to him at some bagpipe festival, though."

"Maybe he's back in the joint."

"No, I checked not long ago. Unless he left the state."

"Do you suppose he and Mom stayed in touch?"

There was a long, long silence. Finally Duncan said, "I wouldn't put it past them. But no. Dad was too…forlorn when I saw him. I guess he could have hunted her down through Aunt Patty, but she always hated his guts so she probably wouldn't have told him where Mom was even if it was the next room."

"No, probably not."

A few times in his career, it had occurred to Conall that he could conceivably end up in the position of arresting his own father. He'd been relieved not to be assigned to the Northwest.

"You glad to be home?" his brother asked.

He glanced around. "Can't say this feels like home. I've actually been away more than I've been here this past year."

"The boys sorry to see you go?"

"Yeah." He had to clear his throat. "Yeah, that was rough." Damn. His sinuses burned.

"Lia know what'll happen to them?"

"No." Now his voice was thick. "No, uh, she says placing kids that age isn't easy, especially when the agency is trying to keep them together."

"They wouldn't separate them?"

"I hope not."

After another silence, Duncan asked, "You ever think of…"

No. Goddamn it. No! How could he?

"I almost got Brendan killed."

"You know that wasn't your fault."

On a burst of self-directed anger, he asked, "Whose fault was it?"

"He's a kid. They do idiot things like that. Besides—"

Conall was squeezing the bridge of his nose so hard the cartilage creaked. "Besides what?" He managed to get the words out.

"If you left the DEA, you could live a more normal life."

He laughed in disbelief. "What would I do? Sell cars?"

"Come to work for me."

This laugh held genuine amusement. "When hell freezes over."

Duncan chuckled. "I guess maybe that wouldn't work."

"It's a miracle Niall tolerates you as a boss."

"That might be because we don't actually have a lot to do with each other on the job."

"It's a little weird, though, you've got to admit."

"Maybe." Duncan went quiet again. "I'm glad you called."

"Yeah." Conall swallowed. "Listen, you might

check in with Lia. Make sure…" He was hunching his shoulders, as if… He didn't know.

"She's okay? Sure." Pause. "Conall—"

"I've got another call coming in," he lied. "I've got to go."

"All right. I've missed you. Don't make me miss you again."

"I won't," Conall said, and knew he was telling the truth. One good thing: he'd reconnected with his brothers. He hoped he wasn't stupid enough to lose them again.

He ended the call, thought about checking out his freezer to see if he could find something edible, but couldn't work up any interest. Lia had spoiled him.

In a thousand ways.

He could stay connected with his brothers long-distance and be okay with that. Suspecting he'd never see Walker and Brendan again…that hurt was unexpectedly powerful.

But knowing he'd never again be able to get up in the morning anticipating the sound of Lia's voice, never hear her laughing in the kitchen or see her kneeling between the rows in her garden, never again stroke his fingers through the thick silk of her hair as he freed it from the braid… Never kiss her, never touch her, never *be* touched by her… Conall didn't know how he'd get himself out of bed tomorrow morning, or the next, or the next.

Pictures of her tumbled through his mind. Sensations, textures, scent. The fit of her body, the feel of her smile against his lips. The extraordinary color of her eyes and the fascinating way it changed depending on light and mood. The recognition that they shared the crippling knowledge that they'd never quite belonged.

Until I took her in my arms for the first time.

Shock struck, followed by pain so acute he doubled over. He might as well have taken a bullet.

He'd been wrong. What he was feeling wouldn't be wearing off like a bad drug reaction given a few days or, at worst, a few weeks.

Unless passionate, desperate, I-would-give-my-life-for-her love could be subdued by willpower alone.

I used to be good at believing I didn't give a damn.

He made a raw sound he didn't even recognize. The trouble was, now he'd figured out that he'd been faking it. After that, sincerely believing became a hell of a lot harder.

But what were his choices?

CHAPTER SIXTEEN

SORREL'S PARENTS CAME to Lia's to pick up their daughter.

It was the right thing for them to do. Sorrel showed them her bedroom, introduced them to Walker and Brendan, Pepito and Copper the horse. Lia watched the way she touched everything as she went: doorknob, dresser, footboard on the bed, fence post and soft muzzle. *See? This is part of my world.*

Goodbye.

The boys cried again when she was gone. So did Lia, but not until after they were in bed asleep.

I can't keep doing this, she realized drearily, around three in the morning. *It hurts too much.*

Why she'd once been able to handle it and now no longer was, she didn't understand. Maybe it didn't matter. Social workers often suffered burn out. Probably that was all that was wrong with her.

It was time, Lia realized, to look for a job again. That wasn't to say she couldn't continue to take in foster kids, but perhaps she'd do it informally. Only the Arturos and Julias, the ones who had been separated from their parents or *abuelo y abuela* by outside forces, not abuse or knowing abandonment. She didn't have to get so attached to those children, because they were already loved. They simply needed a temporary place to stay.

Conall had been gone two weeks when she called Walker and Brendan's caseworker to ask whether she might be considered as an adoptive parent. The caseworker, a man, was surprisingly receptive. If she was serious, he said, they could begin the process.

Yes. She was serious.

She also didn't know if she'd be enough for them. They had reverted in many ways, painful to see, since Conall left. Not entirely; she'd been right to encourage him to befriend them, but they were suffering in his absence.

She thought they would have been suffering more if he'd disappeared entirely. As it was, he emailed both every few days and had called a few times. They knew he still cared. Their voices sounded different when they were talking to him than any other time. If he'd wanted them, she would have let them go.

The first time he called had been bad. Her home phone didn't have caller I.D., so she had no warning.

"Lia," he'd said, and she would have sworn her heart had stopped.

It resumed, of course, because life did go on. Time passed whether you were happy or unhappy.

"Conall," she had managed to say pleasantly. "Let me get the boys." She set the phone down before he could say anything and hurried to call Walker and Brendan. Anxiety—or something else—tingled through her the entire time the boys excitedly talked to him. What she should have done was go out of earshot, but it didn't even occur to her to do that. And somehow she wasn't surprised when Brendan told her Conall wanted to talk to her now and she had to take the phone back.

"Is Bren really okay?" Conall asked without preamble.

"Yes, I think so. He doesn't like to talk about what happened. The other day Walker asked what it looked like when a person got shot and Brendan got mad."

"What did he say?"

"He wouldn't tell Walker what it looked like."

"I can't imagine that anything is worse than watching their mother die inch by inch was."

"No."

"Lia…"

The way he said her name made her feel lightheaded. It was what she thought of as his nighttime voice, low, husky, intimate. Tender.

She felt a sudden surge of rage that he would use that voice.

"Oh, gosh," she exclaimed, "something is boiling over on the stove. But I'm glad you called. The boys loved hearing from you."

But I didn't. Which was self-deceit, of course.

She dodged his second call entirely, making an excuse to the boys about why she couldn't come to the phone.

A week later, he called again and didn't ask to speak to her.

Niall and Rowan had her and the boys over for a couple of casual gatherings, which helped. Jane called twice. Even Duncan came by one day, midmorning, driving his black SUV and dressed in a well-cut charcoal-gray suit.

"I was in the neighborhood," he said with a shrug so casual it immediately made her suspicious.

"Were you."

He studied her face for a moment, then flashed a grin so like Conall's it made her heart squeeze. "Conall says you're not talking to him. He wanted to be sure you were all right."

"Exactly why is it he thinks I wouldn't be?" Then her breath quickened. "This doesn't have anything to do with the people next door, does it?"

Duncan smiled at her and said gently, "You know it doesn't, Lia."

Struck mute, she stared at him.

"You blindsided my brother. He's having to work through it."

She'd blind-sided Conall? "Sure I did."

Duncan only smiled again, chatted about some community happenings, and departed. Lia was left wondering what he'd report to Conall. Was she all right?

Not really, but it would get better. It had to.

She was occupied filling out reams of questionnaires about why she wanted to adopt and why she thought she could provide the boys a superior home.

She'd also been browsing for job openings, but didn't see anything that felt right until Rowan called to let her know the middle school psychologist had resigned unexpectedly.

"I thought of you," she said. "I don't know if it's anything like you have in mind, but just in case…"

"It actually sounds interesting. I like kids that age." Although she hadn't worked in a school before, her graduate degree and experience working with kids might qualify her.

"I know you do." Rowan laughed. "Just think. Brendan is only a year away from middle school."

The realization took Lia aback. He seemed so young. But he was turning eleven in August and starting sixth grade this fall. Oh, heavens; almost a teenager.

She applied right away, liking the idea that her

working schedule would be so similar to the boys'. Her days would be a little longer, but they could go to after-school care or simply walk over to the middle school and do their homework there while they waited for her.

Assuming, that is, they were still with her. Their caseworker said everything she'd submitted looked good, but she heard the reservation in his voice and, when she asked, he admitted there was concern that she was a single woman.

She was mad enough to respond. "Have you found that perfect couple who are dying to adopt two boys the ages of Walker and Brendan?"

"You know we haven't." He paused. "I wanted you to know it might be a problem, that's all."

She managed to thank him, even though he'd scared her.

Oh, dear God. What if the boys are taken away from me, too? She felt hollow, thinking about it.

A month to the day after Conall left, she weighed herself and discovered she'd lost nine pounds. Given that she hadn't been trying and tended to be skinny, that wasn't a good thing. She had to stay healthy.

She watched the boys picking at their dinners that evening and felt a flare of alarm. Were they looking thinner, too? It might be only that they were growing, she tried to reassure herself; boys did that, stretching out without filling in. She remembered Conall talking about how little and skinny he'd been until—what had he said? Sixteen? Seventeen? He certainly wasn't anymore.

She would take both boys in for checkups this summer. In the meantime, she'd let them snack more.

They were so subdued this evening, they didn't argue when she vetoed another TV show and suggested an early bedtime.

"You can read in bed," she told them firmly. When she checked on them half an hour later, they were both asleep. She kissed them both, lightly so as not to awaken them, closed Brendan's book and set it on the nightstand, and turned out his lamp. When she slipped out of their room, Lia left the door slightly ajar.

The house was hot tonight. The temperatures had reached the nineties today, truly uncomfortable in the Puget Sound area where the humidity stayed high. She'd opened windows earlier, but there wasn't enough breeze to stir the air. As she often did at this time of night, she went onto the porch and sat with her back to the newel post, savoring the cooler air.

A soft low sound came from the darkness, an answering whicker from the other direction. Lia wrapped her arms around her knees and wondered where Conall was right now. Usually, she tried not to wonder, given how high the odds were that he was in danger.

Maybe, she thought wryly, what she ought to wonder was *who* he was right now. If he disappeared undercover for weeks or months, would he have to quit phoning the boys? Probably. She prayed they'd understand.

Sound traveled at night. Was that a car on her gravel road? Of course it wasn't very late—some people actually enjoyed the nightlife. She stiffened when the car didn't turn into any of the first driveways. As far as she knew, nobody had moved into the house beyond hers although repairs had been made. Surely nobody would be coming *here*…

Headlights pierced the night and she instinctively scooted into the shadows of the porch. Her heart drummed. Who could it possibly be?

The car—the moonlight was bright enough for her to see that it *was* a car—parked in front of the barn.

In Conall's spot.

She should go inside, lock the door. No, wait and see who it was. Strangely, Lia was dizzy with anticipation although she couldn't imagine why she thought even for a minute—

A man got out, slammed the door. He seemed to be looking right at her, which meant she wasn't as hidden as she'd thought. His deep voice was low, but it carried.

"Lia?" Conall said.

HE'D FELT SICK with apprehension ever since he'd left his SUV in the parking garage at Miami International Airport this afternoon, having chosen a late flight deliberately. He'd had the probably delusional idea that he could show up after the boys were in bed, talk to Lia, and if she rejected him, no one else even needed to know he'd ever been here. He would go straight back to SeaTac, get a hotel room and fly out first thing in the morning.

Now he realized he'd *expected* her to be sitting out on the porch. It had never occurred to him that he might have to knock and wait to see who came to the door. He'd known, somehow, that he could walk across the yard and there she'd be. What he hadn't anticipated was that a strange car arriving at this time of night would scare her. Of course it would, given the isolation of her house. That was stupid of him. He spoke her name immediately.

"Conall?" she said disbelievingly.

"Yeah. It's me." Oh, damn, what had made him think this was a good idea? Why hadn't he called her? Asked whether it was okay if he came?

Long strides took him across the yard. She was standing by the time he reached the bottom step.

As usual, no porch light, but soft light fell through the open front door and the living room window.

"I can't believe you're here."

"All day, I thought about you sitting out here." He had to dislodge a lump in his throat. His voice came out hoarse. "Waiting for me."

She made a sound, a strange hitch of breath. "I think I was," she whispered, and he took the steps two at a time.

Conall didn't know if he reached for her first, or if she flung herself into his arms. All that mattered was that she was there, her face tipped up to his, her lips already parted for his kiss.

He took her mouth voraciously. All that tenderness was inside him, but the hunger was stronger. The hunger, and the fear.

She might still push me away. But she wasn't, he realized exultantly; she was kissing him, her tongue tangling with his, her arms holding him as tightly as he held her. She gave a small sob when he broke off for air, and to look down at her.

"God, I missed you," he said huskily, and kissed her again. He wanted to relearn her body, stroke her from butt to nape, throat to belly, but all he seemed able to do was grip her hips and grind them against his pelvis. He was blind and deaf with need, because—*yes!*—she still wanted him, too.

Reason was barely a murmur, almost drowned

out by driving lust, but he made himself listen. This wasn't all he wanted. He had to talk to her, find out whether there was the slightest chance she could imagine committing herself to him despite everything she knew about him.

Reason might not be loud enough to stop him, but a serious case of nerves had him gradually gentling the embrace, softly kissing her jaw and nuzzling her neck as he loosened his grip on the curve of her buttock, kneaded the small of her back. God, he loved that spot, where the fragile string of vertebrae met the flare of her ass.

He sucked in a breath. *Talk.* They had to talk. He might yet be turning around and walking back to his car, driving away, heading for the airport.

"I should have let you know I was coming."

She nuzzled his neck. "Are you in town because of the case? Or to see Duncan?"

"No." He brought his hands to her upper arms, squeezed and said, "I'm here to see you."

She went very still, like a wild animal caught in the open.

"You," he repeated.

"Walker and Brendan—"

"No."

He couldn't tell if she said "Oh" or only exhaled.

"Can we, uh, sit down?"

"Yes, of course."

Her head turned toward the Adirondack chairs,

but he said, "How about right here? I don't want to let go of you."

This time her "Oh" was distinct.

They sat. He held her hand; interlaced their fingers so they were palm to palm. He'd never noticed before how sensitive the palm of his hand was.

The night was awfully quiet. He discovered he was next thing to panicked. Give him a drug raid any day. At least he'd have a weapon in his hand, be wearing a Kevlar vest for protection. With Lia, he had nothing.

He gulped. "I want what I had here with you."

Her lashes fluttered as if she'd blinked a couple times in quick succession. Startled at his eloquence, no doubt, he thought grimly. He could do better than that. He *had* to do better than that.

"You know what I am," Conall said. "I've told you more about myself than I've ever told anyone."

He'd give anything to know what she was thinking. Her eyes were huge and dark, her lips slightly parted as she gazed at him.

"You said something once. That you thought I had it in me to be a better man."

She shook her head and his heart quit beating. But she told him, "I never said that. I wouldn't have. I said there's more to you than you believed. That all the business about you being incapable of being a good father or husband was nonsense. Do you know how much those two boys love you?"

"I love them, too." It was the first time in his life he'd ever said the word aloud with him as the context. He listened to himself with amazement and thought, *That wasn't so bad. Yeah, okay, then do it.* Big breath. "I fell in love with you, Lia." It sounded raw and awkward to his ears. "And, uh…" His hand tightened unconsciously on hers. "I had to tell you that in person. And find out whether you think you can feel anything for me."

God. He'd gotten it all out, but now he was in freefall. *Parachute, you can open any time. Any minute. Like now.*

Her mouth was trembling. Lia lifted her free hand to it, pressed her fingertips to her lips. She was making some strange little sounds, like whimpers. And then he saw that her eyes were wet, about to overflow.

"I'm sorry," he said on a groan. "I shouldn't have done it like this. You don't have to feel bad—"

"I love you so much. I never thought—" She laughed, but she was crying, too. "Oh, Conall." She dove at him and buried her face in the crook of his neck.

He held her fiercely, his cheek against her head, his eyes closed tight. They were burning. He didn't even know what he felt, it was such a tangle. But it was good, so good. And it hurt like hell, too. He'd cried that day he had to say goodbye to her and the boys, and he was about to cry now, too.

Why was happiness as agonizing as grief? Conall didn't know, but he wanted more of this anyway.

He rocked her, the way she'd rocked Sorrel that day on this same porch, and it seemed to work because the tension gradually eased from her body and his, too. She wiped her cheeks on his shirt, sniffled, laughed again and pulled back a few inches so she could see him.

"You didn't know I was crazy in love with you?"

"I hoped." He grunted at a memory like a body blow. "Do you have any idea how I felt when you informed me that all you were to me was an extension on kitchen and bathroom privileges?" He gave her a small shake. "You didn't really think that."

She huffed. "You didn't give the slightest indication you were falling in love with me."

"Do you really think every time I go out on a job I spend more time hanging around a woman and her kids than I do working?"

"Um...no?"

"You're right. No."

"I'm sorry if I hurt your feelings," she said softly.

No one in his life had ever apologized for hurting his feelings. No surprise when he'd done his damnedest to convince everyone he didn't have any.

"Not your fault." That came out gruff. He nudged her braid to one side and kissed her neck.

Here came the hard part. "Lia... Do you love me enough to marry me?"

For a second she didn't move, didn't breathe. Then she lifted her head and looked into his eyes. "Are you sure that's what you want?"

"I'm sure."

She searched his eyes; he waited.

"Yes," she whispered. "Yes, of course I will. Only..."

Conall tensed. "Only what?"

"I've applied to adopt Walker and Brendan."

He stared. "Well, of course we'll adopt them." Then he said sheepishly, "Well, I guess I shouldn't make assumptions. You've chosen to foster and not adopt, and that's okay if you want to keep taking in kids, but Walker and Brendan... They need us."

"I think they do, too."

He sighed. "You'll have to quit taking in kids that are in this country illegally, though, Lia. I enforce the law. I can't be involved in breaking it."

"No, I understand." She smiled crookedly. "It would be hard to keep making connections wherever you get sent anyway."

Conall realized she didn't know what he'd really been asking of her. She thought he was keeping his job, that he'd be uprooting her and the boys whenever he got transferred to a different field office, that she'd often be left behind coping alone when he disappeared on operations like this one and others far more dangerous. The fact that she'd been willing to do that, to give up her home, her friends, everything she knew for him, left him stunned.

"Lia, I'm turning in my resignation."

"What?"

"When I said I want what I had here with you, I meant it. This house feels more like home than anyplace I've ever been. The yard is great for the boys. What would you do with the horses if we moved? We can get a dog," he said with sudden enthusiasm. "I wanted a dog when I was the boys' age."

"But what will you do?"

He grinned. "Did I tell you Duncan offered me a job?"

"You'd do that?" she said in astonishment.

"Like I told him, when hell freezes over. But the idea of local law enforcement appeals to me." His mouth trailed along her jaw. "I want to come home every night."

"You won't be bored?"

He lifted his head, taking her question seriously. "I don't think so. I used to get a charge out of what I did. I loved drug buys, walking that tightrope, knowing each time that you have to act like you've never acted before, otherwise you're dead. I liked busts. I liked danger, I liked winning." He gave a short laugh. "Truth is it was like a grown-up version of a video game, me at the controls yelling, 'Yee haw.'"

A frown puckered between Lia's eyebrows. "When I asked, you said you liked the adrenaline."

"I did. Past tense. I've been struggling with that for a while. Maybe as much as a couple of years. Discovering I didn't get so much of a charge out of the same things anymore. Planning, strategy had gotten more interesting than being one of the players. I told myself I needed higher stakes, bigger busts." He paused. "I was wrong. I needed something, but that wasn't it."

Her eyes were so dark, he couldn't see the green at all. "What did you need, then?"

"You. The boys. A home. The first week here I told myself I was a stranger in a strange land, but at some point I knew I'd found heaven. Except I had a hard time making myself believe it could be real. It was pretend." His arms contracted, probably squeezing her too tight but he couldn't help himself. "I have hated every minute since I drove away."

If he was hurting her, she didn't let on. Instead she burrowed even closer. "I've hated every minute since then, too. Oh, Conall."

They kissed slowly, tenderly, then passionately. He'd dreamed damn near every night about this— the two of them out here on the porch on a warm summer night, the front door open so that they'd know if one of the kids needed them, that fat braid flopping against his chest as if asking to be unraveled.

"I love you," he whispered.

It was quite a while before she said, "If you won't work for Duncan, what will you do?"

"I've already had a phone interview with the county sheriff's department. They have an opening for a detective. I figure I'd like that." He found himself smiling. "As Niall once put it, I'll be arresting neighbors and friends instead of strangers."

"You've already arrested our neighbors."

That sobered him. "Killed one of them, too."

"Things like that surely don't happen often around here."

He shrugged. "Niall has shot and killed two men on the job. And, yeah, that's unusual. Duncan has only drawn his gun a few times, but it happens."

"Twice?" She gaped.

He told her the story of Niall saving Jane's life when a crazy stalker had a knife at her throat, and then about the bank robber who shot up the parking lot when he spotted a cop.

"All Niall wanted was to deposit a check."

"Oh, no." She hugged him. "I think I'd rather you never had to shoot anyone again. Unless—" She hesitated. "Well, I don't want you to change too much."

Conall threw back his head and laughed. "So if I get bored, it's okay if I shoot someone?"

Lia giggled. "If it'll make you happy."

Voice low and husky, he said, "*This* makes me happy. You. Knowing your bedroom door will be open tonight." He pulled back slightly. "It will be, won't it?"

"Yes." Her voice came out husky, too, the effect being sultry. "Do you think we need to keep pretending for the boys' sake that you have the bedroom across the hall?"

"Maybe until we get married. Unless it's okay to live in sin these days when you're under scrutiny by an adoption agency."

He loved the way her nose crinkled. "Oh, fine," she muttered.

"I want to get married soon." He didn't like to say this, but had to. "I'm only here for two days, Lia. I have to give a month's notice and finish out an operation I'm involved in. I kinda thought, though, that maybe you and the boys would come visit me for a few days or a week somewhere in there. We could take a boat out, do some snorkeling, maybe some fishing—"

"That sounds wonderful. Of course we'll come."

"So." He smiled at her. "You ready for bed yet?"

UPSTAIRS SHE STOOD in the doorway to the boys' bedroom and watched when Conall went in and stood silently looking at them. Their covers were rumpled; Walker had kicked his off entirely. After a minute Conall stepped forward and gently ran his knuckles over Walker's cheek, then did the same to Brendan. Who stirred restlessly, then opened his eyes.

"Conall?" he whispered.

"Yeah." He cleared his throat. "I'm here."

"I'm not dreaming?"

"No." Conall sat on the edge of the bed; Lia couldn't see his face anymore.

But she heard the aching hope in Brendan's voice. "Are you…are you staying?"

"Yeah. I have to go back to Miami for a few weeks, but then I'm here for good. Lia and I are getting married."

"Oh." He sounded heartbreakingly wistful.

"You'll be staying, too." Conall bent and enfolded the boy in a fierce hug. Brendan's arms came up and wrapped around his hero's neck. "We want to adopt you two. If that's okay with you."

Lia hadn't told them she'd applied to adopt them. She'd been afraid she would be denied and thought it was better if they never knew it had been a possibility. But now…of course they'd be approved. Of course they would.

"Yeah! We want that more than anything." She thought maybe Brendan was crying then. Finally he sniffed. "Walker's still asleep. Nothing ever wakes him up."

"That's okay. I'll surprise him in the morning."

"Yeah!" Brendan exclaimed again.

Conall said something to him, so softly she couldn't hear. Brendan whispered something in return. Lia backed into the hall, tears streaming down her cheeks. She hurried to the bathroom, where she brushed her teeth and scrubbed her face until her cheeks were pink. When she came out, she saw that Conall had picked up his duffel bag and gone on to his bedroom with the narrow twin bed.

Smiling, she went into her own room, stripped to her panties and camisole and got into bed, leaving the bedside lamp on.

And her bedroom door open.

EPILOGUE

A STIR AT the head of the aisle turned heads in the church. Seizing the moment when no one was looking toward him, Duncan gently rubbed the heel of his hand against his breastbone. Too much was going on inside him, and it was pressing for release.

He'd never expected to see Conall get married. Duncan suppressed a grunt of near-amusement. He'd resigned himself to never seeing his youngest brother again at all. Hearing his voice on the phone had been miracle enough. But this...

His gaze touched on Jane, who sat holding Fiona in the front pew. His beautiful wife and their child. Fiona met her daddy's eyes and grinned, her face lighting with delight. She bounced on Jane's lap, arms flapping, causing his wife to look at him, too. Her smile was warm, accepting, knowing. She guessed what he was feeling, even though he hadn't said much.

He hadn't had to say much. Jane knew him.

The organ music swelled and shy Anna started down the aisle, carrying her basket and strewing rose petals as she went, concentrating and careful not to look at the audience. Duncan smiled at the sight of her solemnity, her shiny patent leather shoes, skinny legs and the wide frilly skirt of her dress. She'd been thrilled to be invited to be in the wedding.

Jane craned her neck to see, as did Niall and Rowan beside her. Desmond, sitting on the end, grinned encouragement at his sister. Niall had a seemingly casual hand on his back, which was probably all that kept the kid's mouth shut. Des and Anna were MacLachlans now, officially having been adopted by Niall.

By all of us. They're family. My family.

The single attendant, a friend of Lia's, appeared and started her turn down the aisle.

Chest still aching, Duncan turned his head to look at his little brother standing beside him, all grown up. Conall was almost handsome in a tuxedo, but Duncan could feel his tension. Was he half afraid Lia would chicken out at the last second? Duncan had had a chill himself in the same spot; trust didn't come easily to any of the MacLachlan brothers.

But there Lia was, an extraordinarily beautiful woman who never took her eyes off Conall from the moment she began the slow walk down the aisle escorted by two skinny, big-eyed boys in suits and ties. Duncan had the passing hope the getups weren't left from their mother's funeral, but he immediately relaxed. Lia would have made sure Walker and Brendan had something new.

Her parents were here today, in the front pew opposite the one that held the MacLachlan family. She'd made the decision to have the boys give her away, though, and Duncan suspected they'd felt about it the way he had when Conall asked him to be his best man. He'd been stunned speechless, so choked up he couldn't get a word out for a good minute.

"Not Niall?" he'd finally managed to ask.

Conall had given him a wry grin. "Come on, we've always known you're the best man. I'm bowing to reality."

"You're sure?"

"Yeah." Conall had had to clear his throat. "I'm sure."

Of course neither of their parents were here today. Duncan felt something unexpected: pity. It was their loss.

Gaze moving from the awe and love on Conall's face to Niall as he wrapped an arm around Anna and then lifted her onto his lap, Duncan remembered that long-ago day when their mother had walked out after Dad was sentenced to ten years in the pen. Duncan had come home from his summer job hoping for dinner and found Mom packed.

"You're...leaving?" His voice had cracked.

"Yes," she'd said with so little emotion, he knew she was already gone in all but body. "You should, too."

If he'd left for college the way he had planned, Niall would have survived. Maybe. "But...Conall," Duncan had croaked in protest. No, begged.

"There's nothing either of us can do for him, or Niall either. Face it." And somewhere in there, she'd said, "Conall's not your responsibility."

Duncan had made a decision that day. He'd given up his dreams because he'd believed she was wrong.

He'd known for a long time that he had done the right thing. He'd even figured out that he felt a hell of a lot more than responsibility for his brothers.

Today, watching Conall hold out his hand for the woman who had taught him to love again, then smile at the two boys and murmur something to them before they stepped awkwardly aside and retreated to the pew with their adoptive grandparents, Duncan felt his eyes burning.

His brothers hadn't only survived, they'd become good men who had responded in their turn the same way Duncan had that day. When they were needed, they'd stepped up to the plate.

Have I ever told them how proud I am of them?

He wondered what expression was on his face right now. *Am I going to* cry?

Yeah, he thought in astonishment and some embarrassment, maybe.

He met his wife's eyes again and felt as if his chest might split open. All he could think was, how rare was it in a lifetime that a man had the chance to know how lucky he was? To have everyone he loved in one place? All well and happy and surrounded in their turn by people who loved them?

Conall and Lia, hand in hand, had turned to face the pastor, who smiled at them with warmth and wisdom. His voice filled the church with a natural resonance. "We are gathered here today to witness the joining of this man and this woman in the bonds of holy matrimony."

Duncan swallowed the lump in his throat.

My family.

* * * * *

LARGER-PRINT BOOKS!
GET 2 FREE LARGER-PRINT NOVELS PLUS
2 FREE GIFTS!

✦ Harlequin®

Super Romance®

Exciting, emotional, unexpected!

YES! Please send me 2 FREE LARGER-PRINT Harlequin® Superromance® novels and my 2 FREE gifts (gifts are worth about $10). After receiving them, if I don't wish to receive any more books, I can return the shipping statement marked "cancel." If I don't cancel, I will receive 6 brand-new novels every month and be billed just $5.44 per book in the U.S. or $5.99 per book in Canada. That's a saving of at least 16% off the cover price! It's quite a bargain! Shipping and handling is just 50¢ per book in the U.S. or 75¢ per book in Canada.* I understand that accepting the 2 free books and gifts places me under no obligation to buy anything. I can always return a shipment and cancel at any time. Even if I never buy another book, the two free books and gifts are mine to keep forever.

139/339 HDN FEFF

Name _____
(PLEASE PRINT)

Address _____ Apt. #

City _____ State/Prov. _____ Zip/Postal Code

Signature (if under 18, a parent or guardian must sign)

Mail to the **Reader Service:**
IN U.S.A.: P.O. Box 1867, Buffalo, NY 14240-1867
IN CANADA: P.O. Box 609, Fort Erie, Ontario L2A 5X3

Not valid for current subscribers to Harlequin Superromance Larger-Print books.

Are you a current subscriber to Harlequin Superromance books and want to receive the larger-print edition?
Call 1-800-873-8635 today or visit www.ReaderService.com.

* Terms and prices subject to change without notice. Prices do not include applicable taxes. Sales tax applicable in N.Y. Canadian residents will be charged applicable taxes. Offer not valid in Quebec. This offer is limited to one order per household. All orders subject to credit approval. Credit or debit balances in a customer's account(s) may be offset by any other outstanding balance owed by or to the customer. Please allow 4 to 6 weeks for delivery. Offer available while quantities last.

Your Privacy—The Reader Service is committed to protecting your privacy. Our Privacy Policy is available online at www.ReaderService.com or upon request from the Reader Service.

We make a portion of our mailing list available to reputable third parties that offer products we believe may interest you. If you prefer that we not exchange your name with third parties, or if you wish to clarify or modify your communication preferences, please visit us at www.ReaderService.com/consumerschoice or write to us at Reader Service Preference Service, P.O. Box 9062, Buffalo, NY 14269. Include your complete name and address.

HSRLP11B

The series you love are now available in

LARGER PRINT!

The books are complete and unabridged—
printed in a larger type size to make it
easier on your eyes.

Harlequin
Romance

From the Heart, For the Heart

Harlequin
INTRIGUE
BREATHTAKING ROMANTIC SUSPENSE

Harlequin *Presents*

Seduction and Passion Guaranteed!

Harlequin
Super Romance

Exciting, emotional, unexpected!

Try **LARGER PRINT** today!

Visit: www.ReaderService.com
Call: 1-800-873-8635

Harlequin

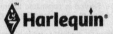

A *Romance* FOR EVERY MOOD™

www.ReaderService.com

HLPDIR11

Reader Service.com

You can now manage your account online!

- Review your order history
- Manage your payments
- Update your address

We've redesigned the Reader Service website just for you.

Now you can:

- Read excerpts
- Respond to mailings and special monthly offers
- Learn about new series available to you

Visit us today:

www.ReaderService.com